The Underpainting

Abbe Rolnick

The Underpainting

Abbe Rolnick

Sedro Publishing
Burien, Washington

Published 2024
Printed in the United States of America
ISBN: 978-1-7360878-3-1 (Trade Book)
ISBN: 978-1-7360878-4-8 (Electronic Book)
LCCN: 2024915241

Sedro Publishing
15100 6th Avenue SW, Unit 521
Burien, WA 98166
sedropublishing.com

The Underpainting

Prepress by Lisa Dailey
Cover design by Andrea Gabriel
Copy Editor: Ariel Anderson (www.arieledits.com)

Other Books by Abbe Rolnick
River of Angels, 2nd edition, Book One in Generations of Secrets (2018)
Color of Lies, Book Two in Generations of Secrets (2013)
Cocoon of Cancer: An Invitation to Love Deeply (2016)
Founding Stone, Book Three in Generations of Secrets (2020)
Tattle Tales: Essays and Stories Along the Way (2016)
Bubbie's Magical Hair, Children's Illustrated book (2021)

CONTENTS

Part One
Sizing Up

It's for the best. How many times was she going to hear those words? Even now the echoes reverberated in her heart. Her hands shook. She folded her arms across her chest. Placed her hands under her armpits.

She knew this self-hug too well. It had followed her since infancy. She closed her eyes, and still a teardrop slipped out. To hell with the *best*. In what rule book was it written that best equaled better—oh yes, she remembered: grammar. *Good, better, best.* She wanted to issue a complaint.

She wrapped in tissue, and then in newspaper, four miniature white clay sculpted dresses that hung on a pretend closet wire just six inches long. A gift from her mom's treasures. At eighty-six her mom hadn't missed a beat, until her time was up. Too many questions remained, too many mysteries unsolved. Who was this woman, now gone for almost a decade?

Sealy pulled a hair tie off her wrist and whipped her gray speckled hair into a bun. It did the trick. She smiled at her reflection in the wall mirror. Twisting the strands into a bun did two things: gave her power, and gave her the illusion of seeing a glimpse of her mother.

As if in agreement, the wind picked up and the maple, dogwood, cedar, and quaking aspen answered with a frightening hiss. Sealy paid attention to wind whistles. She stared out the living room window watching what was left of the leaves sway. A crackling in the air, and then a burst of rain. The thunder hid the wind's rage. Off in the distance, a tree thudded to the ground, roots upended.

Sealy shook her head. She pictured the gravel driveway that wound its way to the road and the ancient cedar that had been listing. She sighed. If it lay across the road…she'd…

It didn't matter, just like it didn't matter that she was alone, left to pack up and rediscover herself. Soon she'd be gone, and a renter would have to deal with the debris.

This wasn't about death, this wasn't about endings, this was about living. Sealy looked at all the art pieces. The ones worth thousands of dollars were her own creations. It was these trinkets that set her off. Damn the photo.

Sealy pulled the black-and-white photo out of her skirt pocket and held it toward the light. The back had been stamped, *April 1951, Maine*. Her mom stood tall in high heels, a tight one-piece jumpsuit, a string of pearls around her neck, and a smile that jumped out of the picture. An inside photo of a library room filled with books and artwork. Next to her stood a stranger—dressed in a dark pinstriped suit. His arm rested on her mom's shoulder. His smile matched her mom's.

The doorbell rang. Sealy tucked the photo back into her skirt's fold.

"I'm coming. Give me a second." Without a peephole to peer through, Sealy reverted to an old trick. She called, "What's the magic word?"

"It's your sister, Sealy. You knew I was coming over to help you pack. Open up the door and stop playing games."

Sealy ignored her sister's tone and greeted her with open arms. "Time got away from me. You know me, always cautious."

"It isn't like you to not answer my calls. Were you avoiding me because you failed to tell me about the For Rent sign? I thought you were going to wait."

"Just reminiscing. I'll be gone for who knows how long. No matter what you think, I have to figure this out. I can't live in limbo. Renting the house out is my best solution." Sealy noticed the stiffening of her sister's shoulder. "Jeannie, I didn't mean to sound ungrateful. Sorry if I hurt your feelings."

Jeannie answered through tight lips, "I may be older than you, but I'm not senile yet. It's the photo, isn't it? I wish I'd never found it."

"But you did. Mom must have planned for you to find the photo. It was with her jewelry, part of the inheritance. You know her, whenever there was a hard topic, she'd divert us. Later we'd find a note, or a gift, or a book about the subject, even when it was personal, like when we wanted to talk about sex. Maybe she hoped you'd have discovered it sooner."

Jeannie picked up a stack of books and piled them into a box. "Would finding it sooner have been better?"

Sealy laughed. "Better for who? I'm nearly sixty, and now I have to question who I am? I hated growing up, being a teenager, always wondering why you and I saw the world differently."

"We love each other, isn't that enough? Why does it matter? Just because Mom had an admirer doesn't mean she cheated on Dad. Does it?"

Sealy let the question linger, settle onto the trinkets. The carved wood figure of a naked woman with a belly had always been her favorite. The rich veins of red and chocolate in the wood cradled the unborn baby. What a shock to see the photo with the figure and the miniature dresses on a mantel in a different home. "Of course not."

"Remember I can read your mind. I know how you think. Spit it out."

"Just a vague memory of a man visiting on one of the summer vacations we took. Mom and I went to Maine on our own for a week, and you were supposed to follow with Dad."

"Sealy, that was so long ago. I remember you arguing even then about being separated. I had a gymnastics tournament to go to. That was real, not an excuse."

"Real doesn't mean that the man didn't visit. That he didn't have a son with him."

"Stop it. You're crazy. In a tizzy, packing up your life, for a photo taken over half a century ago?"

Sealy sat down on an overstuffed ottoman, an antique from another time. "Even this beautiful sofa makes me wonder. Dad never sat in it. Mom would read to me in this corner. You can see the wear and tear on the armrest."

"I can always come with you. You don't have to be alone."

"Don't worry. I'll keep in touch. Let's have a cup of coffee and a treat."

"I should have known; you always bake when you're uneasy."

Obsessions weren't her style, but Sealy had studied the photo repeatedly as if it held the key to all life. If Jeannie knew how fanatical she had gotten, Sealy was sure she would have stopped her from leaving. No reason to alarm her.

Besides the original photo, Sealy had found a postcard sent to her mother.

My dearest Mary,

Summers will never be the same. Children make a family. Take care of Sealy.

Yours, R.

The address was a blur of ink. With care she had used her magnifying glass to tease out three letters stamped across the postage: *OQT*. The only result from her internet search came up with a Native American coastal town in Maine, shortened from Ogunquit. The name meant *beautiful*. It had to be where she went for the summers. There were no hotels to speak of, just families that boarded people, cabins, and an old pub that served as an inn. The town's website offered a list with email addresses. The only response she'd received was from the Hawk House. The email offered her accommodations for as long as she wanted. She would find it to be a nonfussy place to experience the coast as a member of their family.

With no more information, Sealy relied on the town's website, which needed a makeover. Everything was about the past and little about the present. The water and mountain scenes were stagnant photos. She had clicked on them, hoping for a montage of the area, something to trigger a memory. None came. One line at the bottom of the website mentioned new tourist developments in the future for the artistic and the eclectic. *Stay tuned for descriptions of our newest addition to guesthouses and B&Bs, the Hawk House.*

Sealy thought the email odd. She really wasn't looking to be part of a family, just to understand her mother's life. She booked her room at the Hawk House for three months and a one-way flight.

After two connecting flights and a layover due to fog, Sealy descended the plane's steps directly onto the tarmac. It felt good to stretch her long legs, to be in fresh air. She followed the passengers past a welcoming sign, "OQT: Where Nature Meets Art," into the only gate, and through to a rolling baggage claim. Her stomach flipped and growled, a sign of her nerves and that she hadn't eaten for hours. She grabbed her carry-on and headed to where she believed she'd find taxi service. The overhead sign of a bow and arrow and hearts painted in graffiti must have been a jokester's design meant to make a newcomer laugh. Despite the silliness, Sealy smiled. Even with all her research and the statistics spelled out, Sealy hadn't believed that the town would be so small. A blip on a map, almost nonexistent. Her cell phone didn't even have bars.

A midnight-blue Oldsmobile with a taxi sign affixed to the roof waited at the curb. The driver jumped out to open the car door. "Ms. Sealy Morris?"

Sealy noted that all the other passengers had disappeared. "Yes, how did you know?"

The driver's grin took up his entire face. "I'm not psychic, if that's what you think. It's a small town, and besides, it says so on your luggage tag."

Sealy guessed that the driver was in his mid to late thirties and knew everyone in town. "And you are?"

"I'm a Morris too. Dan Morris. You can call me Danny. My grandfather said you'd eventually show up. Just expected you a decade ago, since the time he put the Hawk House on the website listing."

Sealy dropped her carry-on and leaned against the taxi. She felt Dan's eyes on her. "Apparently, your grandfather was right. Just that I had no idea I was expected. I'm known to be slow. Do you want to fill me in?"

"Hop on in. I brought hot cocoa and a cookie to make you feel at home."

It was Sealy's turn to stare at Danny. A vague memory, of eating cookies and drinking hot cocoa after swimming in the cold water of the Atlantic Ocean, emerged. "Do all visitors get this treatment?"

Danny shook his head. "Nope. Only the special ones."

"Oh, then in that case, I can't refuse."

They drove in silence, passing a few dirt roads that turned down driveways, and then past a main road that held quaint shops, a post office, and what Sealy thought looked like a coffee shop and gallery.

The town disappeared as rugged berms of sand-covered rocks came into view. As the scenery passed by, Sealy swirled the ends of her hair around her finger. She peered over the narrow road to see a beach and dark waves rolling into the shore. "No one seems to be out today. Is it always this quiet?"

"It's busier in the towns closer to the big city, if that's what you mean. Most folk leave for the city early in the morning and return late at night, commuters. They drive or take the train. Brave folks like us stay and attend to the sand."

"You're pulling my leg, aren't you? I know it's been decades since I was here as a kid."

Sealy sensed a shift in Danny. "More like a half a century. The world changes. Not for the better. Sand is a thing, if you didn't know."

"Ouch, sounds like I gave you a sour lemon to eat. I didn't mean to offend. Do you want to tell me about the sand?"

"Nope. You'll hear more later. Just think about the name of the town, Ogunquit. It's the Abenaki word for 'a beautiful place by the sea.' No one mentions the storms, the effort to protect the cove."

Sealy silently repeated the town name, trying to let the pronunciation roll around her tongue. The last thing she wanted to do was offend those who lived here.

They rode in silence until the scenery changed to green. A breeze that sounded like the echo of the ocean below greeted them to a postcard of tall trees majestically saluting on a hill. Sealy gasped at the view.

"You okay? I know it's beautiful, but most guests don't react that way."

Sealy nodded. "Most guests haven't painted the scene from a lost memory."

Danny answered as if he had that same sour taste in his mouth. "A painter. That figures."

She tried to make a comeback, but she had none. Did Danny know something about her life that she didn't? That was why she was here, to find out more about her mother. Tears welled up in the corner of her eyes, and she chose to let them fall. The last time she'd cried was at her mother's funeral; the time before that was when she was five. Sealy heard her grandmother's rant: *Tell her to stop. Don't spoil her. The girl needs to learn her place.*

As they rounded the hill and came to a low spot in the road, the trees fell back and a driveway with a manicured hedge led them to a modest brick house with white trim. Sealy had no memory of the house, never painted it. If she had, it would have been two stories, with a gabled roof. The brick made sense, but the landscape required wood to blend in.

Danny parked in front of the entrance. By the time he'd come around to help Sealy, she had already gotten her bag and walked up to the porch. Two kids peeked out from a window. Sealy heard their laughter.

"Don't mind those kids. If they are a problem, let me know."

Sealy took a deep breath. "This is your place? You drive the taxi, book and serve guests, and watch out for the sand?" She should have realized this from the email. Hawk House was a family home, just like it said. Sealy would be part of this if she chose to stay.

"Yep, and I'm a dad too. Anything else you want to know?"

Sealy listened to Danny's intonation, the tightness behind the words. It sounded so familiar. She had offended him again. "You're irritated. My father sounded the same way when I asked too many questions. Are you more patient with your kids than you are with a lady guest turning sixty?"

Danny smiled in reply. "To tell you the truth, this is still new to me. My father made me a deal I couldn't refuse: take over and it's yours. So I did. Our home isn't a business yet. I'll work on being more patient."

Sealy felt a weight in his answer. "Is your dad still alive? Why would he give this up? You don't have to answer me, I'm simply curious. Especially since you expected me here ten years ago."

Before Danny could answer, a tall, well-dressed elderly gentleman appeared at the door. "No sense you two staying out on the porch. This will be a bed-and-breakfast; you're supposed to enter."

Danny took Sealy's one bag from her hand, and the two entered a hallway lined with paintings of the seascapes. Sealy stood gaping at the variety. Even though the house didn't spark a memory, the paintings did. The scene of a young girl swimming out to the surf's edge caught her off guard. Sealy felt herself in the waves, overcome by their strength, knowing she was far away from shore. In the painting an older man swam parallel to the girl. Sealy listened as if words came off the canvas. *Keep breathing, even strokes. That's it. We're almost back.*

She turned to find the same elderly gentleman offering her his hand. Close up, he looked frailer. His clothes hung loosely, as if he'd lost weight. His blue eyes sparkled and the dimple on his chin winked with his smile. Sealy clasped his offered hand.

"I'm Danny's grandfather, Richard. Welcome to our humble abode. Glad you finally found us on the internet. That was my son's idea to offer our home. When you get settled, we can talk. Danny's kids, Roxie and Reese, can show you to your room. We're a family, so I hope you don't mind children."

Overwhelmed, Sealy didn't know what to say. Nodding, she let Roxie lead the way upstairs with her sister in tow. The girls hurried while Sealy took each step upward as if it were a mountain leading from the ocean to the cliffs. Along the staircase were more paintings. Sealy noted the signature at the base of each, *RM.*

"Ms. Morris…" Roxie's voice pulled her back into the moment.

"You can call me Sealy. Ms. Morris makes me feel like your teacher."

"Okay, but my teacher is really nice too. She's almost as tall as you but younger. Here's your room. Poppy said you should have the view out to the blue green of the ocean, not the rocky shores. He said that you would like it best. He baked more cookies too. We already had some."

Sealy took in their banter with serene delight. Kids were a gift—one she had never experienced. "Thank you, I'll come down in a bit."

Roxie held Reese's hand. "I guess it's your nap time. Daddy said you'd want to rest. You're not as old as Poppy, so maybe you won't sleep too long. We haven't had a lady visitor in a while. If you need a stuffed animal there are some old ones in the closet."

Sealy listened to the patter of their feet as they descended the stairs. Roxie's mind followed her own sense of logic. Sealy needed that same simplicity as much as she needed a rest. After placing her luggage on a shelf under the window, she opened the screen, smelled the salty air, and stared at the blue green, a vision apparently only gotten from this room. The room sat high enough to see beyond the rocks, to shimmers of the ocean waves.

She pulled herself away from the view and hung her clothes. Not knowing how long she would be here, Sealy had brought two of every combination of clothing. This was a trick she used when she traveled in the corporate world. Scarves, necklaces, jackets would transform an outfit. Make it simple—colors opaque, splashed with patterns, interchangeable, always presentable.

A wave of tiredness hit. Roxie was right: three stuffed animals looked back at her. Sealy grabbed the lamb with the blue ribbon around its neck and left the two monkeys. She fell into a deep sleep hugging an old friend.

Sealy woke to the sounds of clamoring pots and pans. She jumped out of bed. Disoriented, she panicked when she walked into a door, expecting it to be her bathroom. Holding her bumped head, she made her way to a thin line of light shining through the window. Her only clue to the hour was the sun lying on the horizon, bright pink over the deeper blue. Richard Morris, the grandfather, the painter, and who knew what else, made sure she'd see this view. Why else assign her this room? She hoped that the noises below weren't a call to dinner.

She found the bathroom and freshened her tangled hair, washed her face, and then grabbed a black shawl from her stash of "must" clothing. By the time she descended the stairs, the house had quieted. She found a door that opened to a garden and stepped out.

Near a small bonfire, Richard, Reese, Roxie, and Danny sat in lounge chairs; two seats remained empty. Sealy took the one by Danny.

"Did I keep you all waiting?"

Roxie smiled. "Your nap was short, just like I thought. We always sit here before dinner. Dad calls it our ritual."

Sealy noticed Danny's smile. His sour taste must have disappeared. "Is this a new ritual or an old one?" she asked. "I feel like I've sat here before."

Richard cleared his throat. "Yes, this is an old tradition. A way to come together. I'm not sure if families do that nowadays."

Danny continued, "With the kids and bedtime demands, it's easier to pause and take in the beauty, discuss the day. Otherwise, we don't connect. My father made sure I gave thanks in this way. Been doing this since Reese's age, even when I was a teenager."

Sealy couldn't help but notice the pride in their voices, but also dread. As if it might be taken away. "Is the extra seat for your father?"

Danny remained silent. A look passed from him to his grandfather.

"Oh my, did I take your mother's seat?" Sealy asked.

Roxie jumped on her great-grandfather's lap and said, "Don't be silly, Ms. Sealy. We leave two seats open, always. One for my grandpa and one for a guest. You never know who will show. That's another what do you call it—ritual? Do you have rituals like that where you're from?"

Sealy looked out at the stars, the twinkling of light. Roxie's simplicity had saved the awkward moment. "Yes, I do something similar. My dad died when I was little. I hardly remember him. So my mom insisted that we leave his chair empty. Now that she passed, I have two empty seats to fill."

Reese stared open eyed. "Well, that's silly. Almost the same. But my grandpa should be here soon, and you're the guest."

Yes, Roxie had it right, she was the guest. None of it seemed silly. Danny had said they had been waiting for her for ten years.

Sealy unconsciously pulled at a strand of her hair. She had questions she feared to ask. Why had Richard insisted she take the bedroom with a specific view or save a dilapidated stuffed toy. She glanced over at Richard, a man the same age as her mother.

As he if knew her thoughts, Richard stood. "Sealy, I'm going in as I'm chilled. You can stay outside if you'd like. My son, Paul, should be here soon to join us. Is your shawl warm enough?"

Sealy hugged the shawl as if it were a protector. "It's my security blanket, a warm gift from my mother. She always wore it at night."

"Do you know that even though it is black, there are strains of midnight blue in the weave? Painters, like weavers, mix colors to give depth with the change in lighting. A little bit of trickery adds spice."

Embarrassed that she hadn't noticed the variation of colors before, Sealy pretended to study the weave. "I should know. Do you weave as well as paint?"

Richard nodded and left. Sealy sensed the mood of the group had changed. Reese and Roxie pulled at their father's arms. The outdoor spell had been broken. Within minutes they all went inside. Unsure of what was expected of her, Sealy remained facing the colorful sky.

Sealy hadn't meant to be rude. It was late, past the dinner hour. Instead of returning to the house, she took a walk down a lighted path to a flat area beyond the gardens where an enclosed gazebo awaited her discovery. She had taken refuge from the wind and mist only to find a set of wicker chairs and tables like the ones she grew up with at her mom's house. The coincidences seemed plausible. Paintings of the ocean with a swimmer, old stuffed animals, and the wicker furniture were dated pieces from a past period. Everyone her age would have had mementos like these.

Sealy wished she had brought her painting supplies. The gazebo would catch the perfect lighting for evening and morning spots to paint. The stars against the clouds, the fading moonlight, she imagined with dark blues and grays, a touch of silver to add spark. It didn't surprise her to find a dried paintbrush left on the windowsill.

By the time Sealy returned to the house, it was dark except for a light in the kitchen. She found a plate of food wrapped in foil and a note: *If you are hungry, you can warm this up in the microwave—RM.* Richard had set a bottle of red wine on the table with an accompanying glass.

Sealy appreciated Richard's thoughtful gestures. She ate slowly, letting the heat of the spices in the vegetable fish stew warm her insides. The recipe was one her mom loved, taken from a cookbook from Maine. Her mom's time in Maine had made a lasting impression.

After a glass of wine, Sealy felt another wave of tiredness hit. She rinsed her dish and placed the bottle of wine on the counter. The label caught her eye, a painted rendition from the view beyond the gazebo. In small print the label stated, *Red Blend distributed by RM Inc.* Another business, another talent to attribute to Richard. Suddenly chilled, Sealy draped her shawl over her shoulders and tucked her hands inside. Feeling around the bottom edge, she found what she suspected: blue and black strands embroidered together, *RM.*

Bed called. Sealy looked forward to quieting her thoughts. Whatever she expected from her visit, the Hawk House offered a colorful palette. She mounted the stairs toward her bedroom. One light remained on in the living room. A reflection from the window revealed a man reading the newspaper. Sealy assumed he was Danny's father.

After a week, Sealy had developed her own rhythm within the household. Since Danny usually took Roxie and Reese to school after breakfast, she hitched a ride into town with them. When Danny returned from shopping or to pick up the girls, Sealy would get a ride back to Hawk House. Most days she went to the library and read about the town's history. She had found pictures going back to the 1940s of the post office, the bank, and the grocery store.

Except for a few upgrades it all looked the same. Danny had been right about sand. With the changing patterns of the climate, there had been more storms, the oceans had risen, and the once protected shorelines were washing away. Politically the town had become divided. Many wanted to invite developers to create a tourist spot with quaint shops and high-rise hotels to promote the coastline. The environmentally concerned took the line of preservation.

Danny removed his taxi sign when he shepherded his kids to school. He knew better than to embarrass them. Sealy had offered to pay for her trips, but Danny insisted that he was off duty and the rides were part of the package. Everyone had a seatbelt in the upgraded Oldsmobile, but the wide seats crackled with a clear plastic over the leather. Instead of a mileage counter to track the distance for customers, Danny posted charges based on areas, homes, and stores. His only concession to modernizing was a CD player.

On the rides into school, the girls buckled up in the back seat, and Sealy sat up front. She listened to the girl's gossiping and learned about their dance class, the boy who threw paper airplanes and had to stay in during recess and the new science project they had to prepare. Rarely did she engage Danny in any substantive conversation. But today, after Roxie and Reese had been dropped off, Sealy couldn't hold her tongue. "Danny, I don't mean to pry, but I worry about Richard. I haven't seen him any mornings and only rarely in the afternoon when I'm walking on the property."

Danny pulled off into the school parking lot, let the other cars go by, and to her surprise, turned off the car. "You really don't know, do you? My granddad is sick. He's been sick for years. Seeing you means so much to him. He thought for sure you'd have come after your mom died."

Sealy bristled at the accusation. "You're upset, but don't take it out on me. I'm thirty-some years your senior. Show some respect. He hides his sickness well. What does your granddad have, cancer?"

Danny tried to smile, but his lips quivered. "Of course he has cancer. At his age, everything fails. He's been mourning so many losses. All he talks about is when your mom left with you. In a way, the diagnosis of pancreatic cancer is a gift, his way of letting go. It sounds perverse, but it's true."

She rummaged through her pocket for the photo that brought her to this beach town in Maine. Breathlessly she pushed it in front of Danny. "This is all I've got, no other message from my mother. I wouldn't even have made a connection to this place but for the sculptures on the mantel. They must have belonged here."

Danny shook his head. "That was taken a long time ago. You should ask my father or Richard. They'd know."

"What is with your father? I've been here a week and our paths have never crossed. Do you think he's avoiding me? I'm not sure if he's upset with having me here or any guest. I don't want to be a burden at the Hawk House, especially since Richard is ill."

Danny started the car. "I'm not my father's keeper. Watching the kids is enough. I have to run errands."

Sealy could kick herself. Her motives hadn't been as pure as she thought. She sounded more like a prying gossiper than a concerned person. "If you don't mind, can I tag along? I could help with shopping. I came on this trip to find answers about my mother's life, but I want to help."

"You might try going into some of the shops beyond the library. Lots of old folk still around to jog your memory. I'm sure your studies from the library will help. But books are just words without the real people. You only see what one person has to say about a place. There is always more."

Sealy nodded even though she didn't know if she agreed. As a painter, she absorbed the colors of feelings. Pages in books also described a picture. The essence had to be real. History had many versions. Hers and her mother's were what she had lived by. As they drove to the OQT Grocery, her hand curled into the door's handle. She held it tight as if she could ward off the next realities.

Danny took his shopping list and handed it to Sealy. "If you want to be helpful, can you get the stuff on the grocery list? I've written down the amounts. I'm off to the hardware store. Just get the food and put it on our account. Meet you back here, if not before."

Immediately as Sealy walked through the doors to the grocery store, she smelled the vanilla. Instinctively she turned to the right, by the cash registers, to find the homemade ice cream section. A flash of her younger self holding a vanilla ice cream cone and holding a boy's hand. The bottom of the sugar cone had a hole in it, and the two of them raced to suck out the ice cream before it melted.

Her hands shook as she read the list. She looked around to see if any of the patrons were watching her reactions. One older gentleman studied a cereal box as if it held a key to nutrition; a young mother with her baby in a snuggly carefully selected vegetables. Neither paid attention to her. Sealy perused Danny's list of bread, flour, meats, and fresh foods and then searched the headings of the five center aisles.

Even though Sealy didn't have kids to feed or a large household to maintain, she had mastered the art of entertaining and food shopping. Grocery stores followed the same pattern: the outside was for fresh, and the inside was for packaged good. Not so at the OQT Grocery. Smack in the middle of the third aisle, Sealy found the meat section. Sealy peered at the refrigerator display. Danny requested various cuts of beef and a whole chicken as well as bone powder. The bone powder stumped her, so she approached the counter. In the back, a gray-haired gentleman, wearing an apron, gloves, and a chef's cap, stood cutting meat.

"Excuse me, sir, I was wondering if you had ground bones for sale?"

"Not many people ask for that. You must be staying with the Morrises. I have a bag of pulverized bone powder ready to go. I'll get it."

Sealy noted his name tag. "Mr. Curly, if you don't mind my asking, what's it for?"

"Oh, that's a family secret. What's your name?"

"I'm Sealy Morris. Not the same Morris, but I'm staying with them."

As soon as she made that statement the gentleman gave her the once-over. Her cheeks pinkened under his scrutiny. His gaze was more into her soul than under her clothes. She had dealt with innuendos many times in her travels, but his examination made her uncomfortable.

"Just call me Curly. Nothing wrong with being part of the Morris family. They are our rock. Both Richard and Paul have served as the town manager. Paul is still serving—among his other duties. If you don't claim to be part of our Morrises, then I can't tell you the family secret."

Sealy hoped he was joking with her. The politics of her visit had suddenly become more layered. She placed the bag of bone powder in her basket, finished the shopping list, and made her way to the register.

The meat counterman caught up with her. "My wife made a card and a pie. Everyone loves her apple pie. Please send my regards to both the mayors. Hope they are healing."

Sealy reached for the pie.

Curly grabbed her hand and held on to her wrist. "Be their family. They need help and don't accept much from others. They're the private type that give and, well, you know…"

He was gone before Sealy could reply.

Sealy walked to the hardware store, two blocks past the grocery store. Each step felt like decades rolling back and slamming into the present. Danny had parked the taxi right outside, leaving the doors unlocked. She placed the groceries inside. Rattled by her earlier conversation with Danny and Curly's request, Sealy coiled her hair around her finger. She wiped tears that had accumulated in the corners of her eyes, catching them before they arrived at her cheeks. Talk of illness and needs triggered memories of her mother's cancer.

She caught a glimpse of her reflection in the window. Nothing gave her feelings away, just an elderly lady shopping with a burdened face. If she wore lipstick, she'd try painting on a smile, but she didn't. Instead, she pinched her cheeks, an old trick of her mother's. *Pretend, put some color into your face, the world won't end because you don't understand.* That was when she was a teenager going for an art school interview after she'd failed to get into college. The world hadn't ended, but today she wondered about alternative worlds. Whose life had she been living?

A man tapped at the window and waved her inside. When she didn't respond, he poked his head out. "For goodness sakes, you don't have to worry about entering. What do you need?"

"Sorry, I got lost in my thoughts. Is Danny here? I'm supposed to meet him."

"He's in the back room. Can I help you with something?"

Sealy looked around at the neat shelves, labeled and aligned. Hardware stores gave her confidence, as if some putty, nails, and a fresh coat of paint could fix all problems. "Do you have painting supplies?"

He pointed to a sign, *Outside House Maintenance Section.* "The colors can be mixed. What house will you paint?"

"I don't mean to paint a house. Do you have oil and watercolors for canvas?"

"Well, I placed an order a while ago and the customer decided he didn't want it. You're in luck." He guided her to the art section, small but with sketch pads, charcoals, chalks, and a selection of oil and watercolors. "We're more of a general store than just hardware. You'll find the people who live here are do-it-yourselfers and a creative bunch."

"And the gentleman's order. Is this it?"

"Nope, Richard's order is in the back. I was hoping he'd change his mind or that his son, the town manager, would want it later. But I can sell it to you. Let me bring it out."

He disappeared and returned with canvases of various sizes, a palette, and three sets of paint tubes of various hues.

"I'll buy them, and if you have some brushes, I'd like them as well. I'm staying at the Hawk House, and it's a painter's dream."

"I should have guessed. Danny mentioned you. Seems right to have another artist up there."

By the time she had paid for her purchase, Danny appeared. He had his arms full and a pencil in his mouth. He looked at her stash and tried to talk. His garbled words made her laugh.

"If you have something to say, take the pencil out of your mouth."

He handed her one of the bundles and put the pencil behind his ear. "I knew the painting bug would get you. I was hoping to be spared another artist in the house. Only kidding. I was worried about my grandfather's order sitting in the back. Glad you found it."

"Really. I feel like you planned this, but that's impossible."

"Nothing in my life is planned. Not even the meals."

Heartened by Danny's reception, she let down her guard. "I'm a great cook. If you don't mind, I could help."

"Only if you know the health codes of a commercial kitchen. Even though you're the only guest, I have to follow the rules."

Sealy smiled. "I used to cater and work as a waitress. Does that qualify?"

"I'll let you know if I need you. But you're welcome to look at the kitchen and make yourself comfortable. Bake if you want to. I won't complain."

Sealy waited two days to put her plan into action. Determined to talk with Danny's grandfather and father, Sealy decided to take control. The only way to find her own comfort was to do what she always did. With Danny's okay, she found the kitchen. For a bed-and-breakfast, the kitchen was well organized. An older gas stove had been converted to include six burners with an oven below and one on top of the range. The bottom oven contained three shelves and a dial for convection heating. An upright freezer sat next to a double-doored refrigerator. The rest of the kitchen showed the wear and tear of use. She smiled at the labeled cutting boards, *Fish*, *Meat*, and *Vegetables*, lined alphabetically along the wood countertop.

Sealy could hear her mom's voice in her head. *The kitchen makes a home. Keep it simple, keep it useful, keep it clean.* Intuitively she opened the lower cupboard to find the flour and baking supplies. She smiled at the order, a mirror of her cupboards at home.

Within a half hour she had whipped up a batch of her favorite comfort food—a cross between a sweet cookie and a biscuit. Made from ground nuts, honey, butter, flour, eggs, and almond and vanilla extract, the dunk-in cookies were her yearly gifts to friends. She double baked them and washed dishes while waiting for them to cool.

Careful to leave the kitchen spotless, she noted the time. The girls should be back from school soon, and she'd be out of the way of the cook for dinner preparations. Sealy heard footsteps and then a deep voice.

"Hmm, something smells good. Looks like we hired a new chef."

Sealy turned to see Danny's father and froze. Tall, wide shouldered, with a slight graying of hair, he greeted her with a smile that was an older version of the one she'd seen in her mother's photo. Richard and his son had the same blue eyes, the same narrow, dimpled chin.

Her voice shook. "We haven't met yet. You must be Paul. I'm Sealy, your houseguest."

"Of course you are. And I've been impolite. Either you don't like our food, or Danny hired you."

"Neither. Danny seemed overwhelmed. I mentioned that I used to work in a restaurant and catered. I love to bake and thought I'd learn the kitchen. I'll get out of your way now." Sealy moved to the right and Paul moved to his left. They collided. The awkward moment passed, and they both laughed.

"I apologize for not meeting you the day you arrived. You're our first real guest. Pleased to meet you, Sealy. Thank you for baking and making yourself feel at home. Obviously, you guessed that I am Paul, father to Danny and grandfather to the girls."

Sealy offered her hand. Paul cupped it with both his hands and smiled. "That's okay. I figured you were working. Danny told me that Richard is ill. Normally I don't jump into the kitchen, but I wanted to make life easier."

Paul nodded, but his easy smile had vanished.

Sealy noticed the worry lines around his eyes, the stiffening of his shoulders. The tired spiders etched along his jaw that deepened with his seriousness. Not knowing what else to do, she walked out of the kitchen. "I'll get out of your way."

Paul followed. "I'll be at the dinner table tonight. Maybe we can talk afterward. Did you leave any of your cookies out? I'm known for my sweet tooth."

"Of course I did. A baker always leaves temptation. There are some on the counter. I'll see you at dinner." The aroma of the cookies had at least drawn one of the Morrises out. She'd have to figure out when Richard took his walk.

For the briefest of moments, Paul felt lighter. Usually, he didn't pay attention to the kitchen; finding a stranger there should have worried him. Sealy had made herself at home and for the first time in years, he felt a different warmth emanating. The aroma of baking triggered sweet memories. He carried his cookies back to his home office. He tugged at the knot of his tie, removed his suit jacket, and sat back in his leather swivel chair.

He'd been hiding behind work for nearly a month, using it as an excuse not to face his father's illness. His worries had accelerated with Danny's plan of creating a bed-and-breakfast. He sighed. Instead of a diminishing pile, his desk held mounds of research on every topic under the sun: climate change, beach erosion, dikes, development, pancreatic cancer, ancestry, adoption, and marketing a bed-and-breakfast.

He took a bite of cookie and let the sweet honey flavor meld with the taste of almonds and butter. Burying himself with work didn't change the dynamics of his father's illness. Time to come out from his self-imposed quarantine. His dad needed him, as did Danny and the grandkids. Sandwiched in between generations, Paul had no choice but to engage. He had no idea that the ad on the town's website for houseguests would add another layer. He felt like the old cartoon character Dagwood, with a sandwich that reached the sky. If only his worries for his father and son tasted as good as Dagwood's creation. Remembering Sealy's smile, he laughed at his conclusion.

Paul arranged each pile according to priority—he left his father's medical file on top. Soon he'd have to hire help, as the cancer had progressed to the painful stage. He called the list of hospice and advanced home care places, making notes and times for appointments until he reached his mental limit. Being the town manager gave him insights and knowledge, but the selection had consequences. He feared his selection of one facility over another would be seen as an endorsement by the town manager. All he cared about was his father's comfort. He wouldn't show any favoritism. Paul removed his glasses, let the tip tangle in his hands. He could hear his father's old warning: *As soon as cynicism enters your thoughts, you have lost your power as a leader.* Best to wash up before dinner and prepare to truly meet their guest.

Sealy wound her way down to the gazebo. Her walk was more of a waddle than a stroll, weighed down with painting supplies, the awkward-sized canvas, and a plate of her prized cookies. She made a mental note to carry less, to remember her physical size. She scanned the gardens for the patriarch of Hawk House. With the sun lowering its mast, Richard would be out, if only to look at the shades of color, the change in the sky. That was, unless he was too ill.

Sure enough, Sealy spotted Richard on the ridge above. After depositing her painting paraphernalia, she hiked up a well-worn path to his viewing point. "Richard, hello, it's me, Sealy."

Without turning, Richard replied, "Yes, I knew it was you. The girls would be laughing, and Danny and my son don't get out much to enjoy the view. Who else could it be? Come sit with an old man."

Sealy plopped down on the wooden bench and took a catch-up breath. "I'm out of shape. It's a workout getting to this spot from your outdoor art studio."

"You're still young, I doubt this wore you out. Before I got sick, I used to paint at the gazebo and then have lunch here. Now, when I'm up to it, I take all morning to walk from the house. Exercise is a luxury. I come to see the sun's reflection and the clouds as they change forms—the lighting affects the colors on the water, the shade of the trees. Hmm, I smell something with almonds. Young lady, what do have in that backpack of yours?"

"A treat I baked. Thought you'd like some."

Richard's eyes moistened; his dry lips parted with a smile. "I remember those cookies from another time. Did your mother give you that recipe?"

This was her moment to find out more about her mother and the picture in the Hawk House. Sealy's throat seized. "I've always made them, a hand-me-down recipe." And in a whisper, she added, "Did you know my mother?"

A gentle breeze came off the water, seemed to encircle her question. Richard stared out at the sun sparkles. He finished one cookie and then a second. "I don't eat much anymore. My system doesn't digest well, and I've lost my taste buds. But I can smell these cookies, taste the honey and nuts. They triggered a memory of deliciousness. Best food I've eaten in years."

Sealy offered Richard another cookie, but he shook his head no. She wrapped them up. "These are for later. When my mother was ill, she said the same thing. She claimed she devoured memories, which sustained her."

"That sounds like Mo." Richard lowered his voice as his hand covered his heart. "Was her death painful?"

She couldn't tell if Richard was hiding something. He ignored her direct questions and answered with more questions: "Very few people called my mom Mo. Only my grandmother when she was angry. You must have been a good friend."

"I wouldn't have wanted her to be in pain. My pains get worse daily. I'm tired. Can you walk with me back to the house? No one will touch your painting supplies."

"Have you been watching me? You seem to know everything about my whereabouts.

"Well, yes, I have kept an eye on you. I want to make sure you feel at home. Have you taken the path down to the shoreline? It's a rugged walk even if you're in shape. Maybe my son can take you. He's back from his conferences on the receding coastline. That always puts him in a bad mood. I'm sure you can convince him to take you down. Besides, it's a little dangerous if you don't know where you're going."

They walked slowly. Sealy held her arm out for support, but Richard leaned on her shoulder to keep his balance. Halfway up to the house, he stumbled and motioned to another bench. Before Richard sat down, Sealy noticed a plaque on the back of the seat: *To my first love, Lorraine.* Relieved and disappointed, Sealy wondered if the other benches had markers. She didn't dare ask if her mother was memorialized as well.

After a few minutes, Richard motioned her to get up. "I'm okay now." He rose slowly, stared at the house as if counting the steps needed to make it back.

Worried, Sealy measured the distance with her realtor eyes, judging the pavers and the rails. She tried to distract her concern. "You made the gardens beautiful. Do you have a secret? Maybe ground bones?"

"You've been talking to the butcher. Yes and no. I only use the leftover grounds for the garden. The other use is my secret formula." His voice went down to a whisper, his eyes smiling sadly. "My son helped perfect it. If you promise to keep it in the family, I'll tell you. I grind what the butcher gives me into dust and mix it in my oil paints. Alchemy of sorts, to purify the colors. If I have time, I can show you."

Richard knew he was dying. Sealy felt his acceptance and defiance wrapped simply in the truth. She knew better than to contradict or to pretend it wasn't true. Her mother had been just as matter of fact.

Before they parted, Sealy stood on her tippy-toes to plant a kiss on his forehead. "I look forward to trying your secret formula on my next painting."

After they parted, Sealy rushed to catch the last of the sunlight to paint. Already lower in the sky, the sun had lost its brilliance. No sparkle off the water, shade darkening the woods. She sensed the same was true for Richard. Lost in thought, Sealy focused her vision on one spot along the coast, a set of trees in the foreground. If she painted the same scene at different hours, she might get a glimpse of its diurnal patterns.

When she returned to her room, she found a letter from her sister.

I tried calling you, but your damn cell phone won't work. Call me when you can. I found a stack of letters in Mom's hat box. They are all signed, Yours, R. Let me know what is going on and if you need me.

Love,

Jeannie

By the time Paul arrived at the dinner table, Danny and the kids had already filled their plates. The noise level had reached a fever pitch, with Roxie telling Reese that the birds and the bees had to learn grammar. Danny looked over to him for help.

Paul chuckled as he watched his son squirm. "Danny, I'm sure you can explain grammar to the girls."

Danny's face turned the color of the beet soup that sat untouched as they waited for Sealy to arrive. "Reese, isn't it your turn to say the dinner blessing?"

"We have to wait. Tonight is special. Grandpa is here and I want Sealy here too."

Paul reached over to squeeze Reese's hand. "Shh, if you lower your voice and count to five, I bet she'll walk in." He closed his eyes and counted softly. Like magic it worked. Sealy entered a silent room, all eyes upon her.

"How did you do that, Grandpa?"

Sealy sat down facing Paul and next to Roxie. "Do what?"

Reese bounced in her seat. "He made you appear just when Daddy was going to explain about birds and bees and grammar. I don't think he knows the answer."

Paul noted Sealy's serious face relax; a smile replaced the lines of worry. He took a chance and included her in the discussion. "Perhaps you could shed light on the subject, as it seems that the men at table haven't a clue."

"Mm, let's see. Bees and birds, start with the letter…"

"*B*," the girls chimed in.

"Yes, and if you add two *e*'s and put a *t* on the end, you get the word *beet*, just like what is in our soup. Or if you change an *e* to an *s*, you get the word *best*. No, I don't think that is right either. What do birds and bees both do?"

The girls giggled. "They fly."

"Yes, and they sing. I think we can leave it at that today. Just know that when the birds and the bees sing, they fly."

Paul couldn't help himself. He laughed so hard he almost choked on a piece of bread. "Why didn't I think of that?"

As the meal progressed, Danny and the kids bantered on. Paul watched as Sealy moved her food around her plate but ate nothing. Worry lines reappeared along her brow. He wondered at the change. She'd seemed so settled, relaxed in the kitchen.

He approached her after dinner. "You impressed me with your alphabet grammar lesson. Where did you learn to twist words like that?" He couldn't imagine what had happened in the last few hours to upset her. "You seem distracted. We can talk another time."

Sealy placed her hand on his wrist. "No, I mean, yes. I'm distracted but the answer is simple. My mother was a stickler for words, maybe it was because she worked for a lawyer. Anyway, I play games with words all the time. They have so many meanings, just like colors when I paint. They are layered."

Paul walked with her through the living room to the back porch. He wasn't ready to let Sealy leave. It had been so long since a woman had been at their table. She was their first guest at Danny's new venture. But it was more than that. Sealy seemed to fit. "Do you have time to sit with me for a few minutes? I don't want to impose on your time."

"I have lots of time. Nowhere to go but up to my room."

Her response circled the issue, just like her finger curled her hair. Paul pulled two lounge chairs to face the setting sun. "Well, I don't have anywhere to go at this moment either."

Sealy laughed. "Do I sound that bad?"

Paul grinned. "Just a little pathetic. But I get that. Something is bothering you. Do you want to talk about it?"

"I'm not sure. I'd rather hear about your work as town manager and about your project with Danny to make this a B&B."

Paul appreciated Sealy's frankness. "What do you want to know? The job of town manager is boring to most people. Danny can tell you about the B&B."

"If I wanted to hear about the B&B from Danny, I would ask him. If I wanted to be bored, I could read a newspaper."

Paul swallowed. "You aren't making this easy. I guess I usually leave my job at the office. To use your words, I'm not sure if I want to talk about the B&B's future. A new business is complicated, and this is my time to relax."

Sealy nodded. "Well, we agree on that. My mother always stuck to the facts. She figured that anything beyond that would get her in trouble. She left me with all her troubles, unfinished business."

Paul stared up at the stars. "Is that why you wanted to get away, come here?"

"I guess so. And you, why don't you want to talk about the B&B?"

"This house, our livelihood, our history in the town, weighs on me. I want my father to see his legacy go on. I want my son to be happy."

"Are you happy?"

Paul laughed. "Are you breaking your mother's rules—seeking facts or wanting to hear feelings?"

Sealy blushed. "Did I say I was like my mother? We always disagreed. I often wondered if she was really my mom. But as I grew older, her habits have seeped in. I'll rephrase my questions. Do you want to keep the legacy going?"

"I love this town. I've devoted my whole life to it. I love our home and worry that the town and my life will wash away. Oops. Here I go, talking about work issues."

"You mean, the shores and sand vanishing because of climate change? That's a heavy load to carry."

"Well, I'm not alone in this. The entire coast is facing stronger storms, more hurricanes, and shifts in the climate. My job isn't to save the world but to find options for our town."

"Do you ever talk about this with your father? He was the town manager here as well."

Paul knew he was lying to himself about the burden. He didn't have a confidante to bounce ideas off. He missed his father's clear head. His father, like so many of the old-timers in the town, acted like an innocent in terms of the land, greedy for what was. "My dad is so ill. All he wants is nostalgia, to return to life how it used to be. He talks incessantly of raising me, of keeping the wine distribution alive, of the beautiful gardens, painting, and of old loves."

Sealy gasped and turned her head.

"Sorry, I didn't mean to pour out private stuff. I should take your mother's advice. Stick to the facts."

"That's okay. I asked. Let's call it a night."

"Yes. But before you head upstairs, my father mentioned that you would like to walk along the path down to the shoreline. If the weather is good on the weekend, I can find time."

"I look forward to it. Good night."

Sleep eluded Sealy. She tossed and turned thinking about Jeannie's letter. She dreamed of the alphabet, birds and bees, and *u*'s and *r*'s flying, and felt a stinging sensation. She woke to find a spider in her bed and her arm throbbing from its bite. Reality. She stripped her bed down and headed to the shower.

The drone of steaming water, the creaking pipes, the cleansing actions helped wash speculation down the drain. Sealy knew the only cure to worry was action. Without it she fixated. After dressing she wrote a list: *call Jeannie, find out about the letter, talk more with Richard, research Mother's family.*

A silly list. She should have asked her mother more questions. She should have wondered about her father's death. She should have paid attention. Was it her fault for not asking, for trying to be perfect and fit into the ways of her family?

Sealy stared in the mirror. Her features were nothing like her mother's and nothing like anyone in the Morris family. The brush tugged at knots at the base of her hairline where she had failed to apply the cream rinse. Her thick hair had always been a problem. Memories of her mother's long nails picking through the tangles, the tears, and the sighs of frustration had left an imprint of distinction. *What am I to do with your hair? You look like a ragdoll.*

Over time Sealy learned to work with the curls. The longer it grew, the softer it became as the curls unfurled to waves. Years later, work colleagues complimented her on the weaving of gray through her hair as if she had gone to the beauty parlor. Jeannie's hair was the same as her mother's, light brown, straight with no bounce. Even as Sealy's hair tamed itself throughout the years, her family still joked that she was their clown.

Danny and the girls were quiet on the ride into town. Roxie and Reese busied themselves putting the last touches to their homework. Sealy, lost in thought, half listened to Danny's whispered goodbyes to the kids as he dropped them off at school.

As they arrived downtown, he broke the silence. "Thanks for saving me last night. We usually do okay, but with my wife gone all these years and no other women around I felt awkward. Do you think they are ready for 'the talk'?"

Confused, Sealy searched her brain for what he could mean. "Oh, I'm not the expert. I only have myself and my sister to compare the girls to. I would check out what the school offers. If Roxie has a sex-ed class, you better tell the girls what you want them to hear. Validate what they know. Go slow."

"Got it. If you are ready to come back at lunchtime, I'll be heading that way."

"Thanks, but I have some research to do. I know where to find you."

Sealy headed to the OQT Inn, the oldest pub in town, hoping she could use their landline and pay for the call. The outside brick showed age, but the new awning and sign drew her in. The architect and artist captured a bygone era with a rendition of an old-fashioned lady clad in a drawstring dress that bellowed out from the waist, a gentleman in a top hat, suit with the traditional black-and-white spats, alongside a nostalgic scene of lobster fishermen pulling in their haul. She liked the display, a brilliant feat in marketing as there was something for everyone.

The woman at the lobby counter smiled. "What can I help you with?"

"I'm staying at the Morrises' house but don't want to tie up their phone as my cell phone doesn't work there. Spotty reception. Is there a way for me to use the inn's phone and pay?"

The woman seemed enthused. "You're welcome to use the phone. First call will be free. Anyone staying with the Morrises has my approval. That family is great. If you are calling long distance, I can start a bill for you."

Once again, the magic name of Morris opened doors. She felt like a fraud taking advantage of small-town hospitality. "That's so kind of you, Eloise. I don't hear that name often."

"It's on my name tag, but no one really calls me that for long. You can call me Elly. And you are?"

"Sealy Morris."

Elly's eyes widened and her jaw dropped. "Your mom wouldn't by chance be Mary, would she?"

Elly's reaction unnerved her. Her mother must have made an impression to be so well remembered after all these years. She answered in her most confident voice, "Yes, why do you ask?"

"Oh, I just thought so. If you go into the next room down the hall, there's a phone. Just dial 1 and the area code. No need to worry about the bill this time, even if it is long distance."

Sealy wondered about Elly's change of heart with billing her. She made a mental note to circle back to the front desk on her way out. Elly looked to be about her mother's age, by the way she adorned her dress with layers of necklaces over a pinned scarf. Her full face of makeup and the pearl earrings marked another holdover from the past generation.

Danny's quip about learning the town's history outside of her library research had been right. Photos along the hallway depicted events from the town's inception. They went from black and white to full color by the time Sealy arrived at the next room. And there it was, a photo of her mother with Richard at a cocktail reception. The same one-piece jumpsuit, the same pearls worn in the photo burning in Sealy's pocket. A caption below the photo marked the celebration—the grand opening of the inn and the inauguration of the new town manager.

Sealy sat down on an unoccupied red velvet sofa opposite the photo gallery to collect her thoughts. Elly had sent her to the meeting room for local businesses. Low walls separated the space into private areas; with each section came four comfortable chairs, a small table, a phone, and power outlets. Murmurs of hushed conversations filled the room.

Sealy glanced up to study the photo. Her mother's smile radiated just as it always had when her mother held court at their house. Her elegance and control hadn't wavered over the years. Sealy had had to learn the art, but for her mother it was all instinct. She felt her mother's eyes peering down on her as if to send a message. *Find your place, rule over it with love.* Had her mother found her place here, or with her family?

Sealy dialed her sister's number. The phone only rang once before Jeannie picked up.

"Hello, Jeannie, it's me, Sealy."

"I've been worried sick. You haven't called in a month. Did you get my letter?"

"My cell phone doesn't get reception at the B&B, and yes, I got your letter, that's why I'm calling." Sealy heard her sister's quick breaths, her sniffles. "You're crying. Gut it out. I'm fine. If you're not careful, you'll trigger your asthma."

"It's just that I need you. I know you think this is just about you, but Mary was my mom too. I need to know what is going on."

No matter what she said, Sealy worried that Jeannie would take it the wrong way. All these years when she'd been searching for her place in the family, Jeannie had been the star. Now her light seemed to be dimming. "What we have together is ours. Just because there's new information about Mom doesn't mean we aren't connected. I've been trying to come to peace with feeling left out for years. Damn it, do I have to give you the lecture, the one we hated when Mom would rant about expectations and gratitude?"

Jeannie laughed. "I think you got that lecture each time you tried to take an art class and didn't want to study. I was luckier because I could memorize things. I only remember the blow-up when I wanted to take a class trip that would have me gone for a week. I backed down. You were the fighter."

"Tell me about the letters."

"They all start out, 'My dearest Mo.' Mostly the letters talk about sending money and checking in on the situation. I can't piece together what the situation is. They all end with 'give my love to the family, especially little Sealy. Yours, R.' I don't know what to think, but to be honest, I'm a little jealous."

"Jealous of me? You've got to be kidding. When was the last letter?"

"Let me check. From what I can tell, it was close to forty years ago."

Sealy mentally calculated her own age. "I was just turning twenty-one. I'm guessing, but did the letters start sixty years ago?"

"Not exactly, but close. What do you think it means?"

"That Mom had a secret, and I was part of it. Beyond that I don't know. Do you remember anything? You were little, but maybe this will jog your memory. I don't understand where Dad was in all this."

"Stop pushing so hard. I want our life to remain how it was. Tell me what you've been up to for the last month."

Sealy felt the familiar closing of doors, the abrupt change of topics. Jeannie didn't like her boat rocked. Neither did she, but her world had always felt rocky. If the answers weren't in the letters or her sister's memory, then they had to be here in Maine with the two town managers.

To keep the peace, Sealy described the town's beauty, Danny and the girls, the bed-and-breakfast, Richard's illness, and that she was painting again. Drained, she said her goodbyes. "Got to go, don't worry."

"Do you want these letters? I'd rather you had them."

"Okay, maybe I can find out something you didn't see. Could you also send me my special technique brushes and my sketch pad, the one marked *Landscape*, and my stack of packing supports for mailing?"

"I guess this means you'll be there awhile. I miss you."

"It was right that I came. You know that. Love you." As she hung up, a sense of guilt washed over her. She hadn't mentioned her mother's photo on the inn wall or anything about Richard's son.

Paul finished his meeting with the local shoreline committees and the federal EPA. They'd been gathering at the OQT Inn for the last six months, and still the squabbles continued. Emotionally drained, he closed his computer, shook hands with each group participant, and prepared himself for interviewing caregivers for his father. From the corner of his eye, he recognized Sealy in the main section of the meeting room. Her hands were moving fast as she talked on the phone.

He held back until she'd hung up.

"Sealy, what a surprise to see you here at the inn. Is everything okay? You seemed agitated when you were talking on the phone."

Her reaction wasn't what he expected. She placed her hand over her heart and stared at the photo on the wall.

He followed her eyes, trying to figure out what she saw. "You look like you've seen a ghost."

"In a way I have. It's that mural. What do you know about the photos?"

Paul felt like Sealy asked the question to bait him. He shrugged. "Not too much, as I was just a baby when it was taken. Why the interest?"

"Just curious. I recognize your father. Do you recognize anyone else?"

He felt a shift in Sealy's tone. "I barely know you, but one thing is clear: you could never play poker. You held your heart when you were looking at the photo. Who do you recognize?"

Sealy's smile warmed Paul's heart. He had judged correctly.

"I'm that transparent? I hope that's a compliment. In the real estate business, when one of my clients gets an emotional reaction to a listing, I make sure the owners aren't there. Everyone has their tells."

"I'm sure you are a great realtor. I can see you'd make a great politician with your redirection."

Sealy's face reddened. "I'd rather paint. I recognize the lady who is smiling. Do you know her?"

Paul shook his head. "No, please tell me. She's beautiful and lights up the room."

"That's my mother, Mary."

Paul kept his face neutral, but he felt a chill run through him that froze his heart. His father's ramblings about a lost love were real. "I didn't expect you to say that. She is lovely. I knew your mother had visited here. It seems to be an ongoing topic of conversation between my father and Danny."

"And not you?"

Paul paused. "I'm more concerned about the present. My father needs an in-house nurse. His cancer has advanced. Danny and I can't do it all. He's obsessed with the past. I can only deal with the logistics of his comfort."

"That makes sense. I guess it really depends on your father. He seems worried but not about his physical self."

Paul looked at his watch. His interviews were about to start. "Listen, I'm going to interview some caregivers. Do you want to sit in?"

Still staring at the mural, Sealy's breath deepened. Paul sensed her unease. He must have crossed some line of familiarity.

"I shouldn't ask that of you. You're a guest. Forget I said anything."

"No, really, I have time. I only came into town to talk with my sister, Jeannie. She worries when we haven't spoken in a while. I've been remiss in my communications because I don't get cell reception at the Hawk House."

"I apologize. It's on my list for the community. The whole town needs better access to the internet. Out our way, we need more towers or an underground line. Danny has been talking with a provider, but it's too expensive to do just for us."

"I'm not complaining, just explaining. I'm fine without the distraction. It's a good opportunity to paint. I asked Jeannie to send me some of my specialty paintbrushes."

"So you'll be staying longer?"

"Yes, I mean, at least for the full three months I booked."

Paul's eyes lit up. "Are you sure I'm not imposing on your time? I do need help with these interviews."

"I can stay for a bit, if you think it will help you choose the right person. I couldn't afford a caregiver for my mother. Jeannie and I spelled each other."

"Is Jeannie older or younger than you?"

"She's a few years older."

Paul stored that information away with the new knowledge of Sealy's mother, as well as a strange sense that he had met Sealy before.

The day had disappeared, and Sealy found herself at odds as she left the inn. She felt the pathways in her brain folding and unfolding her mother's past. If she left her mother's past alone, her own life seemed flat. If she pursued her mother's relationship to the Hawk House, the flatness would take form—like an origami swan. She wanted to know, yet she feared the future. The consequences would be more permanent than a paper creation.

Paul had asked her to stay for lunch after the four interviews. For the most part they talked about each contender's character and personality, trying to match it with Richard's needs and demeanor.

As she finished her salad, Paul had inquired about her own life. Sealy held back, just like she had held back from telling her sister about Paul. Separate views of herself seemed safer. But Paul was able to relax her guard. She told him of her love for art, her struggles in school, and how she found her way into real estate— a compromise in her mother's view, not entirely professional enough for her liking but respectable.

Sealy bristled at his question about significant others. Her answer, no, had come off defensive until she looked up into his eyes. His curiosity and care had made it simple. She added to her reply that she wasn't currently in a relationship and was thankful when he didn't probe. He told her that his wife had died in childbirth, just like his mother had.

The afternoon light reminded her of walking out of a movie theater, when the transition from the character's world to one's own life created a jolt. Sealy felt like she was playing a part in a life she might have lived.

The streets were quiet with the lull between lunch goers and employees ready to leave work. She laughed knowing that rush hour here meant you had to wait for five cars to pass before you crossed the street. Sealy thought of her mother sauntering down these same streets half a century ago. Who knew her besides Paul's father and the woman, Elly, at the inn registration?

Sealy knew where to find answers but resisted taking advantage of a dying man's memory. Paul had already given her a warning. He preferred not to encourage his father's obsession with her mother. She wondered if it was a rewriting of the past Paul worried about or the fixation with a woman long gone. The double injustice of Paul's wife's death in childbirth like his mother's pained her. She had come here looking for clarity about her upbringing, not someone else's. She could almost hear her mother's voice: *Sealy, why do you care that you are different, why would you want to be the same as Jeannie or me? It is you I love.*

Maybe she should leave well enough alone. But her mother wouldn't have left the photos or the letters if she didn't want them discovered. Mary, the former legal assistant, never let anything dangle.

Sealy did an about-face and returned to the OQT Inn. She found Elly behind the registration desk checking in a long line of guests. When her turn finally arrived, Sealy had second thoughts on asking about her mother. "Sorry to bother you again, is this a good time to talk?"

Elly appeared frazzled. Her face had transformed since early this morning. Her makeup couldn't hide the worry lines on her forehead or her lips that formed a solid line, and she answered in a monotone, "What can I do for you, Ms. Morris?

"Nothing really, I was curious about how you knew my mother. She never talked about her life."

The worry lines on Elly's forehead contracted as she moved in closer and lowered her voice. "That's a shame, she was so well liked here. Mary used to visit with Richard's brother, Barry, her husband. I think she brought you here a few times. That was a long time ago."

Sealy repeated Elly's comment in her head until the words made sense. Barry Morris, her father, was Richard Morris's brother. Another group of guests formed behind Sealy. Sealy's voice caught in her throat. "Thanks. Um, maybe we can talk later. You're busy today. I'll let you help the others."

Elly nodded. "A group of developers are here vying for our pristine town's attention. Let's hope that the young Morris can hold them off."

Sealy rushed to catch Danny's last trip back to the Hawk House.

Paul returned home later than he anticipated. Danny and the girls had already turned in. He thought he might find Sealy in the living room reading, but the only light on was in the kitchen. He discovered his dinner wrapped in aluminum foil, with a note from Roxie and Reese:

Dear Grandpa,

The spaghetti is green today. Dad says it came from Mars, but we don't believe him. Sealy says it has pesto on it, her mom's recipe. Love you more than the rings around Saturn. We are studying that in school.

He warmed his plate in the microwave, poured himself a glass of wine, and carried his dinner upstairs to visit with his father.

Paul found Richard still dressed in his ritual khaki pants and polo shirt, sitting at his desk. "Dad, you're busy. What are you doing?"

"Just reminiscing. I'll make space for you to eat. Late day at work?"

Paul didn't want to talk about the developers, the shoreline, or any of the town issues. After talking with Sealy, he was more curious about what he hadn't seen all his life. "Yes, one of those crazy days when it is best left in the office. I'd rather hear about you."

Richard looked up with a smile. "I remember saying that same thing to you when I came home late and you were doing your homework. We've changed places. I'm not envious. Should I make you probe by asking me questions like I used to do to you? All you wanted to do then was paint. Whatever happened to that urge?"

Paul laughed. "You're doing it again. Leading me down your path of inquiry. Tell me about my mother. You don't talk about her."

Richard reached for Paul's glass of wine. "Your mom liked to drink wine. She was studious, sweet, a great cook, and my best friend. What else do you want to know?"

Paul gauged his next question with care. "You and Danny have been compiling your memories. I haven't paid too much attention, but now I realize there was another woman in your life. You said as much to Danny."

"Son, that's not a question. Be direct. You know I dated a little while you were growing up. Nothing ever came of it. You should try it sometime. Or you'll be an old man like me and never find that special woman."

For some reason Paul thought of Sealy and he blushed. "I was at the inn this morning, meeting with the shoreline committees. Sealy was there using the landline. She noticed the photographs on the wall. I'd never paid attention to them before. She recognized her mother standing next to you."

Richard took another drink from Paul's wine. "And your question is?"

Paul swirled a forkful of spaghetti on his plate. "Can you explain this? Sealy came here searching for clues about her past. You told Danny that you'd be waiting for Sealy to appear. What don't I know?"

After another sip of Paul's wine, his father's face looked pained. Not angry or surprised, but a darkness appeared in his eyes. "Sealy's mother was married to my brother. She was a good friend to your mother."

Nothing could have prepared him for his father's declaration. Paul's heart sank like a boat taking on water. Confused, he tried to make sense of what he knew. "Dad, I haven't heard you talk about your brother. For some reason I thought he died when you were a kid. What happened to him?"

Richard moved away from the desk and knocked over the wineglass. The neat piles of his sketches turned a pale shade of crimson.

Paul realized he'd hit a nerve and instantly regretted the question. "I'll clean that up. Here, hold on to my arm and I can bring you over to your bed."

Richard looked confused, weak; the apparent normalcy of the visit dissolved. Paul mopped up the wine. When he shuffled the papers to dry them out, his father barked, "Don't touch. Leave me alone."

Paul counted until he heard his father's breath slow down. The doctors had warned him that as the cancer progressed, his father would appear normal and then his brain could switch at any time. They weren't sure if it was a form of dementia, toxicity, or side effects from medications. *Let him find his balance; let him find his way back.*

Sure enough, Richard regained his composure and fiddled with an old cigar box. "Paul, my brother died young. But old enough to make a mess of his life. I've tried to make amends. The dark stain on our name remains. Here, maybe you can make it right."

Concerned, Paul took the cigar box from his father. "Dad, why are you upset? Your brother is long gone. If anything, you found his daughter. I guess this means I have a cousin?" Even as Paul said this out loud, he felt his heart sinking further into his stomach. "Does Sealy know?"

Richard shrugged. "She's here, but I don't think Mary ever told her. It's complicated."

Paul brought his father his pajamas, helped get him settled. "Let's talk tomorrow. I interviewed some people to help out when I have to travel or Danny is too busy with the kids."

"I don't like this part of getting old. I still have so much to do."

Sealy carried her canvas and supplies with care up through the gardens and in through the back door. She'd taken to a more con-templative lifestyle, exertion with physical tasks and concentration on seeing within.

Even though Sealy spent most of her time at the gazebo, she painted scenes from her memory. Her latest series included small canvases of the town hot spots—the ice cream parlor inside the grocery store, the inn, and one of the library buildings. She no longer painted the views of the horizon from the gazebo. They seemed distant and stalled, stuck on pause. Since finding out that her father was Richard's brother, Sealy's sense of nature's cycles appeared trivial.

Absorbed in her thoughts, Sealy hastily mounted the stairs to her room. She looked up to see Paul racing down the stairs. They collided. Paul grabbed her just before she fell.

"So sorry, I didn't see you coming down."

"No, I was in a rush, hungry and preoccupied."

It had been a few days since Sealy had seen Paul. He looked rumpled, a little wild with his hair uncombed.

"My thoughts exactly. I missed dinner again. I was trying to get upstairs to change and sneak back into the kitchen. Danny leaves me something to eat if I fail to show up at dinnertime."

"Maybe we can meet in the kitchen and eat together? Danny makes sure to leave me something to eat too. He's a good son." Paul didn't wait for an answer as he picked up Sealy's paintings. "These are good. You've captured something that isn't there in the real. I mean, the ice cream parlor doesn't look like that now. I went there when I was a kid. That's how I remember it."

Sealy felt chills crawl up her arms, a touch from the past. She avoided Paul's comment and his eyes. "I'll be down after I change and put these away."

She showered quickly, as the hot water had run out. Dressed in a green jumpsuit, she pulled her hair up in a bun and gave the room a quick review. She had hoped that Danny had left her mail, but the bed and dresser were empty.

Sealy smelled the food from the hallway, then watched as Paul dished out dinner.

"Smells good," she said. "What did Danny cook tonight? Smells like my mom's chicken potpie."

Paul looked up. "Wow, that was quick. You look better. I mean, you look more relaxed. Never mind, let's sit down. I don't think Danny cooked tonight. But you guessed correctly, it is chicken potpie. I hired a cook and a house cleaner to help with the chores. The cook is a little green with experience, so I showed her my father's recipe collection. You were right, my dad needs us to care for him, and someone else can do the rest. Besides, a wise woman told me we must listen to our parents before it's too late. Thank you for reminding me of that."

Sealy raised her wineglass. "Yes, a toast to listening and sharing the past. Thank you for bumping into me on the stairs. It seems like forever ago that we had lunch."

They talked about the changing weather, the fickleness of coastal living. How storms rose quickly, lingered, and circled back. Eventually Sealy found an opening to say what was on her mind. "I went back to the inn the other day and spoke with an older employee. She knew my mother and told me my mother was married to your father's brother, Barry. Did you know?"

Paul put his fork down and looked into her eyes. She noticed a tear form in the corner of his eyes. "To tell you the truth, I only just found out that same night when I spoke with my father. I asked him about Mary, your mother. He explained that she was my mother's best friend and Barry's wife."

Sealy shrunk at the sadness in Paul's voice. She bent her head and fiddled with the food on her plate, making the mashed potatoes into a field with fork-furrowed rows and peas lined up in the grooves. "My dad died when I was little. I didn't know he had a family. I still don't know anything about him."

"I'm sorry. I don't understand Richard's or your mother's reluctance to share knowledge of our families. I never met your father. Did your mother ever comment about my dad?"

Sealy tried to smile, but instead she pushed the peas and potatoes together and then shoved her plate away defiantly. "Don't you remember our visits here? Was that memory lost too?"

Paul reached over to Sealy's rejected dish and realigned the potatoes and peas. He added strips of carrots along the sides. "No need to be angry with me. I'm trying to draw the same picture. We need to support one another."

"Is that why you added the carrots?"

"They belong there, don't they? A farmer always plants peas and carrots. But seriously, we have to open this up. My dad gave me a box of photos, drawings, and papers last night. He told me to make amends."

Sealy took a deep breath. "Well, I have a photo in my pocket that shows my mother at your house with Richard. Some of the artwork she gave me came from here. I found it ten years after she died."

"So that is why my father said you suspected something. I guess we begin with what we have."

Sealy sipped the last of her wine. "Can't you just ask Richard? I mean, he's still alive."

"I'll try, but he wants something from you. He thought your mother had told you about our family."

Sealy thought about her mother and then Jeannie. Jeannie needed to know; she was part of this story too. "I have to talk with my sister. She never wondered about anything, thinks I'm on a wild-goose chase because of the photo. I was the one who sensed something different with my relationship with my parents."

Paul cleared their plates and poured them more wine. "We can't figure this out tonight. I'll clean the dishes if you promise you won't keep avoiding me."

"You noticed, didn't you? I changed my schedule, getting up early to paint, missing meals with the kids. I'm too connected already, and I feel like an intruder."

"I haven't slept since my father told me. I'm confused. I didn't know that you already belonged."

Sealy nodded. "Yes—that's a conundrum. Time for bed. Good night."

"Oh, before you go, I found your mail on the kitchen counter. A big box."

"Thanks, Jeannie promised to send me my paintbrushes and stuff." Sealy grabbed the box and rushed upstairs, but not quick enough to escape Paul's eyes.

Paul left Sealy and headed to his office. The cigar box his father had given him sat isolated on his bookshelf. Half-opened, with papers spilling out, the box greeted Paul with a magnetic pull. Richard wanted a resolution, but Paul worried at what he'd find. Life had been simpler when he taught school. He created lesson plans and mental stimulation. He'd given that up when he followed in his father's footsteps, graduating from teaching young minds to stewarding a community.

Curiosity overpowered his reluctance. Paul turned on his desk lamp and sifted through the contents. His father had been meticulous in all matters of business. The papers, yellowed with age, had been folded so many times that Paul feared they'd disintegrate in his hand. Many of the pieces were payment receipts, with Richard's and his mother's signatures. Some were from the Morris Winery, ledgers of accounts receivable with red marks crossed off. The most curious findings were newspaper articles about his uncle. At the bottom of the stash, he found a photo of a baby girl with dark hair. *Sealy?*

He shook his head and turned off the lights. Mounting the stairs, he thought of the pile of issues facing him at work. Perhaps that would be easier than unraveling the past.

Sealy had risen late and rushed to catch a ride into town with Danny. He was waiting in the driveway for her.

"Here comes the night owl. If I didn't know better, I'd say you were out drinking."

"You've got to be joking." Sealy got into the cab and checked the mirror. "Oh, you mean my sunglasses. I was up late reading. Thanks for waiting. Can you drop me off at the library?"

"Sure—just remember that on Saturdays the library closes by noon. We have a guest that I'm picking up. Seems that the inn is full, with a wedding and two conventions."

"That was nice of the inn to send a customer your way. Does that change my status?" Sealy waited a few minutes. Maybe he hadn't heard her question. "Danny, will you need my help?"

He answered with an edge in his voice, "You've been here one month and now you want to take over?"

"Oh, no. You misunderstood me."

Sealy expected a chuckle to indicate he'd been kidding, but instead she felt that sour mood again. The one that told her to tread lightly. She stared out the window to calm herself and refocus. When they were out of the trees, the view of the coastal waters and the sky startled her. A mixture of sun and storm with dark shades of black over blue, the scene was both ominous and dramatic with a light piercing through the clouds.

"Danny, can you stop for a minute? I'd like to take a photo, maybe capture this scene later in one of my paintings."

"Best hurry, as the cloud formation means a downpour. If it gets too bad, I'll pick my clients up early and head home."

The rain caught Sealy on her way back to the car. The dark clouds let loose droplets that stung her skin. By the time she returned, she was drenched. Danny handed her a towel and continued driving.

"Thanks." She dared not say more as the rain's intensity shrunk visibility and made for a slick drive.

Danny broke the silence as he let her out in front of the library. "You won't be needing the sunglasses for the rest of the day. Once the gray clouds of rain settle in, it will feel like nighttime. I'd go to the general store and buy an umbrella if I were you."

Still annoyed by his earlier inference of her taking over, Sealy felt a sarcastic comment rising from within. It took years of training to turn the words around. She drew her glasses down onto the bridge of her nose. "Good idea. Thanks for the tip." Without pause she opened her purse and pulled out a miniature umbrella and held it up. "Let's hope that the sunshine will return soon."

Danny tooted the horn as she turned to leave. "I could use your help back at the house, but promise me that you won't hurt Richard and my father."

Sealy's couldn't hold back her frustration at his comment. "I don't know why you would say that."

"Got to go or I'll be late. I hope you get some rest; it looks like your eyes are still puffy." He smiled. "Maybe you should put your sunglasses on again. Pretend you're a movie star."

Sealy rushed into the library and headed to the bathroom. Overwhelmed by anger, she sat in one of the stalls until she had regained her composure. When she was sure the room was empty, she washed her face, applied cream under her eyes, pinched her cheeks, and put on a smile.

Only one month ago, when she had arrived, Danny had brought her hot chocolate and a cookie as the special guest. What had changed the designation? Had Richard or Paul said something to make Danny wary of her? She'd traveled this far to find out about her mother, never thinking about her father.

She tackled the microfiche section with old newspaper articles. Even though she had read and reread her mother's letters, she had found nothing to explain the exchanges between Richard and her mother other than deep caring. Most of it seemed to be in code. Dated exactly one month apart, the letters never mentioned her father or her sister. Sealy knew so little about her father. She typed in *Barry Morris* and began reading.

Barry Morris finally settles down to marry an outsider.

Barry Morris is arrested for a DUI.

Barry Morris takes over the Morris Winery distribution.

Barry Morris is implicated in a fraud scheme.

Richard Morris states that his brother has been ill and is taking a permanent leave of absence…

Sealy visualized her mother with her father together, living in Maine, running the winery, and then what—banishment? As far as Sealy knew, her family had always been on the Pacific Coast. Her mother's mother was a fixture, living with them. Sealy had always thought her grandmother was there to save money. She could hear her grandmother's voice: *You must make things work, no one needs a person who gives up. Failure isn't a choice.* The two often were at odds. Her mom's intense stare at the end of a workday, when her grandmother had left a long list of necessary chores to do because her father was off on a business trip. When her father was gone permanently, the bickering had stopped.

Another article caught Sealy's eye: "Richard Morris announces his bid to be the next town manager." *This is a hard decision, but one I take seriously. My heart is with this town, keeping it healthy for all. We must protect this pristine area...* According to the date, it was seven years after his brother left. That would mean her father was long gone, and her mother would have no reason to be there celebrating at a party. Sealy sat in contemplation, letting her fingers twirl her hair around and around the sequence of events. As she had done with the other articles, Sealy snapped a photo so she could reread the information and mull over the meanings later.

An announcement over the loudspeaker startled Sealy out of her rationalizations: "We are closing now. There are severe storm warnings. Get home as soon as you can."

Danny was right about the weather, Sealy thought as she scrambled to put things away. *What else was he right about?* Hopefully, he hadn't left for home yet. True to form, Danny had parked the blue Oldsmobile in front of the library. A gust of wind caught her umbrella and almost blew her away. Soaked again, she opened the front door to the cab only to find a passenger already seated. Taken aback by the switch in seating, Sealy quickly opened the other door. "Oops, I'll get in the back."

Danny looked at her through the rearview mirror. "Sealy, Mr. Jewels prefers the front seat. Thanks for sitting in the back. I have another passenger to pick up, my dad. He also needs a ride home."

"No worries, I appreciate your fetching me."

At least she hadn't been relegated to the back of the cab because she had lost favor with the Morrises. Sealy listened to Danny explain the layout of the town to Mr. Jewels. He murmured appreciatively but without enthusiasm. She noted Mr. Jewels's hands holding the dashboard as if he could ward off the rain and inconvenience.

Paul stood outside of city hall dressed in jeans, boots, and covered with a rain parka. He shook the rain off before getting in beside Sealy. "Thanks for the ride. Looks like a nor'easter is blowing through. I want to get back to the house to make sure everything is buttoned down."

Mr. Jewels fidgeted; his hand had moved from the dashboard to the door handle as if he wanted to bail. Neither Danny nor Paul noticed. Sealy tapped Paul's shoulder and pointed to the passenger. She whispered, "The new guest is nervous. Shouldn't you or Danny reassure him?"

Paul bent over and whispered back, "I don't think I can. I'm anxious, but not about Danny's driving. I may need to get the truck and come back in case of flooding. You'll be okay at the Hawk House. Our guest might not be okay anywhere with the storm, judging from his hand clasped against the door handle." A sudden gust of wind rattled the cab, and it veered precariously toward the edge of the narrow road. Paul raised his eyebrow and glanced over at Sealy as he bent over the front seat. "Mr. Jewels, before we head up to the bed-and-breakfast, are you okay? You look concerned."

He cleared his throat. "I never travel in bad weather. Not my style. I purposefully tried to be in town. There must be a place closer to town than your bed-and-breakfast. Too many conventions. Maybe you can contact Richard Morris, I've worked with him in the past. I'm sure he can find me a room."

Sealy looked over at Paul for his reaction. If he were concerned, no one would know. He remained calm, contemplating his response.

Before Paul could answer, Danny spoke up. "Mr. Jewels, this is one of our nor'easters blowing hard. The safest place for you is at the Hawk House. In town you might face more problems. We have a generator, food, and comfort. But it's up to you. Maybe one of your colleagues at the inn can share a room with you, if that is your desire."

Mr. Jewels shook his head. "Nope, I want to stay in town."

Sealy felt tension for the first time in months. Danny had done his best with offering an alternative, but she felt Paul's body stiffen. He sat forward on the back seat and tapped Danny on the shoulder. "Danny, why don't you turn around and take Mr. Jewels to the Rockport Lodge? It's just a couple of miles out of our way. The lodge is being renovated, but they may have a room. We all do our best in this town. With less than a thousand people living here, we can't afford to have a guest inconvenienced."

Without a word, Danny headed back to the lodge. Sealy waited in the cab with Paul, who sighed as Danny and the guest left.

"What is going on? You seem tense. Do you know that man?"

Paul shook his head. "At first, I thought Mr. Jewels assumed that in a small town we would know everyone and everything. But he clearly knows my father. He wants something enough to travel in bad weather. This may not physically be one of those *perfect storms,* but the weather is more severe than normal. Best keep Mr. Jewels in town. He's on a mission. I'd rather find out more about him. I don't want him bothering my father. I have enough worries."

Danny came back. "Dad, they'll rent him a room. I'll get his bag and computer. Be back in a flash."

Paul answered, "While you're inside, see if you can find out why he is here. Or ask the receptionist to find out and give you a call."

When Danny returned, drenched from another downpour, he revved the motor and gently pulled out of the driveway.

Sealy held her breath as the visibility was zero. "Good thing you know these roads. It's treacherous."

Paul moved in closer to Sealy. "You can breathe. Danny knows the turns by heart. He's worried about the girls and Richard. We must get back to the Hawk House. I'll think about Mr. Jewels later. He's safe. Whatever he wants can wait."

They rode in silence as the dart like rain pellets splattered the windshield. The constant roar of the wind overcame even the sputtering of the motor. Sealy accepted Paul's hand when they swerved on a curve. She didn't let go and neither did he for the rest of the ride. As they turned down the driveway and saw the house lights on, all three let out a sigh of relief. Danny parked the car, and they ran between gusts of wind and rain to the safety of the Hawk House.

Exhausted, Sealy felt the heaviness of the storm. On their return Danny had scurried around the house to make sure the generator would automatically turn on if the electricity failed and cleared the gutters of debris. He dug some ditches that led downhill in case the soil wouldn't absorb the rain. Paul had fastened down the windows, stored extra water, and kept in contact with the town. Sealy had played with Roxie and Reese, drawing pictures, reading, and building structures, until it was their bedtime.

Her worries about her role in the Morris household vanished in the emergency. When Danny and Paul headed back into town,

Sealy found herself in charge. She carried a tray of food to Richard's separate suite as he no longer tried to join the others.

Even before she knocked, Richard called out, "Smells good. I'm starved."

Sealy hadn't seen Richard since their encounter in the garden. Their talk seemed so long ago. Knowing that he might be her uncle shifted the dynamic. Ignoring her nerves, she opened the door with a flourish. "Good evening, Richard. The cook whipped up a cheese soufflé for you. It still hasn't fallen." Her enthusiasm kept up an act, a cover for what the family knew. As the days closed in on the past and the present stormed forward, the cancer multiplied its destruction. Richard's eyes had dark circles underneath the lashes. He sat at his desk in a terry cloth robe that had seen better days. His skin had yellowed and the loose folds under his chin revealed a loss of significant weight. Based on her mother's decline, Richard would not be with them for long.

"Well, don't just stand there. Bring it over. I won't bite."

"Danny did warn me that you were getting ornery. But I figured your kinder self would appear again." Sealy felt Richard's eyes bore into hers. He needed something from her. She set the tray on the desk, placed a napkin on his chest, and sat down. "Thought I'd drink a glass of wine with you. I need some company after Paul and Danny headed back to town. I've never been in a storm like this."

"Your mother always enjoyed storms. One summer a doozy hit us—blew the roof off the guesthouse she was living in."

"Oh my, was she living there alone?"

Richard took his time to answer. "She lived there with my brother, Barry."

Sealy held her breath as she tried to reconcile this information. Respecting Richard's age, illness, and friendship, she kept her questions to herself.

Richard moved the soufflé around on his plate. He took the smallest of bites and nearly choked. When she went to help, he raised his hand, warning her off. "Your mother told me you had an overly curious streak. But her words were more compassionate. I think she said you could be too direct."

Sealy subconsciously twirled her hair. "She also told me not to apologize when a feeling came out as an accusation. Just correct it. Tell me about my mother and father."

Richard readjusted the tray, took a drink of wine, and finally replied, "When did you realize that Barry was my brother? Did Paul tell you?"

"He didn't. I found out from a woman working at the inn in town. Besides, my mom's photo is displayed on the walls of the conference room. I didn't see my father's photo."

Richard pushed his plate away, pulled the napkin off his chest to dab at his eyes. His voice trembled. "I had hoped Mary would have talked to you. Let you know more."

"Did you love her?"

"Yes, I did. She loved my wife too. They were best friends."

The words stuck in Sealy's throat. Here she was badgering an older man who once loved her mother. "What about your brother, my father? When did the affair start?"

Richard sighed. "You have it all wrong. I need Mary to tell you." Pain contorted Richard's face.

Sealy had pushed too hard. She tried to soften her words. "But Mary died. You know that. My mom was very private, a matter of fact and the belle of a party. She lit up a room. I didn't always agree with her ways, but like you, I loved her. I couldn't live up to her expectations. Maybe I didn't let her tell me. Even now she is a force to contend with."

Richard tried to smile. "Yes, Mary had her ways. But now that you're here, I want to get to know you. I don't have much time. Forgive me, forgive your mother, even if you don't understand. I apologize for my brother's behavior. He made errors that left a stain on all of us. You were so young when he died. We all tried to help. Maybe that was what held us together. At least for a time."

Sealy held Richard's hand. The two sat that way until the phone rang. Richard motioned for Sealy to answer.

"Hello, Morris residence. Mr. Jewels, are you okay at the Rockport Lodge? No, I don't think Richard can speak to you, he's resting." Sealy watched Richard's face tense as he waved off the call. "It's late, I'll tell him you called. Good night."

Richard made his way over to his bed. He kept his back to Sealy. "I'm done. Thanks for the talk."

"Let me help you." Even as he shooed her away, Sealy noticed tears. "You're upset. What can I do?"

Richard's stare unsettled her. "Nothing. The question is, What did I do?"

Paul closed his eyes as Danny drove his truck back to the Hawk House. The town had weathered the wind better than he expected. All the electrical outages had been fixed, except for the homes by the wharf. The downed poles and water over the roads made it too difficult to repair. He was assured by the fire department and the utility department that most would be fixed by morning if the rains and wind had stopped and the flood waters receded.

The city and volunteer organizations stocked two shelters, in the church and the high school auditorium, with food, water, and bedding. Mostly the elder folk and the families whose homes lay beyond the downtown perimeter, where floodwalls protected their properties, filled the spaces. The only residences lost to flooding were older summer cabins and vacation houses. Paul thought of the new legislation on shorelines, building permits, and those on the council who had opposed his recommendations. Perhaps the silver lining of the nor'easter was current evidence of destruction by a mild storm. He crossed his fingers that he could get legislation on the books to save the shoreline and town in the future. Paul knew by the way Danny drove along the curves of the road that they were almost back to Hawk House.

They pulled into the driveway well past the witching hour. Grateful that the lights were still on at the house, Paul said his good nights to Danny. "You were such a help out there. The volunteers took your lead with sandbags and clearing the roadways. You must be exhausted."

Danny knuckled Paul's shoulder, a gesture they used to do all the time. "Felt good to work with the town. I'm not like you, Dad. All the politics drives me crazy, but physical work lets me see the fruits of my labor. It doesn't tire me like the mental gymnastics you and Grandpa do."

"That will be tomorrow, looking at the budget. I don't know if the storm damage warrants a state of emergency. I'll sleep well tonight and leave all that for the council."

"Before you turn in, I forgot to tell you what I found out about Mr. Jewels. One of the adoption centers is sponsoring a small symposium on adoption legislation. Apparently, Mr. Jewels works with an adoption agency. Lots of interest in DNA searches and ancestry nowadays."

"Go to bed—like you said, too many mental gymnastics. I'll see you in the morning. I'll keep my beeper by my bedside."

Paul remembered the stack of papers on his desk. He felt guilty that he had pushed an old complaint filed about an adoption agency to the bottom of the pile. He dragged his tired frame inside. As he eased his slickers off, Sealy appeared.

"Thought you might like hot chocolate and my special cookies before you retired. It's too late to eat a full meal."

Even though Paul wanted to dissolve in his bed, he was touched. "I won't say no. Maybe it will help my body rest." Just the sight of Sealy calmed his mind. He followed her into the living room. "Thanks for keeping the fire going. I feel the rain in my bones."

Sealy sat on the loveseat with her feet curled under her body. She looked like a kid who had stayed up too late, hair tussled into a sloppy bun. Paul consciously chose the stuffed chair across from her. He couldn't remember the last time someone had waited up for him, let alone a woman so caring. Paul stared at the fireplace, lost in the reds and yellows of the flames. He listened to Sealy's voice, a singsong of emotions.

"Paul, are you asleep? I can wait to tell you in the morning. I just thought you needed to know."

"Sorry, I must have drifted off. It's the first time I've relaxed in weeks." He reached over to touch her hand. "I'm all ears. What's wrong?"

"I'm not sure. When I brought food up to Richard the phone rang. It was that man in the taxi. Mr. Jewels asked for the town manager. But this time he asked for Richard Morris. Your father got upset, shook his head that he didn't want to talk. After that Richard dismissed me. He's worried about something he did when he was in office."

Paul closed his eyes, sighed. A wave of sadness passed over him. "I hate this. My dad is on his deathbed, and now he's worried about the past. Probably some error that fell through the cracks. I'm sure I can take care of it."

Sealy wrapped her arms around herself and curled her knees into her chest. "I don't know, Richard was agitated. Like a ghost had reentered his life. I think it's personal. I going to dig into the records at the library, find out more about the man."

"Well, here's a start: Danny found out why Mr. Jewels came to town. He represents an adoption agency and there's a conference scheduled, of all places in our small town. I remember paperwork coming across my desk concerning adoption records. It's in one of my piles."

Sealy rose. "I've worried you now, but whatever the problem is, I don't want your father to hurt like he is. We talked a little bit about my mother and father. Richard is churning inside with a secret."

Paul nodded, stood up, and squeezed Sealy's hand. His words tumbled, one over the other, swallowed by emotion. "Bedtime. Thanks for waiting up, for caring. I'll be up early, heading into town to oversee the cleanup. I'll check on my dad before I leave."

Sealy whispered good night and softly kissed his cheek.

With the continued rains and cloud cover, normal morning signs of the sunrise failed to appear. Sealy rose from her bed unsure if the nighttime had ended. It didn't matter; she'd left markers of time behind as soon as she had arrived in Maine. Living in Hawk House had its own rhythm. Roxie's and Reese's energies were the sunshine. Richard's slow decline mirrored the ebb and flow in cancer's vast ocean. Danny and Paul kept the daily routines moving with a sense of calm. But without their presence as indicators of the schedule, Sealy's nocturnal dreams blended into daytime.

Darkness kept her from walking to the gazebo. Instead, she found her sketch pad and charcoals and headed for the tiny den hidden behind the dining room and kitchen. No one seemed to use the space, and Sealy doubted she'd be discovered.

Black-and-white sketches offered her a challenge. Mood, outlines, details had to be precise. She drew a thin line that curved like a giraffe's *S*—a long neck and bulbous bottom. One of her art professors insisted that from the repetition of shapes in various angles, a face, person, or scene would emerge. Sealy used this method to trick her brain, to elicit feelings that lay hidden inside. Her first drawing flowed into a pregnant woman's body, which morphed into her mother's silhouette. A rendition of her as she aged, with silver-gray hair and set lines around her mouth. Crow's feet traveled in pairs, resting below the almond shape of her eyes. Sealy put more effort into the curves and lines of her cheekbones and chin, continuing the pattern. She'd never seen her mother pregnant, never seen photos of herself in her mother's belly.

Oblivious to the howling wind and rain, Sealy drew pictures of her father as she imagined him. A beard appeared, scruffy strokes like wire that hid the dimple in his chin. She remembered the dimple. The eyes intent, darker than black, with gray circles beneath the lashes. Her father looked hollow. Then she drew Jeannie, long and lean, with brown hair and red highlights, a blend from her father and mother. She, too, had the dimple. Sealy had envied that dimple. She had tried painting one on her face, not knowing that oils remained for weeks and the correct method of facial painting was with makeup.

On one page, Sealy doodled side views of the Morris clan. Richard, Paul, Danny. She began with the nose, long *s*'s but smaller curves. The similarities held true. Richard's gray beard hid the chin, and Danny had little hair anywhere. Sealy searched her memory of Paul's chin, but her heart hurt too much to probe too deeply. Instead, she stared at her drawing of her father, Barry, and laid it next to the others. The wondering saddened her, magnified a void. A tear dropped and stained the page.

When she finally raised her head out of concentration, a flash of lightning struck, and thunder rolled. No seconds to count in between. The overhead lights flickered, then the drone of the compressor started the generator. Still dressed in her night-robe, she rushed to the kitchen. The cook stood shaking with a muffin pan in her hand. Roxie and Reese entered in their pajamas and rushed to her side.

Sealy scooped the two girls into her arms. She whispered, "Time for a thunderstorm party. Aren't we lucky that the new cook, Sue, is already baking muffins?"

Sue gave Sealy an appreciative smile.

"Sue, while you make Richard his breakfast, I'll make whipped-cream strawberry delights for the girls."

"Great. I was feeling rushed. Didn't expect anyone to be up yet. Thanks for helping me." In a whisper Sue continued, "Just so you know, Mr. Morris isn't eating much. I'll bring him his eggs and muffin, but he might like the strawberry delight better."

"Okay, I'll bring it up to him later."

With the smells of the muffins baking, the girls hovered around Sealy. Each one took turns with the hand beater blending a dash of vanilla and sugar into the cream until the mixture came to a head. Roxie and Reese took parfait glasses and layered the whipped cream with the strawberries. Sealy took a spoon and dabbed a dollop onto their noses and one on her own nose. Giggles filled the kitchen.

Sealy wiped the cream off their noses, but their smiles remained. She noticed that Roxie and Reese both had dimples on their chins, like their father, grandfather, and great-grandfather. She patted the girls and sent them off to the dining table while she cleaned up the mess. Another set of giggles followed. From the kitchen, Sealy heard heavy footsteps.

"Hello, who is making all that ruckus?"

Roxie called out, "Grandpa, look at our thunderstorm breakfast. Isn't Sealy great?"

Sealy met Paul's eyes. His normal bright blue gaze had faded, and the red of tiredness gave him an eerie look. Unshaven, with a rumpled work shirt, he looked like he'd been up all night.

Despite his fatigue, he gave his full attention to the parfaits. "Yes, I approve. You suppose Sealy made extra for anyone else?"

The two nodded and dug in.

Sealy returned from the kitchen with Paul's parfait. "Rough night, huh?"

Paul sat at the table and slowly spooned whipped cream and strawberry into his mouth. When he had finished, he licked the spoon. "I needed that. Thanks for waking up early. Looks like you didn't go to bed, or you forgot to get dressed."

Sealy looked down at her robe and slippers and blushed. "You're changing the subject. I just happened to be up when the lights went out and the lightning and thunder shook the house."

Paul turned to focus on the girls. "Time to get ready for the day, even if the schools are closed. Upstairs you go." He planted a kiss on the top of their heads and shooed them away. Once they had disappeared, Paul sighed. "Roxie and Reese have vivid imaginations. Thanks for taking charge."

Sealy accepted the compliment with a nod. "Go on. If you don't tell me what's happening, I'll have to resort to torture. Seriously, your silence is making me worry more."

"I had to go back to town. Charlie, one of the boat owners, had a heart attack and needed to get to the hospital. The roads were washed out in parts, the drive was treacherous. The family called me because both of our ambulances were stuck in a flooded area. We made it to the hospital just in time. Thank goodness his daughter was with him." Paul paused to catch his breath. "When I got back here, Danny was in a panic, Richard speaking gibberish. Danny couldn't tell if he was dreaming, hallucinating, or caught in a different time zone. I was up all night."

A familiar lump caught in her throat. She held Paul's hands in her own. "Oh my, Sue mentioned that Richard isn't eating much. I didn't realize that the cancer was taking over so quickly." When Sealy moved her hands, Paul looked away. "What can I do?"

"I don't know. He's calling for my mother and talking to your mother. He keeps saying your name over and over. Then he yells at a shadow. As if someone is in the room pointing at him. I can calm him a little by singing old songs. He sings with me. Then he'll drift off. But the shadow scares him again."

"This is the tough part when the toxicity takes over. When my mom started ranting, I thought she was caught in a time warp. Begging for forgiveness. Her brain was in a frightening loop. I promised myself I'd resolve my own past issues so I wouldn't relive them as I was dying. For my mom, singing helped as well. The remembered music broke the loop." Sealy thought the insight might help relieve Paul of some angst.

Paul recovered his composure and moved away. "So sorry. I don't think I've been this moved since my wife died over thirty years ago."

His words went directly into the hollow of her heart. Sealy fumbled with her robe and tried to smooth over the show of emotions. "Love gets bottled up inside. Loving your wife, loving Richard. The loss runs deep." Her words felt so inadequate. "I'm going to get dressed. I'll take a parfait up to Richard while you shower or rest. Maybe Danny can help out some more."

"A shower sounds good. Danny should be back from town soon. I sent him in last night to watch over the flooding. I guess all is okay for now, or he'd have called. Would you do me a favor? When you see my dad, let me know if I should call hospice."

Sealy nodded. "I'll stay with him until you or Danny get back."

Sealy sat by Richard's bedside and listened to the depth of his snores. It had been a few hours since he'd made a valiant attempt to eat her parfait. Earlier, he seemed alert but tired. Now he slept peacefully. Sealy studied his face, focused on the eyebrows framing eyes that flitted back and forth as if he traveled on the highway of his life.

She'd come prepared with a book to read and her basic art supplies. Seated at Richard's desk, a stone's throw away from his single bed, Sealy took out her sketch pad and drew her impression of Richard's world within the lines of the lids: scenes from Hawk House, tall standing trees, and in between their footprint, a man peering out, another man peering inward. Using a charcoal pencil, she drew a road that led to the water, another to a faraway world where a woman held a gavel in one hand and an apple pie in the other.

Absorbed in her work, she didn't hear the door open. Roxie and Reese stood there waiting for an invitation to come in. Roxie whispered, "Sealy, we know we shouldn't be here, but Reese thought maybe you'd let us sit for a while."

Sealy doubted that Reese had come up with the idea, knowing that Reese followed Roxie. She put her finger to her lips. "If you're quiet, I'll let you make Richard a card."

"A get-well card?"

"How about a loving card, one that shows all the things you like about your great-grandfather?"

"We call him Poppy sometimes, not like the flower poppy. But he likes flowers. I'll draw his garden. Is that okay?"

"Whatever you draw will be perfect."

Sealy had never witnessed the subdued nature of the girls. All barrettes and ponytails, their outfits matched, black stretch pants with a green and blue horizontal-striped jersey. Either Danny made that choice, or the girls demanded it. Sealy had worn different outfits than Jeannie, an unwritten rule in her mother's book: be an individual.

After a short time, Richard stirred. At first gently and then he tossed and turned, battling the covers. Reese ran to his side and held his hand. "Poppy, are you okay? It's me, your favorite pumpkin."

Roxie chimed in. "I'm here too, your favorite banana."

His tossing stopped and Richard seemed more peaceful. Sealy gently placed Richard's hands under the blanket and redirected Reese and Roxie. "Girls, it's almost time for lunch. Why don't you go outside and play until Sue calls? Maybe your father will be back by then."

"Oh, Daddy came back and is resting. Said he'd be up to help you soon." They left, placing their cards by Richard's side.

When the girls were out of earshot, Sealy began humming. The only tune that came to mind was one her mother had always sang.

One of Frank Sinatra's crooning songs that made her heart ache. The lyrics traced a man's life from young to older, comparing his later life to autumn and vintage wine.

Richard opened his eyes and stared at Sealy as if she had tricked him. "You're not Mo. That was our song. I wish you were Mo."

A tear fell on Sealy's arm. She wasn't sure if it was Richard's or her own. Again she had to rally, push her emotions back. "No, Mo is gone. That was her favorite song. I won't sing it if it upsets you."

"Well, at least Mo did share some things she loved with you."

Sealy chuckled. "You make it sound like I didn't know my mother. We were close, but she never mentioned you and barely talked about my father." Sealy took out her portfolio. "I drew these portraits early this morning. What do you think?"

Richard pulled himself up on his pillow, reached for his glasses. He seemed alert, purposeful as he studied her art. "You've got talent. An eye for detail, and memories. Mo let you go to art school, I'm not surprised."

Was this a clue of Richard's knowledge about her upbringing? "She wasn't too keen on it; afraid I wouldn't be able to support myself. Insisted that I get a career. She was practical and so conscious about society."

Richard nodded as if agreeing with her about her mother's nature. "Poor Mo, she shouldn't have had to worry about money or society. Is that my brother, Barry?"

"Yes, but like you said, it's more memory than real. I make up things when I don't know."

"Barry was always a troubled sort. You captured his eyes perfectly. A darkness haunted him. I don't want to taint your view of him. But it seems that is present in your drawing."

Sealy noticed Richard's eyes glaze over. She hoped he'd stay lucent, help her learn more about what happened.

The lines on Richard's face grew taut. "Barry and I were close once. He banished us after that god-awful mess with the winery. All over the papers." Richard waved his hands as if shooing away a demon. "Mo and Barry left, for a fresh start. I know it wasn't easy on them."

Sealy softened her tone. "But my mother kept coming back. Why? I mean—well, I don't know what I mean. It just seems odd."

Richard gave Sealy that look again. A cross between an old man grimacing and a puppy dog wanting sympathy. Sealy didn't remember if her father had ever shown her that emotional side.

"Barry loved the winery, a little too much. The startup was his baby and his downfall. When he gambled, he drank. He drank to keep the darkness away, and then he gambled more. He never lost the drinking habit even after he moved away. Mo needed a reprieve."

His words drifted off, as did his gaze. As much as Sealy wanted to find out more, she sensed that the memories took a toll on Richard. Heavy footsteps on the staircase told Sealy that Danny was on his way up. She scooped her drawings together. "Sounds like your grandson is on his way up. Everyone loves you so much. I'll be back later."

Richard grabbed her arm. "Has Mr. Jewels called again?"

"Not that I'm aware of. You can ask Danny, he might know."

Danny walked in with a look as heavy as his footsteps.

Richard sized up his grandson's demeanor. "Glad you're here, Sealy needs a break from this old man. I get stuck in the past. I know you do too. So, what has you so sour this fine morning?"

"Just tired. I was up all night in town putting in sandbags, shuttling the townspeople to shelter. Paul called and said he was worried."

Not wanting to interfere, Sealy made her exit. "Before you two start talking, I'll show myself out. Let me know if I'm needed or wanted later."

Sealy was already out the door when she heard Danny. "Pop, you don't owe Sealy anything. You don't even know her. Just don't forget about your real family."

She held her thoughts in check as she steamed with anger. Danny's immature nature cut her to the core. He didn't understand the past or care about his grandfather's demons. The larger question still loomed: Mary, Mo, Mom. Who was this woman she called her mother? She heard her mother's old refrain: *Let sleeping dogs lie, or be ready to deal with their shit.* Her mother had run from something. Her father had abandoned himself and his family. Why wasn't Jeannie caught in this web?

Relieved that his father was lucid and persnickety with Danny, Paul decided to make sure the connections to hospice were made, but to delay their arrival. Instead, he gathered all town-related work from his home and headed into his office. As he had hoped, volunteers had saved the wharf from flooding and electricity was back on. He rolled down his window and felt the moisture-laden air. Without the howling winds, a calm settled over the town. If the air fronts obeyed, they would have a reprieve from another nor'easter.

Paul had forgotten that it was Sunday. The only places open were the inn with its bar and the hardware and grocery stores— the three essentials when it came to emergencies: shelter with a place to commiserate, a place to find supplies for repairs, and food to nourish. The townspeople scurried to these destinations. Some waved and stopped to talk about road conditions, but most ignored him.

His desk was as he had left it, neat piles of to-dos numbered in order of importance. He plowed through the shoreline issues, modified some of his previous thoughts, and wrote a list to various state and federal agencies to apply for infrastructure assistance.

Rummaging through the pile from home, he found the paperwork on adoption. It appeared to be a complaint that dated back decades ago about a query on mutual consent registries in adoption and a request to unlock closed adoptions. Something about evidence missing in the verification process. Since the only adoption agency was nearby in York County, Paul decided to pass it on to the county. With the recent advent of DNA testing, ancestry searches, and medical needs, he figured the complainant would find resolution.

The rest of the pile dealt with requests for more garbage pickups, noise issues, and complaints about rising property taxes due to newer cottages and homes being resurrected in older areas. All problems he couldn't resolve without committee meetings.

Paul stared out the window and thought of the previous evening. Tired, upset, and worried, he was thankful that Sealy had been there. Only now he felt awkward. He couldn't deny the comfort and warmth she projected. He shook his head and went back to work.

From across the street, Mr. Jewels marched toward Paul's office. Apparently, Mr. Jewels hadn't forgotten about the Morrises. As Paul stared, Mr. Jewels walked up to the door and slipped an envelope into the mail slot. A knot in his stomach churned, a sickening feeling that all wasn't right.

Paul retrieved the envelope from the floor. It was addressed to Richard Morris, former town manager. Did he dare open it? Paul walked back to the window. At that moment, Mr. Jewels looked up. Paul waved and rushed down the stairs. "Mr. Jewels, how nice to see you out and about after the storm. I hope you found your accommodation to your liking. You're still dressed in your suit. Are you here on official business?"

"Thanks for your concern. The lodge is adequate. I left an envelope for Richard Morris. Will you make sure he gets it?"

"That depends. If it involves the concerns of the community, I'm the town manager and it should come to me. My father is extremely ill, on his deathbed. He has been out of office for over twenty years."

Mr. Jewels fidgeted, buttoning his vest, adjusting his tie. "It's a private issue. Please give it to him."

"I thought you came to attend a symposium on adoption legislation. You work for an adoption agency. Why would you need to talk to my father? You've called the house and got him upset. I need to know."

"I'm not at liberty to talk to you. Just give the envelope to your father. I won't call again."

Paul watched Mr. Jewels walk away.

After her latest paint session at the gazebo and walk in the woods, Sealy scrubbed her hands and nails as if she were a surgeon ready to operate. Murky brown residue clung to the sink while reds and blues swirled down the drain. She wished that the hurt from Danny's stinging remarks could be flushed down as well.

Sealy dressed quickly and slipped out the back door. Still fuming, she walked to the main road. Avoiding Danny meant she couldn't ask for a ride into town. Walking shoes, a raincoat, and her thumb would work for the four-mile trek and give her a chance to clear her mind. If no one drove by, she'd accept a nice stroll.

Sealy's stride eased as she headed down the hillside. Though protective of her aging hips and careful of the blinding curves, she'd forgotten about the storm's debris. A car appeared out of nowhere, honking at her to get out of the way. Spooked, she jumped back and fell into the bushes. Finally after three tries, she eased herself up, using the brambles as a rope to give her leverage. Just as she did, another car appeared. This one stopped and a woman about the age of her mother called out, "You must be Sealy, staying up at the Morris's. What has you walking on the road?" She gave Sealy the once-over. "Is everything okay?"

"I didn't want to bother Danny for a ride into town, and Paul is already there."

"Hop on in, I'm headed that way. I'm Diane, I live just past the Morrises'."

Grateful for the ride, Sealy slid into the passenger side. "Thanks, I was getting anxious after that tumble."

"Good thing you weren't walking on the other side. It's a long way down the cliff. We've lost some crazies that way, driving too fast or getting caught in the fog. You've been at the Hawk House for over a month. No one has ever been there that long, except years ago, when Barry lived there."

Diane's words slipped so easily out of her mouth that Sealy wondered if she had a filter in her brain. So far, Diane had been the only one to mention her father's name. "Oh, when was that?"

Driving and looking at Sealy, Diane continued, "A long time ago, he used to live there, then moved away with Mary, his socialite wife." She said Mary's name with a hint of disdain, putting Sealy's guard up. "Some…falling out. He only came back for short visits. Odd for a brother, don't you think? How's Richard, heard that the cancer is taking its toll?"

Sealy tried to smile politely, but the probing went beyond normal curiosity. "I'm just a visitor. I'm not privy to those issues."

"You have to wonder what goes on there. Three men without a woman. I tried visiting Richard after his wife passed. He never responded. Same with his son, Paul, and grandson, Danny. You'd think they'd welcome some friendly caring."

Sealy looked at Diane as she drove around the curves, a determined woman, aged but still handsome, and obviously capable. No use speculating. If Diane wanted her opinion or wanted to spread gossip, Sealy was sure that whatever she shared would be spread to the town. Sealy found herself defending the Morris men. "They seem to be doing okay. Danny's kids don't lack for love."

Diane slowed the car as a truck came up the hill. "You married? Not to pry, but why would you pick this town to visit and stay so long?"

Sealy felt the probes going deeper. "It's a great town, small and beautiful. Just what I need to paint and reflect." She regretted the ride. As her mother had so aptly taught her, she turned the stage away from herself. "You must have a pulse on the community, know everything. I appreciate this ride, very neighborly. It's precisely why I came, to find out what a small town has to offer. What keeps you here?"

Diane smiled, happy to have Sealy's attention. "Oh, well this has always been my home. I inherited our property from my parents. When my brothers didn't want to stay, I took it over. They're both in the city, making money. Got to keep up with my blueberries, apples, pears. They're not as persnickety as the grapes. This place suits me well. The Morris families used to be close to ours. The boys and I went to the same school. Lots in common. I dated Richard and then Barry in high school."

Sealy didn't care about her dating habits sixty years ago. Diane still lived in her past. Her mother had wanted to push the past away, and here Sealy was opening Pandora's box. "Did you ever marry and have kids?"

"No, I didn't want to be held back, tethered. I was, and still am, free range. Makes most people skittish. How about you?"

With her questions to Diane, she'd boxed herself in. Sealy laughed. "I'm single, if that is your question. Not free range as you put it. I would have loved to have had a family." Thankfully, they had arrived in town. Sealy gathered her raincoat and scooted closer to the door. "Thanks for the ride. Can you drop me off at the inn?"

"No problem, do you need a ride back?"

Sealy had no idea how she'd return but shook her head. "Kind of you to offer, but I'll find my way. Nice meeting you."

Diane peeled out and tooted the horn. Sealy couldn't help but smile. Every town had someone with an abundance of chutzpah. She tried to imagine Diane and her mother in the same room. They both were fearless, but her mother hid her powers. How many times had she heard "Don't air your laundry for all to see?" Sealy realized that this must have been her silent mantra to survive.

From Danny's and Paul's accounts, Sealy had expected the town to be a mess. But their hard work with the town's volunteers had kept the flooding to a minimum. The restaurant at the inn was busy with locals sharing their stories and waiting to use the inn's phones. She made herself comfortable until the callers disappeared. The last thing she wanted to do was rush her phone call to Jeannie. Worse yet would be to have someone overhear her conversation.

Jeannie answered on the first ring with an overpowering force: "Are you okay, Sealy? I read about the storm and thought you wouldn't be able to call."

"Calm down. I'm okay and so is the town. Good thing it was me who was calling. You'd scare anyone else away. The storm wasn't as bad as anticipated. I hitched a ride into town. Lots of debris on the roads, and Paul and Danny were up through the night taking turns with the volunteers to keep everyone safe."

"I don't like you being so far away. My only sister. Besides, I'm lonely. The kids are grown up, and my friends are busy."

Sealy tried to sooth Jeannie. "That's normal. I miss our coffee dates and our walks." By Jeannie's silence, she knew something was up. "Why don't you visit your grandkids? It will keep your mind off whatever is bothering you."

"Do I sound stressed? Sorry. I'm still going through Mom's stuff and then collecting your mail. I don't like going backwards."

"I'm doing the same thing here. I'm more confused than ever. Can I ask you an odd question?"

Jeannie laughed. "All your questions are odd. Ask away."

The inn's restaurant began to fill up. Sealy turned her seat away from the aisles to face a wall. Her voice shook as she continued, "Do you ever remember Mom being pregnant with me? Or have you found any pictures?"

Jeannie's voice shifted from concern to frustration. "What do you mean with that question? I don't remember, I was little. If Mom had an affair with Richard, I wouldn't know."

"Shh, calm down. Of course you don't know. I just noticed a trait that every kid in the Morris family has, that same dimple in their chin. I found out that our dad is Richard's brother."

Sealy heard a gasp and then every curse word Jeannie could muster. "So what? Of course Dad had a family. We just never met them. Where are you going with this? You are crazy. I'd give you my dimple if that would make you feel better. Who knows about genetics? For goodness sakes, we can get our ancestry lineage done. Anything to stop this fixation with chins."

Sealy tucked that thought away for another time. She'd already upset Jeannie too much. "I didn't mean to get you riled. What did you find that has you on edge?"

"If you must know, Mom's notary stamps."

"What's odd about that? Mom worked in law offices."

"Yes, but the stamp Mom used here isn't the same as the one I found in a box labeled *Maine*. It has her given name, not her married name."

Sealy twirled her hair, thinking. "That's easy. Maybe she got it before she married our dad."

Jeannie continued in a flat voice, "The date on the notary stamp is just about the time you were born. Mom had been married for five years."

Sealy let the date sink in. Unconsciously, she touched her chin. "Maybe Dad insisted. He was in trouble. He left under a cloud of suspicion. He embezzled from his own family."

"I don't want to hear any more. Damn it. Stop sleuthing. Come home."

"Richard is too sick. I can't leave yet. He has something to tell, but he seems to have promised Mom not to say anything." From the corner of her eye, Sealy caught sight of Mr. Jewels heading over to the phones. "Got to go. There's a lineup of people wanting to use the phones. Love you."

Sealy turned away and hid behind one of the tall upholstered chairs. She wasn't as invisible as she thought. Mr. Jewels took the seat next to hers.

Good manners got the best of her. "Oh, Mr. Jewels, you're still here. I thought you'd leave as soon as the storm ended."

Ever the odd gentleman, he shook his head. "That would have been my preference, but I need to talk to Mr. Morris, Richard. Old business."

"I didn't know you were a business partner of his. But then again, I'm just a visitor."

"If you don't mind, it's a private matter. Nothing to do with business at all. Nothing to do with the town. Something odd though. I'm just following up on ends that don't tie neatly."

Sealy nodded. Wasn't she trying to do the same thing? Tie up her mother's life in a neat bow. Only she felt the ribbons unraveling her own life. "Good luck, Mr. Jewels."

She walked outside as fast as she could. Anything to get away from the insistent man and his mission with Richard. Dotting all the i's, going backward, for whom and why? Sealy recognized an investigator, even an old one like Mr. Jewels. She wondered what he'd make of her mother's many names. Sealy said them out loud—Mary Morris, Mo, Mom—letting them drift off in the fresh air. Sealy had never seen her mother's maiden name written out on her documents, except on her birth certificate: Leigh Mary Jones. Jones, a name her grandma didn't even use, feeling it too common. Sealy never understood why the name Morris was any better. Especially if her father had been such a scoundrel.

Paul drove as if he carried a ton of bricks in the back of the truck. The only real added weight was a grocery haul of essentials and a quick stop at the bakery and wine shop. He studied the town in slow motion as if it were the first time he'd ever been there. He tried to imagine it in the mid-fifties. That was when his father took over as the town manager. Paul had grown up here, and the quaintness remained. The town had no traffic lights. Trees and flowers lined the road. The sidewalks had been added and the roads resurfaced, but otherwise little had changed. He believed the issues would be the same as now—development, economy, safety, and health. Why did his hometown feel foreign all the sudden? Why didn't he pay attention to the mural on the wall at the inn? He'd seen it so many times but never wondered why his mother wasn't present. He just assumed she had already died. His whole life had been made on assumptions.

Until now, he had never doubted his father's loyalty to the town or his ethics. Two things had changed—meeting Sealy and Mr. Jewels's presence. Sealy conjured up warmth, intimacy, safety. But Mr. Jewels fed into family secrets, from his dad's brother and now some personal issues.

Just as Paul approached the rise on the road toward home, he spotted Sealy walking. He turned down the radio and pulled over. "My goodness, what are doing?"

Sealy approached the truck with a huge grin. "Wishing that I hadn't hitched a ride into town and now had to walk back. Would you have mercy on me and give me a ride home?"

"You mean Hawk House. Absolutely." Paul didn't know if the home reference was a slip of the tongue, but he loved the thought that Sealy would be a permanent fixture.

Sealy reacted with laughter and a reddened face. She slid into the front seat with a sigh. "I didn't want to bother Danny, and you were already gone. Thought I'd do what I used to do when I was younger."

"You were one of those hippies, a free spirit."

"Not really, not with my grandmother living with us. When I went to college it was the only affordable way to travel. My mom could tolerate my independence, but she always cautioned me about safety. Speaking of free spirits, a woman named Diane gave me a ride in. She's in her eighties and prides herself on her being untethered. Yet she's attached to so much, especially any business that involves the Morrises."

Paul shook his head. "She knows everyone's business. But you're right. My father wants nothing to do with her. After my mother died, she'd drop in with some news about her vineyard and our wine, a false need to talk business. Nosy, that's what my dad called her. I was little, she made me feel weird."

"Edgy." Sealy turned toward Paul. "I didn't like her inquires." I felt like she wanted to know more than gossip. I thought at first she was lonely, but I didn't share anything about your dad, or me, if you're worried."

Paul shrugged, kept his eyes on the road. Having Sealy in the car felt right, but people and issues coming out of the woodwork just as his father's life was ending concerned him. "I'm not worried about what you said or didn't say. I'm used to being scrutinized because of my position in the town, but never personally. I can see why Danny doesn't want anything to do with politics. He's content running the business and the potential guesthouse." At the mention of Danny's name, Paul noticed a change in Sealy. Instead of facing him as he drove, she turned her head. "What's up? Did Danny do something to upset you? I thought you two got along."

"I thought so too. But I overheard Danny talking with Richard. He thinks I'm after something from the family, that your father shouldn't pay so much attention to someone he hardly knows and really isn't part of the family."

Her words had come out in a rush. Paul tapped his fingers on the steering wheel. "Oh, that kid." He veered down a side road that followed the cliff to the coast. "Let's take a break from the drama."

Sealy perked up in her seat, stretching to see the way down. "Is this the spot Richard wanted me to see down by the shoreline?"

Paul parked the truck on a patch of cleared dirt. "We'll have to walk from here. Careful, as it may be slippery after the storm. I just happen to have some cheese and wine from shopping. We can bring it with us. If that is okay with you?"

"I've got my walking shoes and my sketch pad. I'm up for an adventure."

They walked for a good ten minutes on narrow pathways that hugged close to the cliff, switched back, and then opened to a small cement pad with a bench and table, covered by a wooden lean-to. Paul brushed off the bench and sat down on one end, making room for Sealy on the other end.

Paul broke the silence. "Even after the storm and the debris on the shoreline, this place always brings me peace. My father came here every day for years, then he stopped. I'm not sure why. Now he can't make it down, even if he wanted to."

"I guess that's why it's so important for you and Danny to be stewards of the shoreline."

Paul smiled. "Maybe we're just selfish. Nature can have its way, but I don't want development to hurry it along. I respect of all this, the waves, the debris, and eternity."

"I couldn't have said it better. Where are the glasses? We can toast to this as we share the bottle?"

Paul laughed. "Wait a second. My dad made the bench double duty as a place to sit and as a storage unit. He stores his art supplies and some essentials, like a bottle opener, wineglasses, and utensils."

Paul set the table and watched Sealy from the corner of his eye. She immediately pulled out her sketch pad and drifted off into the scene. He envied her concentration. It had been years since he had drawn or painted. Not for lack of prodding from his father. After he gave up teaching and took on the role of town manager, he had no time.

He busied himself searching for the bottle opener. A few of his father's sketches lay on top. Surprise and sadness overwhelmed him. One was of himself, in various stages walking along the beach. From Roxie's age until after he had a son of his own. The aging process told stories of how he had changed. As a young boy he appeared as a free spirit running in the waves, engrossed in the curious study of critters along the way. The sketch transformed him to middle aged, with hunched shoulders, and his hand holding the fingertips of a boy ready to rush off into the waves. Paul skimmed over the most recent version of himself with worry lines surrounding his eyes at half-mast. Another sketch was of a woman with a smile that welcomed you in, hair flying in the wind, eyes sparkling as if a star burned inside. He sat with the images, staring at the waves, until Sealy approached.

"Oh my, look at you. So much emotion on your face. We came here for a break. Are you okay?"

"Just overwhelmed. My father may not say much, but his drawings capture all his thoughts."

"Care to share the sketches?"

Paul opened the wine bottle with a flourish. "Only if you show me yours."

Sealy put out her hand. "A deal, let's shake on it."

Paul handed her Richard's sketches and Sealy placed hers on his lap. "Before we begin, let's have that toast." She smiled in agreement. "Here's to the waves, the debris, and eternity." Sealy clicked her glass against his as they locked eyes.

He felt an intensity, perhaps a reflection off the water. Her eyes sparkled with sincerity and a touch of mystery. Her voice was just a whisper in the wind. "I've been here before when I was little. Being here triggered the memory. I've sketched it."

He waited for more, but Sealy drifted off into the world of his father's sketches.

The breeze left a sandy grit on Sealy's face. She held on to Richard's art sketches as if they would unlock another door. Her hands shook with emotions that defied logic. Paul sitting by her side had only been a vague child memory to her. Not only was Paul real but had a full life as the son of the man who meant more to her mother than her own father had. Brothers, cousins, family, all labels meant to describe assumed love. Greedy, that's what she was. She'd come searching for comfort, but instead she felt selfish as a Peeping Tom peering into another's life.

As she viewed Richard's sequential sketches of Paul, she saw another sadness. The erosion of joy in between the lines. Richard knew that he had passed his burdens onto his son. Sealy knew the technique of drawing within the shadow. One view drew the eye to the faces, shapes, the other added perspective, but sometimes the artist hid other figures within the fading darkness. She noticed a little child gazing between the rocks, a woman walking within the trees.

Unconsciously, Sealy reached for Paul's hand and squeezed. The return pressure of his fingers sent a jolt to her heart. She almost pulled away, but Paul held strong. When he finally let go, it was to remove a tear off her cheek. If only she could draw what she felt. Her words stumbled out. "I can't see where you and I are in all this. The past in these drawings sets us up, but the picture is too dark. Is it this way with every parent, hidden lives that turn into lies?"

Stains of salt residue lined Paul's face, as if the ocean spray underlined his pain. Sealy could barely hear his voice over the waves. "My dad is full of surprises. I wish he'd be more direct. Not hide behind his paintings. I'm not sure I agree with his assessment of me."

Sealy pointed at the drawing. "Do you see me in the drawing? I'm peeking between the rocks. I know because I was there. And my mother often took walks when I swam out into the waves with Richard."

"I hadn't noticed the figures in the shadows. My memory of that time was different. I never learned to swim. I was afraid of the waves. My dad would tire of prodding me on. I thought it was a babysitter who stayed behind walking with me when he would disappear…" Paul pulled out Sealy's sketches. "This sketch you just drew tells more, doesn't it? You're running back from a swim; the waves are chasing you. Richard is behind you, and you are coming toward a boy." Paul pauses, points. "It's me building a sandcastle. I remember the crown, a sea urchin shell. It's in your hand."

Sealy felt her heartbeat quicken; her memory was real. Why had it been concealed? "I once went for therapy. My mom suggested it, which seems odd considering she hid so much of herself. Anyway, the therapist tried to coax my feelings out. I didn't have the words to express anything. The lady handed me a pencil and paper to draw. That was the beginning of my journey with art. I think Richard is doing the same here." She placed Richard's drawing next to her own. "Same rocks, even the cluttered beach with scattered driftwood is there. Only my mother is gone."

Paul poured each of them another glass of wine and sliced the cheese. "If this wasn't about us, would you see this differently?"

Sealy sifted the sand through her fingers. "I'm not sure."

"Well, from my perspective, something is missing. Otherwise, why hide love? My mother passed away; your father died. Love should prevail."

Sealy remembered her conversation with Jeannie. "Something else is going on. Your father relied on my mom to tell me. But she couldn't or wouldn't. Richard told me that my father chose to leave, that he hadn't driven his brother out of the business." Sealy took a deep breath. "And I talked to Jeannie, asked her if she saw our mother pregnant, or if she remembered my birth. Boy, did she get angry. I don't know, after seeing Mr. Jewels today at the inn, I have doubts about everything."

Paul played with his glass of wine. "Mr. Jewels came to my office. He left an envelope addressed to Richard. I ran after him, but he didn't reveal anything. Dogged with his mission. Why does he worry you?"

Sealy continued fiddling with the sand, drawing circles within circles, a spiral with a bull's-eye. Her voice faded as if the wind had taken away her thoughts. "Do you really want to know?"

Paul added a question mark to the sand design. "I've learned to never ask a question I wasn't willing to hear the answer to. In this case, I trust your intuition. You see and feel more than anyone I've ever met."

Sealy curled her hair around her fingers as she answered, "I always wondered why I felt so awkward in my family growing up. Jeannie and I are nothing alike, although we love each other. My own grandmother talked about me in whispers, as if I were a second-class citizen. I might be exaggerating. She watched me like a hawk, but not Jeannie. I noticed during this visit that everyone here has a chin dimple. So does Jeannie. I don't."

She expected Paul to laugh, but he didn't. "There must be a rational explanation. I mean, scientifically, the 'dimple gene' might be recessive or something like that. You're so talented in art, in ways that I could never be. Doesn't that prove something?"

"I guess, but my intuition tells me different. Originally, I thought I was adopted. Then I thought my mom had an affair with a mysterious man. I never knew my father had a brother or more family. Now I find out I'm related to you, a cousin. But like you said, why keep all that secret? Mr. Jewels's insistence on talking with Richard puts another spin on everything." Sealy wrapped her arms in a self-hug. "My mom used to say that if it smelled bad, it was. A refrigerator rule, but I think it applies."

Paul didn't answer immediately. His face melted into concentration as he stacked the picnic supplies away. "I agree, my dad's reaction isn't normal. Whether that has something to do with you, I don't know. I've been tempted to look inside the envelope Mr.

Jewels gave me, but I won't. Whatever is inside isn't my issue unless my dad includes me."

Sealy bent her head in apparent embarrassment. "I've been so obsessed that I didn't take you into consideration. Danny already made it clear that I'm a distraction. I don't want you or him to think I'm robbing your family of time, attention on anything else. I've been selfish, but—"

"Don't second-guess yourself. I'm glad you came. Ignore what Danny said. He's under lots of stress with managing the winery, the kids, and my dad's illness."

Movement in the waves made Sealy jump up. "Something is floating in the water." She ran down to the shore. Paul followed. Out of breath, they scanned the horizon.

Paul pulled out his cell phone. "Danny, call the Coast Guard. I think a piling let loose with part of a boat launch. It's heading toward town, with a what I believe is a baby carriage."

Sealy couldn't settle down after they arrived home. Danny sat by the phone waiting for news from the Coast Guard, and Paul disappeared upstairs with Mr. Jewels's envelope. Reese and Roxie hovered by the window, raced each other across the living room, and pulled at Danny's leg, begging for attention. The energy in the house pulsated with emotions. She'd explode with worry if she didn't do something.

"Reese, Roxie, let's make a surprise for your dad, Paul, and Richard. I bet they'd love lemon meringue pie."

Reese's eyes widened. "You can make a pie with lemons? No way—they aren't sweet."

"Come on, it's magic. The kitchen is where I use a secret ingredient."

The two girls squealed with joy.

Sealy put her finger to her lips. "Shh, your dad is on the phone. Let's go."

Reese grabbed her left leg and Roxie hugged her right one. Sealy waddled into the kitchen dragging two bundles of joy. The perfect distraction.

Before they began, Sealy wrapped the girls' hair in towels, forming makeshift chef hats. Sealy divided up the tasks and within a few minutes the smell of lemon custard filtered throughout the house. Each of the girls studied the recipe, looking for the secret ingredient.

"I don't think you'll find the magic written down, girls, but you'll know when the pie is done."

While they waited for the crust to bake, Sealy showed them how to whip the egg whites into peaks. They took turns assembling the pies and creating mountain crests over the filling. Although they were having fun, she knew they wondered about the magic. As they washed dishes, Sealy took the leftover crust, rolled it out into the shape of a heart, and sprinkled cinnamon and sugar on top. Just as she took the baked heart out of the oven, Danny burst in. She held her breath.

The girls ran to his side. "We're waiting for the magic from Sealy."

Danny hugged the girls and then turned to Sealy. "They found the carriage empty. No one has called in an emergency. At least for now, the panic is over."

Sealy let out a huge sigh and smiled. "Well, girls, in that case, I think the pies have cooled enough to have a slice. I'll get the plates, and then you can tell me where the magic is."

Sealy waited for everyone to take a bite. Reese and Roxie both looked inside the pie, licked their lips, and looked again.

"Who knows the answer?"

Roxie answered with a full mouth, "You, you're the magic. You made lemons sweet and made Daddy smile."

Reese chimed in, "Yeah, smiles and sweetness."

"In that case we have three celebrations—a lemon pie that taste sweet, smiles, and no more worries."

Danny gathered them up. "Almost no worries. My dad is with Granddad, seems he's talking nonsense about a lost baby. This must have triggered a memory."

The days seemed to stretch from one emergency to another. Richard's continual confusion permeated the house. After yesterday's events, she'd slept well but the tension drained her. After lunch, Sealy raced up the stairs. Whatever memories Richard conjured up, she didn't want to know. She ignored the voices and moans she heard coming from his room. Her fingers fumbled with the key to her door—clear sign of panic when her hands and feet went numb. Her cure was to wash it all away. She slipped into the shower and let the water beat down on her back until the heat made her burn. She turned the water on cold and faced forward until her muscles felt like rubber. Finally, she compromised on warm on the verge of hot and washed her hair and body. Satisfied that her thoughts and fears no longer clung to her, she toweled herself dry. One last glimpse of the suds as they drifted down the drain completed the letting-go process.

The shower refreshed her, but still her doubts mixed with new truths made her impatient. After she dressed Sealy found her research. On the back side of the article exposing her father's indiscretions at the winery, Sealy discovered a notification of a baby found wrapped in a towel on an inflatable raft set loose during a storm. Was this baby's fate what triggered Richard's flashbacks?

Not knowing what else to do with her worries, Sealy calculated she'd have just enough time to take a short walk before dinner. Everyone had disappeared from lunch by the time Sealy came back down. The quiet felt unnatural. She went into the kitchen in search of movement, then to the garden outside. No sounds from Richards's room. She thought the worst until she found Paul in the back room off the kitchen. She wasn't the only one who used it as a refuge. Not wanting to disturb him, she made an about-face and slipped out the kitchen through the back entrance.

The chill in the air snapped Sealy to attention. She'd been going around in circles about her mother's old photo. The photo was just a slice of time—not her time, but her mother's. Her mother's actions cast a spell on her. Jeannie had been right; their love should be enough. Sealy stumbled on the loaded word *should*. Even now her mother's reprimands filtered through: *There is no law that includes the word* should. *Go by what is, not what you can't prove or what you want.*

Sealy stuck more with intuition. She wondered if her mother had followed her own advice. If her mother had believed in the law and truth, Sealy wouldn't be at the Hawk House, caught between the pulls of Richard's will and the determined and permanent silence of her mother. Sealy's gut told her that her parents ran away—not from the scandal at the winery, but something worse. If only she could sketch the past and have the truth revealed.

Her exit out the kitchen door led her down a gravel road just wide enough for a truck. She assumed this would lead to the front driveway, a road for deliveries. Instead, it circled the house where the road forked off past the garden hedges and slightly widened.

Fresh ruts meant that someone had used the road during the storm.

She'd left the house without a jacket. The clouds had lost their menacing look and the crisp air brushed along her arms. She walked quickly. With each of her steps the gravel seeped rainwater. Sealy had walked about a mile before she saw any change in the scenery. The woods opened to a field lined with rows of grapevines and another driveway. She walked over a hill that partly obscured one lone wood house. More fields followed until she came to roads with signs. One pointed to Morris Winery.

Sealy could kick herself for not knowing more about her surroundings. The Hawk House had become the center of her world. She saw the town and the area only through this lens. She hadn't realized that Diane's grape fields were that close. For that matter, she hadn't asked anyone to show her the winery.

She decided to turn back despite her curiosity. The last thing she wanted was to cause panic at the house because of her absence. A few minutes later she heard a honk coming from behind her. Danny pulled up in the truck.

"I haven't seen you here before. I assume you just found the path behind the house. Hop in. I'll give you a ride back if that's where you're going."

Sealy detected a tone of sarcasm in Danny's voice. Not wanting to cause more of a rift, she gave him the benefit of the doubt. "I'm slowly finding my way around here." She laughed. "It only took me a month to discover this road. Now I have two more months to find out about the winery and the vineyard."

Danny kept his eyes on the road, but his voice faltered. "You're still planning on leaving? I had the sense you wanted to put down roots."

There it was—the fear that she wanted something. Sealy took a deep breath, looked out the window as they passed the rows of grapes. "Some of the vines look damaged. Will that impact the winery?"

"Why the sudden interest?"

Before she could answer, Diane waved them down from her driveway. "Did you hear about the baby carriage floating down the coast? It's just like what happened years ago. I bet your grandfather is really upset. You know, it was the same pier as before."

Danny's face went white. His fists clasped around the steering wheel, scrunched so tightly that the skin reddened. "This time the carriage was empty, and every child has been accounted for. No need to worry, Ms. Diane."

"Yes, but years ago, a baby floated down on an inflatable raft. It took weeks to find the mom. The whole town was in a state. Your grandfather had just lost his wife giving birth to Paul's twin sister. Such a bad time."

Danny nodded. "Yes, I'm sure it was. I wasn't there. But all is okay today. Do you need us for anything else?"

"Well, not really. Just being neighborly."

Sealy wondered at Danny's tone of voice, his abruptness. She leaned over toward Danny's window. "Looks like the storm wreaked havoc on the grapevines. I asked Danny if your crop will be okay."

"I've seen worse. They're a hardy stock used to the nor'easters. It's the fruit trees I worry about. Just won't be able to deliver as much to the Morrises. Thanks for asking though. Send my best to your granddad."

Danny rolled up his window and sped off.

Sealy lurched and held on as the tires spewed gravel. She waited until Danny had slowed down and the color of his face returned. "You were rude to Diane. She's just an old lady making conversation. Why did you let her get you upset?"

"You don't get it. She's a busybody. I was protecting my father and grandfather. She seems innocent, but did you hear her? Giving out information about our personal life in the guise of being friendly. Jesus, I didn't even know my dad had a twin baby sister who died at birth. Who knows what she said when my mother died?"

"Well, at least we know why the baby incident upset Richard so much. I'm sure that he still feels the loss of his daughter even now. Besides, his memory might feel more real than the present."

"Are you saying he has dementia, or worse?"

"I'm not saying anything. I'm trying to understand why you are upset with me and maybe the world."

Danny smiled. It was the first time in weeks that his whole face relaxed. "Granddad said you were nice. It was what I thought when I first met you. But since you've been here, he's more riled up. Nothing I do satisfies him. He's obsessed. Even my kids and my father seem to prefer being with you."

Sealy nodded. "So you're jealous of a woman in her sixties, who is nice to your family, a guest who apparently your grandfather really wanted to see. That makes sense."

"Now you're mocking me. It's more than jealousy. What do you want?"

"I don't want to upset your life or that of your father. I just want to have some questions about my mother answered."

"We aren't wealthy, in case you're wondering."

"I don't need money, in case you're wondering."

Danny turned toward Sealy. "Good, at least you're not a gold digger. Let's find out how the Hawk House is holding up. My dad is in a tizzy about something. Maybe you can calm him down like you did with me and my girls."

Paul bent his head in frustration. Dang his father and memories. Richard had refused to open the envelope from Mr. Jewels. The news about the floating carriage sent him on a tirade about a lost baby, and then he began ranting about his brother. Before he dozed, Richard made one more comment. "Just because the books look good doesn't mean they're correct. Barry tried to protect me. He left because of me. I had no idea."

After two hours of searching, Paul had found the Morris Winery accounting ledgers from the 1950s to the 1970s. Nothing popped out as embezzlement. He expected to see a drop in cash and gross discrepancies in the bank statements. But the numbers looked good.

His experience in his role as town manager pushed him to look deeper. Instead of looking at the sales and cash, he studied the grape and fruit accounts, then the vendor accounts, and the retail accounts. He noticed a pattern. The grape and apple quantities received by various vineyards didn't match yields. The closest vineyard, their neighbor, at that time sold them the most fruit. Large checks went out in payment for the fruit, but the volume and sales of their blends failed. What happened? Why continue using these grapes and apples if they didn't yield?

Paul found all the canceled checks with Barry Morris's signature. This was his job, but the most curious discovery was in the warehouse ledgers. The incoming weights didn't jive with the numbers on the invoices. If Barry was going to embezzle, why didn't he just take money from the receivables, not pay the vendors, stash money in another account? Why mess with the weights, yields, and production?

Drained beyond words, Paul left the question hanging. He folded his glasses, placed them in his shirt pocket as he left the study. He'd had enough of searching into the past. He needed to take care of the present. As he mounted the stairs to his father's room, he crossed his fingers that Richard would still be resting. Thankfully, he was curled in an S shape, hands wrapped around Mr. Jewels's crumpled envelope. A black-and-white photo of Mary lay by his side. Another photo with his mother, Barry, and Mary lay on his other side. The four were outside of the Morris Winery for some celebration. All looked festive, but off to the side, Diane stood with her arms up in the air, hands curled in fists.

Careful not to disturb Richard's sleep, Paul dislodged the envelope. The sealed flap had been ripped open and the contents removed. There was nothing offensive about the photos, nothing new or surprising. Paul searched under the bed and in the trash for a document. It was too early to wake his father for his next dose of medicine.

He left the photos in place, glancing around the room for a clue. Mr. Jewels was too insistent in his manner for this paperwork to be insignificant. Unless the photos weren't what was inside and Richard was just reminiscing. Paul trudged down the stairs, each step weighted by fears. He'd never met his father's brother, barely remembered Mary, never met his mother. All his life was tied to Richard. What else had his father failed to share?

A whirlwind of noise preceded Paul's entrance into the kitchen. Reese and Roxie each carried a tray with sandwiches and fruit. "What are you two laughing out?"

"Grandpa, we made everyone a snack. Can't you see the design?"

Paul scratched his chin, walked around the trays. "Let me guess. Mr. Peanut Butter jumping over a river of jam and Mrs. Cheese climbing an apple tree."

Another fit of laughter and the two raced outside. Paul followed to find Danny and Sealy seated with cardboard crowns on their heads. "Lucky me, I'm just in time for a royal treat."

Sealy pointed at the seat next to her. "The girls made you a crown as well."

Roxie skipped in a circle. "Yep, something to cheer you up. Sealy said you were having a hard day. No one should have a hard day, especially if they don't want to."

Paul sat down and put on his crown. "And may I ask what kind of day I should have?"

Sealy looked him straight in the eye. "Something more spontaneous, like when we were young and accepted whatever came our way. I know we aren't kids, but watching Roxie and Reese, I envy their free spirit."

"Is that how you remember me when we played on the beach?"

Sealy twirled the tips of her hair. "I remember Sundays and other stay-home days. We called them free days. No matter where or what we did, we were forbidden to work. All our chores and homework had to be done by Saturday. I don't remember the days of the week when my mom and I visited. They were all Sundays."

Paul laughed. "Danny, are you taking Sealy's advice? If you are, then I'm the only one not following orders."

"I had to give in. After seeing Diane on the road. Sealy caught me being rude. A different perspective helps."

"Then I won't ask you why. We can talk about it later. See, I'm learning."

Sealy hid her eyes between her fingers. "I'm guilty of stressing too. That's why I bake. It keeps me honest. And everyone loves the result."

"Is that all they love?" The words had slipped out before Paul realized the inference. He noted Danny's glance at him and Sealy.

Sealy chimed in, "I'm sure they can't be any better than the girls' treats." Roxie and Reese smiled.

Danny grabbed the kids. "I'll let you two relax before dinner. If today is our day of rest, tomorrow is our day to work."

Sealy had taken the next few days to paint. She wrapped up the last of her twelve unframed paintings and carried them out to Paul's truck. With Danny taxiing the girls and locals around, Paul had insisted that he could drive her into town.

"Thanks for this, I owe you."

Paul chuckled. "I thought you had one or two paintings you were sending home. This looks like you could fill a gallery."

"It will. I forgot about a showing I promised to do last year. I could have sent some of my paintings from the warehouse, but since I have all these new ones, I thought I'd send them. Thank goodness Jeannie sent me support kits to shore up the canvas for when I ship them."

"You are full of surprises. I had no idea."

Going by the straight lines of Paul's lips and the way his voice drifted off, Sealy felt tentative. She buckled up, and instead of facing Paul, she looked out the window. The silence hung like an impermeable wall. She rolled her window down and let the breeze blow through. "I didn't mean to surprise you. My artwork is private."

Paul reached over and squeezed her hand. "So is mine. I understand that. Coming from a family of artists, I tend to keep my own work under wraps. I'm not as good as my father. I didn't know you were represented by galleries. That is very public."

"Does it bother you? It really isn't a secret in my family. My mother and sister know. It was my mother's idea. I took a pseudonym, using a combination of my family names. I sign *JMS*, which is *Jeannie, Morris, Sealy*, or it could be my mom's maiden name, Jones, and her first name, Mary. My mom didn't want me to embarrass her. She thought it all folly. That's why I'm a realtor."

"It isn't your success that bothers me. I thought it was just a hobby, not a huge part of who you are. I wish you'd mentioned it."

"My mother had so many rules and expectations. Her opinions have rubbed off on me." Sealy took a deep breath. "I have another confession."

Paul pulled off the road onto the shoulder. "That sounds ominous. I don't want to get in an accident."

Sealy laughed. "No, it's good, but embarrassing." She took another breath. "My mother and grandmother were so worried about my social standing that I hid my artistic profits. I made them believe that I had earned my living totally on my salesmanship. I did win awards as a top realtor in my firm, but nothing compared to the financial successes of my art pieces." The serious look on Paul's face confused her. Sealy wished she had kept her secret.

He sat there studying her.

Sealy whispered, "Please say something. You're making me uncomfortable."

Paul shook his head, touched his hand to his heart. "I can't imagine how you must have felt with that type of pressure from your family. My father always told me to work from my heart.

He's an artist first. Town manager and businessman came second and third. Art for me has always been a hobby. I have other loves. Makes me second-guess my own choices."

"And what would that be?"

"Teaching school. But that door already closed. Now I'm the town manager, part owner of a winery. Thank goodness Danny took that over. I'm content. I'm thinking your secret fame is why my father and son had such a hard time finding you."

"Why would they track my artwork? Do you think Richard knew I was an artist?"

Paul smiled. "Maybe he was hoping you were."

Sealy thought back to the letters between her mother and Paul's father. They had stopped when she was twenty-one. That is when she had painted in earnest, small pieces to add extra cash to her meager wages. Her mother had said she couldn't afford to help her anymore. That would make sense. Richard's checks had eased the way for her to take classes. Only they weren't at university, but to art school.

"Earth to Sealy. We're at the post office. Do you need my help?"

"Oh, sorry. I can manage. You have important meetings. Let me know how it goes with Mr. Jewels. I can find my way back with Danny."

"Are you sure? I'll be at my office till 5:00."

"Good to know."

The post office was the size of a postage stamp. Sealy would have missed it if Paul hadn't dropped her off in front. She'd passed it so many times walking to the library and the grocery store. Scrunched in between the bakery and the bookstore, the double-door entry appeared as if it were a mural painted on from another time. The entrance was real, but the people on either side—one eating a cookie, the other reading a book—were realistic renditions of the townspeople. *Clever.*

As Sealy struggled with the doors, the postmaster rushed to help her. "What do we have here? Your packages are almost larger than you. Paintings, I presume."

"Yes, how did you know?"

"I've worked here for almost a half century. I know an artist when I see one. Besides, I saw Paul drop you off. Are these Richard's paintings?"

Sealy shook her head. "No, they aren't his. I'm Sealy, a guest at the Morrises' house. And you must be?"

The elderly woman looked down at her shirt. "I'm supposed to wear my name tag, but why bother? Everyone in town knows me. That is, but you. I'm Louise. Promise not to turn me in for dereliction of my duties."

"I promise. But I need your help. I didn't have all the packaging supplies. I've brought just the canvases, but they are fragile. Can you wrap them up so they won't get damaged? I think they make special boxes for this."

Louise went behind the counter and pulled out flattened boxes. "This should do. Since the town collects artists, I've done this many a time. I take it you're a student of Richard's and you want to send the paintings home."

Sealy blushed. "Not exactly. I've got a showing in Seattle next month. I hope I left you enough time to get them there."

"This is going to be expensive. Did you paint them here?"

After Sealy's confession to Paul, she felt ill at ease talking about her work. "I can start the paperwork and stuff the boxes. I don't want to keep you from your duties."

Louise looked around at the empty counter and the door. "Nope, I'll help. None of the regulars will be here until lunch. I've already sorted the mail, and it's slow with the storm and all."

As they worked together and developed a rhythm, Sealy began to relax. "You mentioned that the town collected artists. What did you mean?"

"They must not talk much up at the Hawk House. Richard started an art school years ago. An eclectic group came. Art was a loose form back then. That's when Richard also experimented with winemaking from the local fruits—especially the blueberries and apples. After the art school closed, artists still came here. The town has its magic with views and simplicity. Some of the artists didn't like the big-city life." Louise stared out the window as if remembering that time. "Many stayed, but for the most part they left. Lots of couples formed, and when they had kids, the big city drew them back. Families do that."

"Is that what brought you here? You have that wistful look."

"I tried my hand at pottery. Some of my work is in the gallery one street over. I fell in love with one of the painters. But she got pregnant, with another artist. Broke my heart, but not my soul. I stayed here where I was accepted for me. But that was a long time ago. The post office suits me."

Sealy handed Louise the labels and paperwork. "I'm thankful you are here. I've been visiting for a little over a month, and no one told me about the town's thriving artist enclave. The Morrises are busy with their lives."

Louise studied the paperwork. "How much do you want to insure them for?"

"A hundred thousand."

Louise looked up and scrunched her eyes. "Who are you, Ms. Sealy? No one 'insures' their work for that much unless they're famous."

Sensing that Louise would understand, Sealy told the truth. "Can you keep a secret?"

Louise whispered. "It's just you and me and the gossip mill."

Sealy lowered her eyes. "I am famous."

"Let me get this straight. You're telling me that you are so famous that these paintings are worth a fortune. I've never heard of you, and you're in a small town talking to an old postmaster."

"Exactly. It's the perfect situation. Don't you think?" Sealy laughed and couldn't control herself. "You see, I've hidden my identity for forty years. Afraid of what people would think. And here you are, of the same era as my mother, openly sharing that you loved a woman."

Louise marked the packages, stamped them, and rang up the bill. "That will be five hundred dollars, Ms. Sealy. Or as the packages state, JMS."

"Perfect. Can I bother you for a little bit of gossip from long ago?"

"That's my specialty. But you better be quick, as the loyal patrons will be here soon."

"Just two questions. Did you know a woman named Mary from that time, and do you remember a story about a baby found after a storm?"

"Lots of Marys in my life. There was a fine looker, but she didn't have any interest in me. She stayed at the school. She was more an organizer than an artist. I think she married Richard's brother, Barry. Is that the lady you want to know about?"

A tear slid down her cheek. "Yes, she was my mother. She died ten years ago. It's what brought me here."

Sealy thought she'd hear condolences, but that wasn't Louise's style. "Everyone loved her. I could have too. But she was a straight shooter, never crossed a t without dotting an i. We called her the peacemaker. Surprised me when she and Barry left town so quickly. Come to think about it, it wasn't too much later after that baby was found that they left. I always thought Diane had something to do with their departure. Barry and her brothers had a run-in at the winery."

Suddenly the bell hanging over the door clanged. One person after another strolled in. Sealy waved goodbye.

Louise yelled above the chatter, "Sealy, famous lady, I'll look you up."

Inhaling the salty brine, Paul took the scenic way to his office walking along the wharf. He admired the old wooden boats, low-budget one-man operations, organized for utility. The traps and trawl lines each had a spot, the gaff hung near the boat's lip, ready to catch their color-coded buoys. He laughed as a group of kids ran by yelling, "Look at that bug. Biggest lobster I've ever seen."

Not far behind came the boy's grandfather with his leather-skinned face and a smile as wide as a piano. "Morning, Mr. Morris, fine day. Looks like the waves and weather have settled down."

Paul nodded. "Did your boat sustain any damage?"

"We're okay, but some of the other guys weren't so lucky. I'm letting them use my boat after I get a run or two in. No need to be greedy."

"I can always count on you to have a big heart. Just let me know if anyone is in need. I might be able to get some disaster funds."

By the time Paul arrived at his office, his apprehensions about his father and Mr. Jewels had subsided. His father had slept fitfully but without incident. Amnesia seemed to be his elixir for survival. Neither of them had made mention of the envelope. Even so, Paul knew it was a matter of time before his father's body gave out. The number for hospice care lay beside each phone.

He let the wave of sadness wash over him. The loss of his mother was too distant of a memory to cause him pain, just curiosity. The loss of his wife had been buried inside so deep that he had become numb. With Sealy at the house and his father so ill, synapses of love and hope fired inside his nerves.

As always, his staff of two had organized his day. A line of people waited to talk with him, each with coffee and homemade treats to tide them over. Hours later he finally tackled his desk. Buried below the pile he found a transcribed phone message from Mr. Jewels:

> *I must leave today, without your father's response. His signature was crucial to make matters right, easier for all concerned. I'll carry on without it. Give my apologies to all, I did my best.*

Paul gripped his chest; the ache swirled around, filling his entire torso. He took a deep breath, drank a glass of water. His heartbeat was steady, but he felt the blood moving through his system, his stomach queasy, his shoulders shaking. It couldn't be a heart attack; he had just been checked. He stood up and all his extremities worked. Satisfied he hadn't had a stroke, he called Danny. When he didn't answer, he punched in Sealy's cell phone number.

Three rings and then, "Hello, Sealy speaking."

"Sealy, it's me, Paul. Are you still in town?"

"Just going for a bite to eat and then to find Danny. Are you okay? I didn't even know you had my cell phone number. I haven't had good enough service to use it."

"Something has come up. Where can I meet you?"

"Paul, you've got me nervous. How about the café near your office? I'm walking but should be there in ten minutes."

"Great."

Paul took another drink of water. The shaking had stopped, but the ache had settled in his stomach. He took the note with him and slipped out the back door of his office.

By the time Sealy arrived, Paul felt almost normal. She entered with a wide grin and Paul responded in kind.

"Thanks for coming. I didn't mean to scare you. Truth be told, I scared myself and needed to talk."

Without missing a beat, Sealy tilted her head, looked at him from the side of her eyes. He felt her quizzical gaze as one of true caring. "From what I see, you look fine, but not your usual self. Is this about Mr. Jewels, your father, work, or you?"

"I like that about you, you're not afraid to jump in. I think it's all the above. Mr. Jewels left me a note saying he was leaving and sent his apologies. The way it was phrased, it seemed that since Richard hadn't responded, he was apologizing for his next actions. Cryptic—but chilling in a way."

Sealy took her time answering. "We know that something happened in the past that your father doesn't want to talk about. We'll have to face it later, I guess. I suspect that Mr. Jewels wanted Richard to explain something to him and to us. I couldn't make my mother tell me things. But we haven't done anything wrong. What else is there?"

Paul hesitated. "I read the note and then my chest hurt. Not really my chest but my whole body ached. I thought it was a heart attack or a stroke, but the sensation had a vibration that shook my core."

Sealy reached across the table, held his hand by the wrist. Paul's felt a warm sensation run through his skin. "I felt the same thing when my mother was crossing over that threshold between being present and disappearing from my hold. I think we should find Danny and return to Hawk House. Your dad might need us."

Paul whispered, "I called Danny before I called you. He didn't answer. Let's go—that is, if you want to. I'll let my office know where I'll be."

Sealy let go of his hand. "We should go. Everything else can wait."

Sealy spoke with an even, soft voice, but Paul noted the tear sliding down her cheek. He left a tip on the table, even though they hadn't ordered.

Days were a blur and nights tumultuous. Sealy hadn't rested since their return from the lunch they never ate. Danny had already made the call before they arrived. Hospice had swooped in within two hours. Sealy was thankful that Paul had the foresight to pre-arrange all the care. And still, Richard lingered.

Sealy wondered what kept Richard from letting go. For the most part he was incoherent, ranting and then he'd go quiet, as if he heard voices. Even with hospice there to help with medication, bathing, and monitoring his vital signs, they all took turns sitting by his bedside. Danny always brought the girls with him. They painted and drew pictures, Danny read him poetry. Paul took the early morning and after-dinner shift so he could work. Sealy slipped in during the day. Richard often blurted out words, names, and would grab her arm—eyes open, pleading. Then he'd disappear in a fog after hospice administered morphine.

The more agitated Richard became, the more unsettled Sealy felt. She began jotting down his tangential murmurings, a puzzle to decipher. Determined to sort through the sadness and angst, Sealy returned to the gazebo to paint.

She started with wide brushstrokes, laying an underpainting of burnt umber and burnt sienna. This was the heat below the surface, and on the edges and in the center, she added blues for a cooling effect and shadows. The thin layers formed shapes and faces until her mother's arms reached out. Her sister held one hand; in the other hand a small child, locked fingers. The child floated in the breeze, feet lifting off the ground, tangled in the branches of a tree. The wind and her mother's hair hid the storm and shadows of two men. Sealy swirled her brush, fine strokes with white paint to lighten the scene. Frustrated, she put the canvas aside.

She began again, this time with a cool palette of colors, building light, warm colors of greens and yellows, then switching to purples. Quick brushstrokes, thin and precise, created grasses. Scraping with an old toothbrush, Sealy created the illusion of wind ripples swaying the grass. In the distance a building was surrounded by rows of plump grapes hanging from vines. Two female figures walked hand in hand. A group of men stood in the corner, a brawl, and then a serene scene of children rolling down a hill.

Exhausted, Sealy cleaned her brushes and sat with the paintings. They told a story she didn't know. Perhaps this was as it should be. She'd learned over the years to quiet her critical left brain. No stroke is lost, no feeling disappears. Many a time she had painted another painting on top of a canvas, only to bring it back with more depth and precision.

Loud steps warned her that someone approached. Sure enough, Paul appeared, his face stained with salty lines, eyes red.

"Paul, has Richard slipped away?"

Paul shook his head. "No, but he will soon. Could you come and sit with me? Danny is with my father now. He's letting Reese and Roxie say goodbye. I don't want them to see the final moment."

Sealy packed up the canvases. "Let's go."

Paul grabbed her free hand, and they walked silently up the hill.

Paul sat on one side of the bed, watching his father's shallow breath and Sealy's deep inhalations. Sealy dozed in his father's overstuffed chair with her finger hooked on Richard's thumb. Sadness lay like a blanket over his heart. Unlike Danny, he enjoyed sharing his father with Sealy. She seemed to bring out joy even in such misery.

Richard's breath deepened. His lips emitted a purr with each exhalation. The change in pattern woke Sealy. As she fumbled to wakefulness, Paul quipped, "You haven't missed much. Your breath synchronized with my father's. I wondered if you two were in sync with your dreams."

Sealy gave him a slow smile. "You may be right. I was dreaming of painting and art. I'm sure Richard sees his life layered within his canvases. I wish it were true that I could tap into his dreams. Maybe then I could figure out why my father left, why my mother didn't come back here. I wish I could go back in time and be my mother."

"Oh no, please don't. I want you right here, as you."

"I think your father gets me confused with my mother. But I don't get you confused with being Richard. Funny how that goes. You two seem so different and alike. I'm neither like my mother in looks nor actions and I see no resemblance to your side of the family. That's what confuses me. For some reason I thought there would be a familial connection."

Paul squeezed his eyes and opened them wide. "You don't resemble me or my father. Family is more than physical appearances."

Sealy glanced over at Richard. "I think your father is listening. He's smiling at this conversation. I meant that my disposition is different. The only thing I have in common is that I like art, and that I'm Mary's daughter. Your disposition is like Richard's—private, deep, ready to enjoy. My sister, Jeannie, is so like my mother, in her appearance and temperament. She focuses on the details, doesn't always see the big picture. I acquired the business mind by overriding my creative side."

Richard began to fidget, his hand reached out, his eyes popped open. Paul took his hand.

Sealy stood off to the side. "I should leave you two together. I feel like I'm intruding."

Richard bellowed, "No, you belong here. Damn the bloodline. Damn Mr. Jewels. Damn the brawl." He coughed, grabbed Sealy's hand. Holding both of their hands in a tight grip, he whispered, "Promise me you'll stay together."

Before they could answer, Richard gasped his last breath.

Sealy placed her fingers under his nose. "I'm afraid he's gone. I didn't mean to upset him. I'm so sorry."

Paul kneeled by the bed, listened to his heart. Sealy's voice was a distant echo, down in a dark tunnel. He'd been here before, the place where sadness lay. He rested his hands around his father's face, still warm with life. As Sealy tucked the covers around Richard's torso, Paul reached for her hands. The mere touch pulled him back from the blackness. Staring at Sealy through his teary eyes, he thought of Richard's last wish.

Part Two
Stepping Out

Sealy passed the next few days in the background, watching over Reese and Roxie, while Paul and Danny dealt with the details of putting Richard to rest. With no time to shop for clothes for the girls, Danny had asked Sealy to fix them up—a good distraction from the underlying feelings of sadness that permeated through the house and her own struggle between her head and heart. Her twinges of feeling for Paul were not sisterly and neither were their embraces.

Reese and Roxie found Sealy in the living room by the fire. Each had carried dresses from their closets.

"Oh my, how many dresses did you bring down? Remember it's cold out and we have to have sleeves and no bright colors."

Reese sorted her summer fair out from the pile. Roxie struggled with the prints. "Are you sure we can't have flowers. Aren't they given at funerals to make people smile?"

Sealy grabbed them both in her arms. "You two are the flowers. Growing wild and crazy and more beautiful every day. Look, you both have blue dresses—will they work?" With their nods of approval, Sealy studied the dresses. A quick look told her she'd have to make some alterations. "Who knows where your dad keeps the sewing kit?"

The look of bewilderment on Roxie's face and the tears on Reese's told her she walked herself into a minefield of emotions. Roxie answered, "My mom's sewing box is in the den. At least that is where she used to keep it. Poppy gave it to her, but who knows. Daddy has never used it."

"What happens if you lose a button?"

"Oh, that's easy. We pin it. We have pins in the kitchen drawer. Daddy can fix everything else, but not our clothes."

"Meet me in the den after you change into the dresses. Then I can see what needs to be done."

In the time it took Sealy to get a fresh cup of coffee and walk to the den, the girls had already changed. Roxie was standing on a chair reaching for the top shelf.

"Hold on, girls, I can help you. Just direct me, as I don't see a sewing kit."

"Poppy put it up high, behind the books on gardening. I don't think he wanted to see it, and neither did my dad."

With care, Sealy removed the front layer of gardening books and then stared.

"Is it there? We never moved it, promise. Are you okay?"

Her hands shook as she reached for the hidden sewing kit. "Yes, I'm fine." She carried it down as if it would explode. The sewing kit was a basket just like the one her mother had used. Handmade, woven grasses formed the base and cover. The inside held a crafted red wood box with a top compartment and two lower levels that opened on scissor hinges.

Memories flashed by of her mother with pins in her mouth. *Stop fidgeting, this will only take a minute if you stand still. We don't have money for a new dress, but you'll look beautiful.* And her mother never failed her.

Sealy dabbed her eyes. "Okay, Roxie, looks like I have to take your hem out and lengthen the dress. You've grown. I think there is enough material, but if not I can figure it out. And you, Miss Reese, either you lost weight, or this dress was always big. I can tuck it in on the sides."

After the girls changed back into their pants, they both huddled together whispering. Sealy knew they were up to something by the way they kept looking at her. "What it is? I know you want to say something."

Roxie ran over and gave her a hug. Reese sat on her lap. "Reese wanted to know how come you never talk about your kids.

You have some, don't you? Otherwise, you couldn't possibly be so good at loving us."

Sealy bent over and kissed the tops of their heads. "I've had practice, but not with my own children." Her voice quivered. "Sometimes woman can't have children."

Roxie nodded. "Just like children sometimes don't have their mothers."

Paul paused outside the den. He listened to the innocent voices of Reese and Roxie in conversation with Sealy and felt the familiar tightness of emotion inside. The girls came running out, waved, and headed who knows where. He found Sealy on the floor surrounded by dresses and sewing paraphernalia.

"I'm not a good host, am I? Either you are in the kitchen baking treats, sitting with Richard, and now a seamstress. I don't know what I'd do without you."

Sealy's answer came slowly, as if she was far away. "Yes, you are. You let me do what I'm good at. Your father set off a stream of events when he put that ad on your website. Like it or not, I'm entrenched."

Her voice caught at the back of her throat. Paul realized that she'd been crying. He sat down next to her on the floor, careful to keep his distance. She looked so forlorn, like an abandoned child lost within a pile of rumple. The contents of the sewing basket surrounded two blue dresses.

Paul cleared his throat. "Do you want to tell me what's going on?"

She barely looked at him. "Sorry, I'll clean up the mess."

"Not yet. You dumped it for a reason. And you're crying. What triggered this?"

Sealy straightened her shoulders and gave him a side look, as if she wanted to back out the door, leave the situation. "It started with the sewing basket. Then Roxie asked me a question about my children."

Paul held back the urge to hold Sealy. He didn't feel as if she trusted him enough to let her guard down. Instead, he lifted her chin up and looked into her eyes. "I never asked you that, I didn't want to pry. Leave it to kids to blurt out their thoughts."

Sealy gave him a faint smile, twirled her hair. "I told them the truth, that I couldn't have children. But that's not why I'm crying. I let go of that dream a long time ago. The one man I loved couldn't accept my condition and we parted ways. He has four adult children and grandkids. Oddly enough, they live close by and I'm friends with the whole family."

Paul waited. "Are you going to tell me what made you cry? Or will I find the answer on the floor?"

Another smile, another twirl of her hair. "Roxie said some kids don't have mothers just like I don't have kids. I thought of you without your mom and Danny without his mom. I never asked about Danny's wife. So many children without mothers. And then the sewing basket. My mom had the same one."

"Is that why the contents are strewn on the floor?"

"I thought there'd be a clue. My mom was good at that. I feel like she's here nudging me toward…"

Paul softened his voice. "Take a breath and finish your thought. Is she nudging you toward Richard, toward her past, or toward your future? Would any of these be so bad?"

"You make this sound so easy. But you know it isn't. Your world isn't the same with me here. My presence has dredged up skeletons—about my father, the winery, even Diane mentioned to Danny that you had a twin sister who died at birth. He didn't know that."

Paul folded his hands as in prayer. He finally found breath enough to speak. "I guess Richard's code of silence was just as strong as your mother's. This is the first time I've heard of having a twin sister. No one in the town ever mentioned it." He closed his eyes and felt a profound loss.

Sealy stretched her legs and picked up buttons and scissors. Her voice quivered even as she tried to make light of what she had just revealed. "I'm sorry, I didn't know if you knew. Forgive me. I'm sure Richard's friends will come out of the woodwork at the funeral. Richard was well liked. Maybe some of his friends will say something. At least I can pick up some juicy gossip to fill in more gaps."

The thought hadn't entered Paul's mind. The Morrises' history was well known, documented. Their private life had never been a topic of discussion. Upset, Paul dreaded the idea of being the center of gossip. He answered Sealy more tersely than he wanted: "I expect a good showing. Friends and foes will behave. We are a civil group here. I doubt there'll be public revelations. I'm still the town manager for another two years at least."

"You can depend on my help at the reception. I learned from my mother how to deflect a situation. She always worried about what people would say. One of her quips was 'Tattle tales look for an entrance. Make sure your door is closed.' Paul, we aren't the same as our parents. You're not hiding information. You're the opposite by opening the door and letting people in." Pointing to the floor, Sealy sighed. "Besides, look at the mess I've made."

Paul kneeled. "Let me help clean up. Hand me the basket, seems like there is a slot for everything." Paul moved the scissor hinges, stretching out the levels of drawers. The last drawer lay flat without slots, only a nub with a string attached. He pulled the string and the base opened to a hidden layer with letters. After a quick look he whispered, "These are from your mother to my mother."

Sealy reached for them, but her hand stopped in midair.

The shock of their find slowly sunk in. Paul stumbled with his words. "I've never had a window into my mother's life. Do you mind if we share the letters?"

"They don't belong to either of us, do they? Let's finish cleaning up and then read them together. That is, if you have time."

Paul fiddled with the hinges, stared at the basket. "Yes, I have plenty of time. I'll go get us a bottle of wine and some cheese. There's no reason to wait."

Sealy reached for her glass of wine, took two sips, and waited for the numbing effect. Paul sat in the corner reading and rereading each letter. He laid them out as if they were a puzzle. She traced her mother's handwriting, the long *l*'s, the curve of the *s*'s and the fancy *t*'s. She remembered notes of encouragement, love in her lunch box. Her mother never said much, but she had felt her presence at school as a counterbalance to her awkwardness.

Paul finally looked up. "Could you read these three notes out loud? I want to imagine your mother's voice. I wish the notes were dated."

"Scoot over. I'll try. I had her voice in my head when I was a kid, not so much as an adult. When she was serious, her tone would lower. Her voice a whisper, as if each word was for you alone." Sealy began.

Dear Lorraine,

I prefer calling you Lory, which I know makes you smile. Best save that for when we are together. I'm sending a note over as I won't be able to stop by today. Barry has more on his plate with the neighbors feuding. He won't share what is wrong, but it seems to be affecting the winery. He's retreating from the world. Maybe you should see the doctor. You seem so glum.

Mary (Mo)

PS I took care of the paperwork.

"Is that how your mother sounded? Your reading puts love behind each word."

Sealy let the letter fall on the table. "Usually, she didn't let that side show, but in our quite moments I felt that devotion. I'm trying to figure out the sadness in her voice."

"I detect worry on all sides. I wonder if this is when my mom's illness started. Even before I was born. Please read on."

Lory,

Enough with formal protocol. I'm not sure when I will get over to help. You need bed rest. Stop trying to be Miss Perfect. Remember to have fun. I know you look like a balloon, but a baby belly suits you well. It will get easier. Barry started drinking. It's as if the fog protects him. I'll keep you posted with any news about the application.

Mo

"I'm amazed at how open my mother seems with my father's problems. She never once mentioned them to us. I guess she trusted your mother."

Paul picked up the letter and studied the words. "I really wish I could hear my mom's reply. Seems they were working on a project."

Sealy sighed. "Even in these letters, so much isn't said. Maybe this is when my mom became secretive."

Dearest Lory,

Richard is so upset about the art school. Barry thinks something happened with the locals and that is why there was a fight. Barry warned me to stay away from everyone. I feel so helpless. Especially since you and Richard need calm now. Are you sure about helping? You don't need to follow through, I'm sure the family would understand.

Mo

PS I love you no matter what.

Sealy went silent. She felt each word, as if her mother had come back and touched her heart. She turned to Paul. "The letters were emotional. It was as if they were sitting here with us. I don't know what to think."

"Mary's worry for my mother—so overwhelming. Given Mr. Jewels's sudden appearance and my father's reaction, they might have been a reason to worry. Whatever is going on about adoption in these pages, it makes no sense. I wish we had the other side of the equation."

Sealy envisioned her mother's sewing box sitting on the top shelf in her laundry room at home. "I could call Jeannie and have her pick up my mother's matching sewing box. We used to quarrel about it. My mother gave it to me, but Jeannie had more sewing to do with the kids than I did. I felt guilty, so I always volunteered to make costumes for her kids."

"I can see why you offered to help with the girls' dresses. Your mother was wiser than she knew."

"I don't know. I'm tired of wondering and searching. Paul, do you mind if I use the house phone? It's still early enough in the day for me to call Jeannie."

"Go ahead. This is your home for now."

His words sounded weighted to Sealy. Even without Richard's death, finding the letters between her mother and Paul's mother caused her pause. Her heart felt the pain of so many levels. "Let's leave our personal histories aside until after the funeral. You have lots on your plate."

Paul nodded. "Good advice."

Sealy squeezed his hand and left him with the letters.

Exhausted from the week's preparations, Sealy stood in the corner of the garden waiting for the guests to arrive. Richard would have appreciated the low-angle sun with subdued greens and blues. Grateful that she had packed a black dress, Sealy wore her mother's favorite flats that revealed her toe cleavage. They had always joked about the expression. In honor of her mother's flair and Richard's aesthetics, she had added a blue silk scarf that matched the shawl he had woven.

She had come home early from the funeral to help set up the platters of appetizers and sweets. The ceremony included just the family, herself, and Richard's former staff. No one had questioned her presence, and she had steered clear of any conversations of substance when Richard's secretary drove her back to the Hawk House. It had been easy as the elderly woman talked only of Richard. Every word an adulation.

"Such a strong man of character. He raised his son alone. I was with him after his wife, Lorraine, died and until he left the town manager's office. Oh my, I miss him so. You're such a dear for working here, especially to help out with the burial." Her talk drifted into cries of deep sadness. Sealy realized the secretary had been in love with Richard and had mistaken her for an employee of the Hawk House. Sealy ignored the older woman's quick assumptions.

Danny rushed in, out of breath. "Sealy, could you watch the girls, keep them busy? I've got to make sure everyone can park. They've practically closed the town down. Paul's out there talking with Richard's old staff and some folks that used to live near here."

"I'll rescue the girls. Where are they?"

"They're playing in the limousine."

Sealy found them in the back seat of a restored Rolls-Royce stretch limo. Roxie stood on the seat with her head poking out of the sunroof. Reese was inside talking through the sliding window to the driver.

"What have we here? My two favorite girls in a fancy car. I need your help inside."

Roxie poked her head back in the car. "Reese, we gotta go."

The driver stepped out of the car and formally opened the door for them. He even bowed. Sealy recognized him from the meat counter. "Curly, what a surprise to see you without your apron, cap, and gloves. Thanks for taking care of Roxie and Reese."

"Ms. Sealy, nice to see you again. It's an honor to escort the Morrises. Richard always loved my old cars. When I found out he had passed, I made sure that I could take the day off from the grocery store and drive. From what the girls tell me about your cooking and sewing, you took my advice about looking after everyone."

"I didn't have a choice. They wheedle their way into your heart. Danny and Paul have been overwhelmed with Richard and his death. I couldn't abandon the girls."

"Did you ever find out about the pulverized bone powder?"

Sealy chuckled. "Yes, Richard let me in on its use. I've already used it to clarify the paint colors."

"Must mean you are one of the Morrises. Welcome to the family."

Curly's analysis took her by surprise. Was Richard's sharing his paint formula a sign? A tug at her dress brought Sealy back. She waved and turned to the girls. "Okay, time to serve our guests. I'll race you into the house."

Within minutes streams of people entered. Reese and Roxie hovered by her side until they spotted some kids from their school. Off they went and Sealy stood alone. The antithesis of her mother's cardinal rule as host. *Keep moving, this creates a sense of control. Always have a glass in your hand, smile. Stand tall, let your long legs assist your grace.*

Sealy walked into the thick of the crowd. With a gentle touch to the shoulder or elbow, the guests parted, acknowledged her presence, and followed her path. Theatrics worked in all situations, a cover for her insecurity and a redirection to their thoughts. Sealy refused the designation of employee. Yet Curly's description as part of the family left her feeling like an impostor. Either way, she wanted to help.

Danny and Paul stood at the door. As Sealy approached, Diane from the vineyard entered, accompanied by two men. The room quieted and the din of conversations ceased. All eyes followed them, until Paul shook their hands and they moved on. Danny ignored their handshakes and talked with the next guests. Sealy held back, watching the dynamics, worried that Diane would approach her.

Instead, she felt a tap on her shoulder and heard a whisper: "Famous lady, get ready for fireworks."

Sealy turned to find the postmaster, outfitted in her work uniform. "Louise, how nice of you to come. You might be the only other person I know except for Diane."

"Be careful with that one. She's got her fingers in every pie. Not because she's got a sweet tooth, more a hankering to charm her way into your business. I'm surprised her brothers came with her."

"Thanks for the warning. But why? What can she possibly do to me?"

Louise came in closer and whispered, "Either she reconciled with her brothers and the three are up to no good, or the boys are here to claim the vineyard. If they find out that Mary is your mother, they'll try to snare you into some conspiracy theory. Danny knows trouble when he sees it. Look at his body language. He's put up a wall. I'm not sure about Paul. They ruined Richard's and Barry's life."

Sealy faced Louise. She remembered Louise's tale of her father's run-in with Diane's brothers. "You do notice everything. I better pay attention. You're scaring me."

"I hear so much at the post office. The daily chit-chats or silences are my gauge of a patron's state of mind. It's better than a bar. As the postmaster I notice more than anyone through the mail—bills, correspondence, packages. I consider myself a doctor. I've taken my own Hippocratic oath."

With more and more people passing through, Sealy had lost sight of the kids. Louise's talk put her on edge, as if an imminent disaster was about to occur. Finally, she spotted Reese and then Roxie on the floor under the dining table, building a city with paper plates. Relieved, she guided Louise over to the buffet. "Try my cookies. It's a recipe from my mother."

"I remember these. Mary would take them down to the art school at the day's end. I traded her for a weekly delivery in exchange for two baskets. Best barter I've ever done."

Sealy relaxed with the change in tone. "Were they sewing baskets?"

"Yes, Mary got one for herself and one for Lorraine. The two were inseparable. It was hard for Lorraine and Richard when Barry and your mom left."

Curious but not willing to relinquish too much, Sealy steered Louise away from probing conversations. "Did you make them? I loved the outer weave and the wooden interior with all the layered compartments."

Louise's face lit up with the compliment. "It's a Quaker design from my past."

"I'd like to hear about that sometime."

Louise nodded. "We artists need to stick together. Be careful now, the press from the big city of Portland just walked in. I'm sure Richard would be smarting. I wonder why they're here."

Sealy turned to see Diane's brothers with a cameraman and a reporter. "Do you think they're here because Richard was the former town manager?"

"No. Local small towns are more civil than that. We're private people. Especially at a wake. Diane and her brothers are up to no good. You better stop it."

Worried and annoyed at the intrusion of privacy, Sealy caught Paul's eye and motioned toward the doorway. Thankfully, he took her cue. She stepped outside of the room and faced him. "I didn't want to disturb you, but Louise from the post office noticed the Portland press is here. She thought it was suspicious especially since they were with Diane's brothers. Thought I'd warn you."

Paul's reaction validated her concerns. He scanned the room and zeroed in on the brothers. "Good call. Seems old vendettas have surfaced. Diane's brothers haven't been here for as long as I can remember. I didn't recognize them."

"Louise said they left town just about the time my parents departed. She mentioned an argument."

His tone changed, and Sealy detected more than annoyance. "Don't take on our problems, Sealy. I've learned not to jump ahead with only assumptions. Let me dig deeper. I'm more concerned the press is here." He took her hands, bent his head so their eyes met. "I need a favor. Can you find the reporter and cameraman and distract them while I talk with the brothers?"

Reassured Paul's annoyance wasn't with her, Sealy squeezed Paul's hands and reentered the dining area. With a deep breath, she collected her thoughts. Paul's advice to stay out of the Morrises' problems stung. She'd been trying so hard to fit in that she'd forgotten the purpose of the funeral. Richard's death wasn't an end but a beginning. The people gathered in the room were here to honor his legacy and their own. Paul had to play two roles, that of the town manager and that of a grieving son. Her presence added another layer. His words expressed his frustration, but his warm hands told a different story.

Sealy thought of her mother's funeral reception. Only a handful of Mary's friends had attended. They talked more about themselves and how close they were to her mother, and less about Mary alone. Knowing now about the Morrises, Sealy wondered if any of her mother's friends knew her past. And did it matter? Wasn't that exactly what Jeannie had said last night? *Stop this nonsense. Mom was Mom, her past isn't ours. I'll find the sewing box, and if I find more letters, I'll send them. Maybe I'll even find your birth certificate.*

I'm worried about you, sis. You shouldn't care so much. How could she not care? All her life she'd felt unsettled.

As she walked through the room, Roxie and Reese grabbed her hands. Their soft palms calmed her.

"Come with me, I'm off to find a man with a camera and another with a pad of paper and a pen."

Reese laughed. "You mean those two sitting with the woman in the corner? Will they take our picture?"

Sealy recognized the woman from the lobby of the inn, Elly. With the girls in tow, they sauntered over.

Paul watched Sealy dance with his granddaughters. The three swayed, Sealy's long legs and arms led, and the girls followed across the room. He squeezed his eyes closed, refusing to release the tears. He couldn't imagine dealing with his father's death without her.

Diane stood off in a corner. Danny stood to her left. Paul noted his posture, shoulders pulled down, body bent at the hip ready for a sprint. He knew that pose, had seen it on the football field when Danny calculated a play.

Paul approached Diane at the buffet. He overheard her grumbling with the two men: "You could have told me you'd be here for the funeral. It takes a death for my brothers to return after all these years."

So these men were Diane's brothers. They were taller than Diane, more refined. He guessed that sixty years ago, they would have had women swooning. Still handsome, they looked stiff, out of place in the Hawk House. They had come in suits, a little too formal for the town.

Paul eased his way in between them. "You two must be Diane's brothers. Thanks for coming."

The taller of the two extended his free hand. "I'm Geordie and this is Chuck. Your dad always enjoyed shortening our names. Declared our given names were too formal. We came out of respect for your father and family. I'm sure you've heard stories."

As Paul shook the man's hand he felt a slight tremor, curved knuckles, and withered skin. As much as he worried about the secrets his father left unshared, he felt a sympathy for Diane's brothers. Their vineyard and the winery had been entwined for years. "I stay away from gossip, if that's what you mean. I don't recall my father saying much. Your sister is the one who talks."

The brothers nodded, a pained look crossing their brows, followed by a resigned set to their jaws.

Paul moved in closer and patted Chuck's shoulder. "You're here, that's what counts. If you'd like, we could talk later. No worries."

Before either could answer, Diane appeared with a glass of wine. As one of the servers passed, she took another glass. Paul felt a shift. Geordie moved aside and Chuck stepped behind his brother.

"My, my, did I interrupt something? I hate to be excluded."

Paul became a mediator and led the three down a safe path. "No need to feel excluded. It's your brothers who have missed out on years of this town. I only just met them. I'm sure it's nice to have them at home. If you'd like, I can take them on a tour of the winery in a few days. Get them out from under your hair."

Finishing off both glasses of wine, Diane shook her head. "I don't think they'll be here that long. I can't imagine why they came."

Geordie reached back to steady his brother from the verbal slap. "Diane, you needn't worry about why we came. We're staying in town, out of your way. Chuck and I will leave when we are ready to. If you don't mind, we were in the middle of a conversation."

Paul noticed Diane's body cringe at her brother's words. He redirected his offer to the brothers. "Well, in that case. I can meet you two for lunch when I'm at the office. If I can help you feel more comfortable, just let me know."

Diane walked away only to turn and call out to her brother Chuck for all to hear: "Our town doesn't need a loser like you."

Diane's words had an instant effect. A hush fell over the room. Everyone looked at Diane, mumbled among themselves, and then looked away, either out of politeness toward Chuck and Geordie or disgust with Diane.

Paul ushered the brothers toward the patio but made a quick detour when he saw Sealy with the press. Engaged in an animated conversation, she turned in time to wave him off. As she continued talking, the cameraman snapped a few shots, and the journalist took notes. Paul had to admire her. Sealy's knack for diplomacy eased all situations. He hoped that the press's photo and an article wouldn't backfire on her.

Sealy sat alone on the patio. Still in her black dress, she kicked off her shoes, letting her feet dangle over the bench. Too tired to mount the stairs to change, she pulled her hair back and wrapped it with her blue silk scarf. The hypnotic swing of each foot let her thoughts drift.

The funeral reception had only lasted a couple of hours, yet she had talked to more townspeople than she had in the month she'd been here. A mixture of the old guard and the young upcoming professionals shared stories of Richard. Only Louise talked to her about Richard's life before becoming the town manager. Tears slipped from Sealy's eyes, leaving a salty trail along her cheeks. She let them stay.

Chilled by the evening breeze, Sealy drew her mother's shawl around her shoulders. Feeling the breeze talking to her, she laughed and turned to find Paul standing behind her.

"What's this, you're out here alone, laughing and silently crying?"

"How long were you standing there? I laughed because I thought I heard a whisper in the leaves. I imagined my mother and father talking. The tears are for losses—yours, the kids'—and a sadness of not knowing. Funerals are intense."

Paul sat down beside her. He had changed out of his suit and wore old, weathered jeans and a green plaid flannel shirt. They sat close enough for her to smell the peppermint soap from his shower. Their pinkie fingers touched.

"I just came down to check that the house was in order. I thought you had retreated to your room. Glad that you're here. I've exhausted you."

Sealy smiled. "More than exhaustion. I was so worried about Diane after Louise's warning and seeing Danny on edge. I just wanted it all to go smoothly for you."

"Did this add to your tears?"

Sealy curled her pinkie into his. "I just flashed on a memory." Holding up her little finger, Sealy smiled. "Pinkie swear, do you remember?"

Paul shook his head. "No, tell me. What did I swear to?"

"I'm not sure. But I remember I was leaving the beach. My mom was calling, and you came up to me and said, 'Come back, pinkie swear.'"

A wide grin transformed Paul's face. "Wow, I was a smart kid. But that didn't bring on your tears. It's something else."

Sealy shrugged. "I'm not good at articulating when I'm confused. I don't know what I intended by coming here. Maybe clarity. I'm more confused."

"You came here to find out about your mother. All parents had a life before they became parents."

"It's not her life I'm worried about now. The whispers I'm hearing in the breeze are tidbits of gossip. Some good, some bad. I still don't know if they loved each other. I never knew them when that was true. I see the bench your father made in honor of your mother. It's physical evidence of their love. I don't want to ruin your life by revealing hidden secrets and past transgressions."

"Do you mean what Louise said about the fight between your father and Diane's brothers?"

Sealy released her pinkie from Paul's. "Earlier you said I shouldn't take on the Morrises' problems. The problem is, I am a Morris. I read so many unflattering stories about Barry Morris in old papers. Whatever happened back then is why my mother moved away. Maybe it's why she never came back."

"I see. I don't believe this is about you, Sealy. Diane doesn't know who you are, and neither do her brothers."

Sealy nervously twirled her hair. "I saw how you reacted, pulling the brothers aside. You're not sharing something with me."

Paul put his hands together and took a breath. "I found some anomalies in the bookkeeping at the winery. It was hard to find. I had to compare the receivables with the invoices and then compare the quantity of grapes delivered to what was rendered. Something isn't right. I went back years and found something similar when your father was in charge."

Sealy couldn't listen to more negative discoveries about her parents. She turned her head away from Paul. "Yes, my father got into a bind. The articles inferred that. He felt guilty, drank, and ruined our lives."

"No, you missed my point. Please look at me. I don't think your father cooked the books back then, just like I don't think Danny is doing anything wrong with running the winery. My father suspected something all along."

The significance hit Sealy all at once. "If you're right, the only common denominator is Diane. But why would my father fight with her brothers?"

"We'll find out soon enough. I'm meeting with them for lunch next week. They aren't staying with Diane. I think she is furious."

All Sealy could muster in reply was a moan. Holding her stomach, she rose from the bench. "I'm not feeling too well. I've always hated anger. I'd rather make things right, get it all out. Even when I was young my stomach would react. I still internalize the stress."

Paul stood with her. "I can even see it on your brow. It furrows deeper when you're upset. Like when you play with your food at the table or twirl your hair."

Gathering her shoes and shawl, Sealy turned to go.

Paul reached for her. "Don't go to bed upset. I agree with you. Secrets eat away at what is good. I'll walk you back."

Sealy accepted Paul's arm. They walked silently back to the house. As they parted, Paul bent down as if to kiss her. As she looked up, her scarf slipped off her hair and onto Paul.

With an awkward laugh, he kissed her forehead and said good night. "Hope you feel better in the morning."

"I will, thanks for listening. A good night's sleep will help." Sealy waved the scarf and smiled. "See you in the morning."

Paul checked his watch to see if he had overslept. Nope. If anything, he was early. Why didn't he hear little voices or conversations coming from the dining room? He quickened his step and found Danny seated in the corner alone.

"What's this? Where are the kids?"

"They're in the kitchen with Sealy. I gave the cook the day off. She needed a break after all the commotion of the last few days. Besides, I needed to talk to you alone without prying minds."

"Is this business or personal? You have that tense look you always get. Remember business is just business, we will always survive."

Danny nodded. "What happens when business gets personal?"

Paul mentally went through his conversation with Sealy. He hoped she hadn't said anything about his old and new discoveries about the bookkeeping to Danny. "Hard not to mix business into our family life. We're so connected, living together and sharing workloads on two businesses. Are you unhappy with our arrangement? Adding the bed-and-breakfast was your idea. Is it too much with the winery?"

Danny gave him a look of disbelief. "I wish it were that simple. Dad, are you so clueless to what is happening right in front of your eyes? My grandfather, your dad, just passed away, and the past is creeping in on us. Didn't you see Diane swarming around the family? Something doesn't feel right. I never told you this, but before Charmaine passed, she warned me about Diane. Charmaine said she was predatory. I chalked it up to her mental health. Charmaine was in her psychotic stage, paranoid about everything. I needed to protect the girls. I regret not listening to her."

Paul sat down next to Danny. Moved in closer so that his knee was against his son's, their eyes level. "You can't blame yourself. You tried everything to help her. What is it now that's triggered your concern?"

"Diane and her brothers. They're still scared of her. She spews hatred. I don't trust her."

Paul zeroed in, teasing out Danny's issue. "Are you worried about us, the kids, the business, or what happened to Charmaine?"

"I still miss Charmaine. I know it's crazy, but I feel like Diane is haunting this family. Charmaine said the same thing. Little things like Diane's presence on the road when Charmaine walked to the winery. Diane would pop up as if expecting to see her. No matter when I go to the winery, within minutes Diane appears with a delivery, a reason to call, or to distract me. It's as if she has an inside view of the route and our layout."

Danny's intensity increased Paul's sense of dread about the financials at the winery. He lowered his voice to almost a whisper. "Sadly, I think you're right to mistrust Diane. She has an edge that's more than annoying or forward. I used to dismiss her as my father's scorned girlfriend. Not that he ever thought of her that way, but she cooed as if she cared. Too saccharine for my taste. But there's more."

Danny leaned back on his chair. "What more is there to know? I'm worried that with Grandpa's death Diane will try to upset Sealy to somehow hurt you. Just like she did with Charmaine and me."

Paul stood. "You're scaring me, Danny. I've never heard you talk like this. Sealy is strong, mature, not easily swayed like Charmaine."

Danny shook his head. "I didn't mean to compare the two. But Sealy isn't as strong as you believe. I've seen Sealy crying, trying to hide it behind her sunglasses. She's great with kids, can handle almost any situation, yet you know she's vulnerable. Diane and her vineyard…just saying her name gets me upset."

Not wanting to reveal more about Sealy and the vulnerable moments she had shared with him, Paul veered the conversation back to Diane. "I can't speculate about motives, but I can tell you facts. Years ago, your uncle Barry was accused of doctoring the winery books. I found discrepancies that he couldn't have made—if he were smart. Barry is, I mean was Sealy's father. He disappeared from the area and took his family with him. Now, looking at the winery books, I find the same shenanigans. The commonality is our longtime neighbor and vineyard supplier, Diane."

Danny rose from his seat. "This isn't helping me feel any better. How can you be so calm with all of this? Grandpa was so excited when Sealy decided to come. I had no idea about this twisted story."

Paul poured himself coffee. "You'd do anything for your grandfather. He only showed you love, when you were growing up without a mother and when Charmaine left…" Paul paused mid-thought when he heard Roxie and Reese enter with Sealy carrying a plate.

"Daddy, look what we made with Sealy: elephant ears. She said they'd make you smile. We know you're upset. Please smile."

"Oh my, you even wrote our names with frosting on top."

Sealy laughed. "They insisted, to make sure everyone had their own cookie. I made a few extras for seconds. No one can be sad for long with frosting."

Danny grabbed two of the cookies. "That's my clue to get moving. I'll take the girls off your hands—that is, if they cleaned up in the kitchen."

"Go ahead. We're finished in there. I left it just like your new cook likes it. She made a list for today's meals—labeled in the refrigerator."

Danny held Roxie's hand while Reese wrapped her body around his leg. They wobbled out, laughing.

Paul moved his chair under the table and walked toward Sealy. "Thanks for stepping up again and again. Do you have time for a cup of coffee with me?"

Sealy smiled. "Of course. I put my name on one of those cookies."

Paul detected a note of wistfulness in Sealy voice. "Are you okay? Last night you were upset. Did you sleep?"

"Like a log. I showered to wash away the stress and don't remember much after my head hit the pillow."

"But you were up at the crack of dawn baking cookies." Paul stifled a yawn. "I don't believe that is your normal pattern. I had a hard time getting up hours later."

Sealy bit into an elephant ear and breathed in deeply. "Danny talked to me last night and asked me to fill in. It's a good excuse to be with Reese and Roxie. They've been talking about their mother lately. Richard's death reminded them of loss. A little extra love can't hurt."

"I can see the wheels going around in your head, Sealy. Your face is a dead giveaway when it comes to emotions. Now you're worried about the girls, your protective nature. Even last night you acted that way with the press. Care to tell me what you talked about?"

"I'll tell you after you eat the elephant ear with your name on it."

Paul laughed as he uncovered his cookie. "Oh, mine has hearts on it too." As he nibbled at the hearts, he stole a glance at Sealy. "Whose idea was that?"

Sealy's eyes twinkled. "I confess, I added them."

"Your way of giving out a little extra love? Be careful now, I'll get spoiled." Paul caught Sealy's hand as she reached to twirl her hair. A curl slipped through his fingers. "Now that I've swallowed the whole cookie, tell me about the journalists—or did you think I'd be overwhelmed by the hearts and forget my original question?"

"I'm that obvious?"

Paul nodded and waited for her to continue.

"At the funeral reception you gave me the task of distraction. All I could think of was that journalist wanted a good story. I wove a tale that was filled with truths, taking some liberties of discretion. I hope I didn't say anything inappropriate. But I'll let you be the judge of that."

"I'm sure you were diplomatic. They took notes and shot photos. I doubt my position as town manager will be affected unless I decide to run for the council or governorship. In that case you could be my campaign manager."

Sealy laughed. "But I didn't mention you, I told them of my need to rest and paint. That I found a wonderful website of the town with the Hawk House listed as a bed-and-breakfast. The journalist wanted to see my work. I offered to do a show at the end of my stay."

Paul turned his head, confused at Sealy's talk of leaving. "Here I am making you my campaign manager and you're talking about your departure. I guess that says it all."

"Please don't take my words literally. The last thing I'd want to do is upset you."

Paul tried to smile, but his eyes didn't follow through. "Pretend I didn't say that. I know you're here to find out about your family, and you have another life with your sister, Jeannie, and your art. Your time here will end."

Sealy busied herself gathering the cookies and coffee cups. "I'm not my mother. She left and didn't come back. I'm opening doors, not closing them." She shrugged. "I'll let you get on with your day."

Paul noted Sealy's change in tone. "Mind if I join you for the cleanup?"

"Of course not."

Paul gathered the rest of the dishes on a tray and they both headed to the kitchen.

After the funeral Sealy remained at the house for most of the week, making sure the girls were occupied. When Danny told her she had a package at the post office, she hitched a ride into town.

Sealy paced in front of the post office. An elaborate hand-drawn caricature of Louise sitting in a dental chair hung on the door with a note that she'd be back soon. Sealy chuckled. Small-town priorities made more sense than her own rush to pick up a special-delivery package requiring a signature.

Sealy remembered on her last visit to the post office Louise had mentioned galleries two blocks over from the main street. Sealy meandered down the street, noting the storefronts with colorful canvas awnings that protruded over the sidewalks. Each had a long pole extension attached to the wall, enabling the shop owners to wind and unwind in case of a huge storm. New England sensibility.

On the corner of the last block, a gallery invited patrons in with a sandwich-board sign that said, "Step into a painting and find your soul." How could she resist? A jiggling of the door set off a melodic set of bells—do, re, mi, fa, sol, la, ti, and do. Charmed, Sealy entered and an older women stepped out from behind the counter. As Sealy studied the lady's eyes, a flicker of light changed them from green to blue, and they finally settled on hazel. Before Sealy could work out why, the woman offered her hand.

"Welcome, I'll let you wander, and if you need anything, I'm sitting back where I paint. Hope you have an hour to spare. Everything is for sale, all local painters, but the small painting behind the register remains here."

"Thanks, I just heard about the galleries down this way. I'm thrilled to have finally discovered you. My name is Sealy."

"It's a small town. Word gets around when a new artist has arrived. Besides, I've seen you out on the cliffs painting. Glad you found us. Ring the bell on the counter if you want something."

A spell had been cast. Sealy assumed the enchantress was the owner. Direct and to the point, with a jolt of confidence, just like the sandwich board. Each piece had been chosen with care, an eye for color, texture. The more Sealy looked, the more she saw— pottery next to paintings and baskets set in themes readjusting one's senses, playing with the mind, as if to free the Russian wooden dolls that opened always to find another inside.

In the back corner under a subdued light, Sealy spotted a painting of a woman with her back turned toward the viewer. The woman, clad in a flowing blue dress, walked along a road barefoot, holding her shoes. In the opposite direction a forlorn little girl appears, wearing oversized shoes. Sealy stared, holding her breath, waiting for the child to meet up with the woman. The hills obscured the path with dips and turns. She waited and waited until the owner appeared.

"Not many people spot this one, even with the overhead light. It's called *Crossroads*."

Sealy smiled. "I'd call it *Expectations of the Heart*. I didn't notice a price. Is it for sale or is it like the painting over the register?"

"Depends on the buyer. I have strict instructions from the artist to make sure it goes to the right person. Are you that person?"

Sealy knew exactly what was being asked. She often wondered if the buyers of her paintings reflected on the story inside. Did they notice the lighting, the shoelace, the door with the sock stuck in the corner? Could they jump inside the scenery, imagine themselves transported?

Sealy talked quickly. "I worry about the woman walking too slowly, her shoulders pulled back to keep her head up. I can't see her face. Either she's crying or smiling. It depends on the twists of the hills and if they meet again. I think the story will change in different lighting. If you turn the light on the child, I'd see the little girl's story."

The owner took the painting off the wall. "It's yours. Now you have the difficult job of finding the right lights."

As they headed to the register, Sealy looked up at the not-for-sale painting. It was the mirror image of the one she was purchasing. The woman and forlorn girl had changed positions. The owner followed her gaze but said nothing.

"How much do I owe you?"

"It's your lucky day. Whatever cash you have in your purse."

Sealy laughed. "No, I don't think so. I can't accept it then."

The owner's eyes twinkled. "Okay, then all the cash plus a painting from you."

"It's a deal. I'll leave you my number."

"No need, I trust you."

As Sealy left, she turned back to see the owner remove the painting over the register.

Since his father's passing, Paul had been overwhelmed with managing the town. The storm damage, while not devasting, had highlighted inadequacies with their power grid, drainage, and road maintenance. Engineering reports, bids, and photographs covered his desk. Working with the county and state for grants took time, and the fixes needed to be done now.

His meeting with Geordie and Chuck had been postponed twice, once on their end and once on his. Paul waited at a small café three blocks from the center of town. He had chosen the place because it was new with few patrons and out of the public's view.

Exactly at 1:00 p.m. Geordie and Chuck walked in. They had abandoned their suits, but their pressed khaki pants and polo shirts seemed just as out of place for this artsy fishing town. Paul imagined his father would have chided the two brothers for their airs. Not that Richard didn't wear khakis, but the monogrammed initials and brand names signaled wealth. Paul reflected on his own outfit. His striped button-down shirt with rolled up sleeves and his pleated slacks hinted he was out to lunch on a workday.

Paul stood up as they approached the table. "I'm glad we can finally meet. I apologize that I had to cancel last week."

Geordie pulled out his chair. "Keeping a town running is more work than fun. We're both retired, living the good life, or trying to. That's why we're here."

Paul noted the emphasis on the words *or trying to*. Not wanting to hear confessions, Paul slowed the conversation. "No need to rush our talk, let's order something to drink and eat. I put aside my appointments to give us time. I'll get the waiter."

Chuck nodded his agreement and Geordie ordered two Caesar salads and iced teas. Paul opted for the same with lobster. While they waited for the food to arrive, Paul talked about the changes in the town, the influx of tourists, and the push to modernize. Once the food arrived, he maneuvered the conversation to include the brothers.

"My dad wanted the town to keep its quaint nature. His goal was never to make Ogunquit a competitive town, just a thriving one. What do you remember?"

Geordie mused, "Richard was the visionary in our group. He focused on art and creativity. Chuck, you worked with him more than I did. What do you think?"

"Richard lived and breathed the art school. He loved the synergy. I tried my hand at painting, never got far. I was more realistic, wanting to make a living for myself. Others were more into…sharing. If you know what I mean. The social politics and coupling were the downfall of the school. Your dad was devasted by the closure. But he always had a backup plan."

Geordie interrupted, "The plan was more Barry's than your father's. Barry had the brilliant idea of developing a grape to grow in this harsh weather. He was a biologist at heart, not a businessman. Too trusting."

Paul imagined Sealy sitting at the table, pushing her food around, listening to Geordie talk about her father. He felt the same urge to line up the peas on his plate, but there were none in his salad. Did he really want to hear more about Richard's past or that of Barry?

"My father never talked about the art school or his brother, and by the time I was old enough to know anything, the winery was well established. He juggled that and his position with the town with no complaints."

Geordie looked down at his plate, took a sip of water. "We know and we've come to make restitution. Richard and Barry deserved better."

Paul listened in disbelief. His father had been wracked with guilt toward the end. Paul feared what would come next. "I thought our meeting involved town issues. Are you going to expose a long-gone indiscretion involving Richard's good name so you can feel better about yourselves, *live the good life* without feeling bad about the past?"

Chuck raised his voice. "No, no, no. It's my fault. Can't you understand that we have to make amends, or we'd break our promise?"

Geordie consoled his brother and turned to Paul. "Maybe we should meet in a more private setting. Chuck needs to rest. I assure you that we mean no harm. Our proposal will enhance the town. We won't gain anything. You're right, the past remains silent, but real. Nothing we do will change history."

From the corner of his eye, Paul spotted Sealy crossing the street, headed toward the café. She carried an oversized package in her hand and struggled to open the café door. "Excuse me for just a second. I'll be right back." He rushed to open the door. "Sealy, what a surprise."

She greeted him with a huge smile. "This is a small town. I'm here for a latte and snack."

"Looks like shopping made you hungry. I'm just finishing up lunch with Diane's brothers. Do you have a minute? I can sit with you after they leave."

"Are you sure? I don't want to interfere."

"Just an introduction. I promise, nothing more. We were just ending the visit. Besides, you look like you could use help with that package." Paul walked to the table, where he found Geordie and Chuck huddled together, whispering. "I don't think you've met Sealy, our first guest at our bed-and-breakfast. Richard felt very close to her."

With the mention of Richard's name both men came to attention. Paul knew they were upset but politeness overrode their emotions. He hoped that Sealy would work her charm and smooth their ruffled feathers.

Once settled with her package securely placed on the floor, Sealy offered both hands to each of the men. "Paul mentioned he was finally meeting with you two today. Richard must have meant so much to you. So sad that you couldn't say your goodbyes. I was lucky enough to share his passion for painting. He even showed me some of his technical secrets."

Chuck smiled. "Nice to know that he still had that passion and passed it on. I always wondered if he was still into art. Is that what brought you to the Hawk House?"

Paul held his breath, wondering what part of the truth Sealy would share. True to her nature, she revealed just enough to quell curiosity. "Funny you should ask. Tidying up my house, I found an old postcard with the town's name. Ready to take a retreat, I looked the town up on the internet. And here I am. Apparently, it was a long-overdue connection. I would have liked to have met Richard earlier in my life."

Relieved at her answer, Paul saw that Geordie remained intrigued. "Ah a painter, that makes sense. Is that what you have all wrapped up, one of your latest works?"

Sealy glanced quizzically at Paul before she answered Geordie's question: "Well, not exactly. Small towns have their charms and just down the block from here I found a small gallery. I couldn't resist this painting. I bartered one of my own paintings for it. The owner seemed to be waiting for a specific person to buy the piece."

Chuck cleared his throat and glanced at his brother. "Sounds like one of the artists from Richard's art school. All philosophy of finding the match for the meaning and no entrepreneurial drive. I'm surprised you conceded to her wishes. If I'm correct, the woman would be our age. Something about you Sealy…perhaps another connection."

Paul made light of Chuck's comment. "Great news, that means Sealy will have to stay longer and paint more. I'm sure Chuck and Geordie would love to see your work too. Maybe after our next meeting."

At the mention of another meeting, the moment of levity disappeared. The brothers stood, Chuck smoothing his shirt and placing his napkin over his half-eaten salad. "Can we set a date and time? We'd like to keep all this private, away from the prying ears and eyes of our sister."

Paul replied, "As the town manager I have to keep everything transparent. No hidden agendas. Whatever we talk about must be in the best interest of the community and not involve personal issues."

Geordie gave an evasive answer: "We haven't talked with Diane in forty years. I can assure you, we act on our own. We made a promise years ago to give back to Ogunquit. I'll collect our bill."

Paul rose and shook their hands. "How long will you two be in town?"

They both answered, "As long as it takes."

Paul felt a gentle nudge on his elbow from Sealy. Turning, he included her in the conversation. "I see how determined you both are to make good on your promise. Let's meet tomorrow night for dinner at the Hawk House. That should be private enough. Sealy, do you mind?"

Sealy graciously put her hand up. "I can eat earlier and help with the girls if you want Danny to attend. We'll make it a special girl's night and leave you three to discuss matters."

Geordie nodded but Chuck spoke up. "I don't know that Danny needs to be there. That's up to you, Paul. Sealy, I see why you got along with Richard. You remind me of his wife's good friend Mary. You have her grace and the passion of her husband. Funny how impressions last so long with us old folk. They say we lose our memories, but I disagree. I hope we'll see you tomorrow night, after dinner."

Sealy sat outside on the deck with her reading glasses in one hand and the special-delivery letter in the other. She shook her head. *How could I have been so stupid?*

Her not-so-innocent attempt to placate the press at Richard's funeral had had unintended consequences. According to her publicist, someone was snooping into Sealy's pseudonym's work, calling galleries, asking about her and her history. Rereading the letter from her publicist, she cursed the air with the one word she allowed herself to say in anger, *sotarotafa*. Repeatedly she mumbled the word until she shouted it out loud with emphasis on the *fa* syllable: "Sotarotafa!"

From inside the house, Sealy heard the giggles of Reese and Roxie. Switching gears, she turned to face them. Sealy raised her left eyebrow and laughed. "What's so funny? I bet you don't know what I said."

Roxie giggled again and Reese walked outside to sit on Sealy's lap. Roxie shrugged and said, "It's a big word, so it must mean something big."

Sealy nodded. "Yes, I only use the word when I have big thoughts that I can't unravel. It's a nonsense word I invented. Sometimes I mess things up and must fix them. Shouting the word out loud helps."

Roxie gave Sealy a hug. "Daddy sometimes uses bad words and Grandpa kicks him. We aren't supposed to say those words."

"When we make dinner later, you both can make up a word to use when you get frustrated or upset."

From the doorway, Danny interjected, "I don't want to interfere, but I heard you three talking and some gibberish. Is everything okay?"

Sealy smiled. "I'm not sure. Being here has its complications with my life elsewhere. Thanks for asking."

Placing her glasses on top of her head, Sealy laughed at Danny. "No need to stand in the doorway. I won't bite even if my gibberish sounded scary."

As soon as Danny sat down next to Sealy, the girls climbed up on each of his knees. "I decided to take Roxie and Reese out for a drive and then a quick bite at the inn. We need to have some time together."

"You won't be joining Paul and his guests for dinner?"

Danny hugged his girls. "No need for that. I'm sure I'll hear about it from my dad."

"I guess I'm on my own."

Roxie frowned. "Will you be lonely without us?"

"Oh no, don't worry. After the cook makes the guests their dinner, I'll make myself a wonderful stir-fry from the garden vegetables and I'll read. Enjoy yourselves and be sure to tell me about your adventures."

Danny squeezed Sealy's shoulder as he left. "Let me know if I can help."

Caught off guard by Danny's sincerity, Sealy waved the letter in the air. "Business. Nothing too complicated."

Reese tugged at Sealy's sleeve. "'I'll let you know what my big word is tomorrow. I'm sure Daddy can help me think of one."

Paul passed most of the afternoon studying old winery ledgers and rifling through his father's personal effects. Nothing mentioned Geordie or Chuck. He turned off the office light and headed up to change for dinner. He returned to find Sealy sitting outside staring at the trees. "Where is everybody? I thought you were having an early dinner with Roxie and Reese."

Sealy sighed. "They're off with Danny for family time. I think they need it. At least Danny does. He has been edgy lately but today seemed genuinely concerned about me."

"And why would that be? Did something happen I should know?"

"I'm sure you know more about Danny's affairs than me."

Paul pulled a chair next to Sealy's. He laughed. "I wasn't referring to Danny. He's been haunted by Diane for years. I meant, what caused him to reach out to you?"

"Wow—you just said a mouthful. Now I'm more curious about Diane than Danny's actions toward me."

"You're twirling your hair again. I'm getting to know how to read when you're nervous. What happened?"

Sealy stretched her legs out and repositioned the blanket. "I've put my foot in my mouth. I'm not sure, but when I talked with the press at the funeral reception as a diversion, I may have revealed something that might harm my anonymity."

"You mean that you are an artist. The whole town knows that. You bought supplies in town, went to galleries. Small towns notice. Besides, you even told Geordie and Chuck that you came here to paint."

Sealy took a deep breath. "Yes, but no one here would do investigative work and rile up my publicist. They were asking personal stuff about where I was born. I've never been asked that before. If it wasn't the local press, who would it be?"

Paul didn't know what to say. He thought about Mr. Jewels's queries and Geordie and Chuck's need to vindicate the reputation of his father and Barry. He cleared his throat, raised his hands in the air. "You got me. I'm not sure this is connected to your actions here. Being a famous painter isn't a bad thing, is it?"

"Normally I'd agree with you. But it was something I felt that I needed to keep from my mom, even though she knew I painted. It wasn't what she wanted for me. Even though she's gone, I feel guilty for my talent. There, I said it out loud. I'm a talented painter. I shouldn't be ashamed. I just don't know why anyone cares."

"I can't say I have the answer for that either. But I do know you must be hungry. Why don't you join us for dinner? Geordie and Chuck seemed interested in the painting you bought."

"Do you think I need a distraction or are you taking pity on me for my worries?"

Paul took her hand. "Would that be so bad? Besides, our guests knew your mom and dad. They probably know more about my father as well." After pausing for a second, he continued, "I guess the biggest reason is that I'd like you to be there."

Sealy's cheeks turned pink. "In that case I better change."

When Sealy returned, she found Paul in the living room pouring wine for Geordie and Chuck. They all turned as she entered. She pulled her mother's shawl tighter, adjusted her hair and, with practiced familiarity, smiled in greeting. Paul's eyes twinkled his pleasure at seeing her. Geordie nodded, but Chuck stared awkwardly.

Thankfully Paul noticed the stare. He stepped out to meet her and obscured Chuck's direct view. "I was just explaining the change in plans for dinner since Danny took the girls out."

Sealy sensed a bit of tension. "I hope you two don't mind. I don't want to interfere with your conversations. I think Paul felt bad that I was on my own."

Chuck spoke first. "No, of course not. This is Paul's house, and we are his guest."

Geordie sipped his wine. "Is this one of the original bottles from our first attempt at making wine with the new grape variety?"

"I had Danny go to the wine cellar to see if there was any in our inventory. Unfortunately, he couldn't find any. The records show quite a few, but who knows with old records? The ledgers reflect high production numbers, which should have translated into more bottled wine. We did find this bottle with the vintage year 1960. We still bottle something similar with the same label, Jessica's Nor'easter. Labeled for the full force of the wind and rugged soil. I'm not sure where the name Jessica fits in. What do you think?"

Chuck sniffed the wine and took a taste "Not bad, a little sweet for me. Most likely it's blended with some blueberries. Am I correct?"

Geordie nodded. "I remember the blend. Barry worked hard on it, but something happened to the batch. Another flub-up that he was blamed for."

Sealy listened intently to the nuances in Geordie's voice. He seemed genuinely disturbed. "I'd love to have a taste as well."

Paul quickly poured her a glass. "Oh my. I didn't mean to exclude you."

As Sealy reached for the glass, she felt Paul's pinkie finger linger. "No worries, I've been here as your guest long enough that I'm comfortable speaking up." Chuck kept his eyes on her as she drank. Sealy sensed he was searching through his memories. She tried the wine, letting it linger in her mouth. "I'm not a connoisseur of wines, as I only recently started exploring this world. This wine is rich, a deep woody flavor with a hint of something I can't quite make out. I agree with you. I note a bit of cherry."

Geordie chuckled. "For someone who claims to be a novice you have the vocabulary. We had just started growing Léon Millot grapes."

"I'm a quick learner. My mother knew wine, although she rarely drank. What were you saying about this wine's past?"

Paul laughed. "We now age the Nor'easter in French and American oak. Our bestseller is a dryer blend, with Marechal Foch and St. Croix grapes added. Your sister hasn't been able to produce those grapes, so we buy them from another vineyard. Enough of wine talk." Paul steered the group over to the dining table. "Time for the appetizers, something to tide us over until dinner. Please continue with your story of how the wine was ruined. I'm not privy to that part of my father's life."

Chuck cleared his throat. "Do we want to talk about this now or after dinner? I'm not sure how you'll react. This is part of the reason we're here."

Without waiting for an answer, Sealy pulled out each of the chairs and found a spot facing the windows. Paul sat down to her right, Geordie and Chuck facing them.

Paul made a toast: "Here's to the flubs of the past and understanding the present."

Everyone seemed to relax. They drank a bit more and enjoyed the platter. Geordie finally spoke up. "One night after the original tasting, Barry went into the winery. He heard noises and he smelled something potent. He checked the barrels, but the smell made him queasy, so he went outside. He didn't see anyone. The next day one of the workers found a can of wood preservative opened in the back. Being cautious, Richard and Barry decided to throw the batch out for fear of contamination. Barry was overwrought with guilt."

Sealy sat with her hands in her lap, her thumbs rolling around each other as Geordie related the story. She kept her face neutral as the talk proceeded. Not sure if the guests knew she had a connection to Barry, Sealy took her cues from Paul.

When Geordie paused, Paul interrupted, "Back then the regulations weren't as strict, but my father was a stickler. Did he blame Barry?"

Chuck answered, "Not really, but Barry had stepped out for few hours because of a ruckus down by our house. He must have left the winery open, and someone entered. Barry felt responsible. It got worse as time went on. Slip-ups kept happening, mainly when Barry was called out. I suspect Barry knew who was trying to sabotage the wine. He was protecting someone."

Questions swirled in Sealy's mind. "Pardon me for interrupting, I know how important this is to you two. I just wondered if you found out who he was protecting. I'd hate to think of old wounds being opened without any way to heal from them. I wouldn't want anyone else to feel more pain as wrongs are righted."

Sealy felt a gentle nudge on her foot from Paul. Before Geordie could answer, Paul interjected, "I never met my uncle Barry. If he did protect someone, Barry must have valued that person more than he valued himself."

Chuck shook his head. "I wish that were true. I know he was protecting us. We didn't sabotage the wines, or steal, but we turned a blind eye to the problems. We got in trouble with women and drugs. Every time we messed up, Barry came to save us. We let him be the fall guy."

Sealy tempered her thoughts, searching inside for the right words. "Why would he do that? Did he owe you something? There must be a reason."

Chuck countered, "Barry was of another era, and he was male. He protected everyone. I agree that Barry suffered and therefore lost his purpose. He was riddled with pain and responsibility."

Geordie pressed his lips together in disdain. "Perhaps we should leave this conversation for another time. It's hard explaining the past, especially if one isn't from here."

Sealy realized her attempts at neutrality had disappeared. She wrapped her mother's shawl tighter across her arms. "I spoke out of turn. I'll think I'll get some fresh air and come back when dinner is served. That way you'll be able to discuss matters without my interference."

Chuck, Geordie, and Paul rose from their seats. Paul took Sealy's arm. "I'll walk you to the gardens. Excuse us."

Geordie called after them, "Perhaps Sealy would bring down the art piece she purchased. I'm curious about it."

Sealy mustered a smile. "I'd love to. See you in a bit."

Once outside, Sealy turned to Paul. "Don't worry, I'm okay. I apologize. My inner thoughts slipped outside of me."

Paul laughed. "That's something Roxie or Reese would say."

"It's true though. After all these years of wondering why I felt awkward, finding my mother's reality to not be so truthful, my filters have holes."

"I'm sure someone investigating your past makes you squirm too. I've got to get back to Chuck and Geordie. Dinner will be out in a half hour. Let's talk later."

Sealy squeezed Paul's hand. "Promise to fill me in on their confessions. Who knows what we'll find."

Sealy left the gardens and retreated to her room. She closed the door and sat in the chair by the window. The sun had already set, and in the dark sky one lone star flashed its presence. Sealy imagined her mom winking. The thought gave her courage.

As if on cue, her cell phone rang. Jeannie's name flashed. On the third ring, Sealy answered: "Jeannie, I was just about to call you."

"Hold on a second. Let me turn off the news. Must be something in the air. I have had newspaper journalists knocking at my door asking about my artist sister. What have you done?"

"Good to hear your voice, even if you're annoyed with me. I do have something to confess. Let me speak before you interrupt. Whatever happens because of me being here isn't about us. Okay. I've stirred up the past. I don't think Dad was as bad as the newspapers portrayed. He might have been a martyring hero. But that's beside the point. I've hidden my artistic fame from you. Your little sister paints under a pseudonym."

Jeannie's breathing filled the airwaves. Finally she spoke. "Why would you do that? That's the dumbest thing I've ever heard. Who gives a rip?"

"Mom did. For some reason she wanted me to make my way with a profession. Even though I was talented, she was against it. I always wanted her approval, so I pretended it was my hobby, not my profession. I fooled everyone."

"You won so many realtor awards. So that is your hobby, not painting? I don't care. Why would anyone mind that?"

Sealy fiddled with her hair, looked at the clock. "I've got to go downstairs for dinner with some old friends of Richard and Dad. I can't keep up my façade any longer. They don't know who I am, but I sense they know something that happened before you and I were born. Maybe just me. Anyway, I'm going to expose my fame and let whatever happens, happen."

"Are you okay?"

"Oh, Jeannie, send me a virtual hug. Smile at reporters and investigators but shrug the inquiries off. Leave it up to me to unravel my own web. I do have two requests. See if you can find my birth certificate. I haven't seen it in years. Also, could you take a DNA test? After you get yours back, I'll take one too."

"It's a deal. I love you no matter what."

Paul watched as Sealy showed Geordie and Chuck her newly acquired painting. Animated, her hands became brushes describing the duality of the artist, the tender story of a young girl and an older lady, how the lighting changed perspectives. Sealy seemed to have stepped into the painting. He could listen to her forever.

Mesmerized, Geordie turned the painting over. "I don't see a signature on the front or back. Do you know the artist's name?"

Sealy shrugged. "I assumed it was the owner's personal work. She was more interested in my reaction than proclaiming her abilities. I know the feeling. Until just recently, I hid behind a pseudonym with my artwork."

Paul, not sure of what Sealy was about to say, moved in closer. "Has that changed? Will there be a big reveal?"

"I think not, but who knows? I'm tired of compartmentalizing my actions and thoughts. It's exhausting. No need to give the past so much power over the present."

Paul frowned. He remembered Danny's warnings about Diane and Danny's perception of Sealy's mental strength.

Chuck broke into Paul's thoughts. "You look disappointed, Paul. Sealy is probably feeling like we do. At least she's twenty years younger. My brother and I waited too long to set the record straight. Besides, I told Geordie that Sealy reminded me of an artist we once knew."

Geordie shook his head. "Yes, he's fixated on figuring out why you seem so familiar. I guess we're all on a journey to make the present and the future better. Thanks for sharing the painting you bought and your news."

As Geordie babbled on, Paul noticed Sealy stiffen at Chuck's continued stares.

"You two are so kind. I'll wrap my painting and call it an evening," she said.

"We haven't told you about our good news. Geordie and I decided to create a foundation to give back to the community. While you were gone, we talked with Paul to see if the town regulations would allow us to create a center here. We still own property separate from what our sister owns. Our seed money would be the start, but it would eventually have to generate its own financial success."

"Don't get ahead of yourself," Geordie cautioned Chuck. "Paul hasn't agreed to anything. This is just a preliminary talk."

"I agree in principle with your ideas. But in my role as the town manager, I can only provide you with the regulations for nonprofits. Anything beyond that isn't up to me."

Sealy came to Paul's aid once again. "I look forward to hearing more about the project as things progress. It's getting late. I'm sure Richard would have been honored that you are making this effort. Will it include the arts?"

"Not necessarily. Geordie and I were thinking of women and babies. A home of sorts with education."

Paul waved his hands in the air. "My dad would want what was best for the town. The foundation can't rest on your remedying the past."

"Of course, but that discussion is for another time. I'm afraid we must go. Chuck and I aren't night owls anymore. Widowed, we tend to turn in early. Thank you for a great dinner. Good luck, Sealy, let us know when we can see your work. I'm intrigued."

As Sealy stirred the cookie dough, she remembered Geordie's last words, *I'm intrigued.* He hadn't meant for her to stress. But Sealy's knotted stomach said something different. Chuck's stares shook her more than her original find of her mother's photo. Used to being alone with her thoughts, she jumped when Paul's voice called her name.

"Sorry I startled you. We didn't get to talk after Diane's brothers left the other night. I knew you were rattled. Is now a good time?"

With her steaming coffee in hand and the cookie batter mixed in a bowl, Sealy smiled. "Perfect timing. You caught me doing my favorite calming distraction. I'm making oatmeal raisin chocolate chip cookies. Do you want to dirty your hands before breakfast?" Sealy handed Paul a scooper. "Just drop them on the cookie sheet. Don't worry about size, just make sure they don't touch and have room to spread."

They filled two trays before Paul spoke. "I'm guessing Chuck is why you need a distraction. He doesn't mean you any harm. He's more worried about past transgressions. Part of his guilt is letting your father be the fall guy for their pranks as young adults. Unintended but devastating."

"Do you think he knows that my father is Richard's brother? He never indicated that. I don't look like my mother or my father…but still…"

Paul shook his head, reached for her hand. "I suspect that if they don't know now, they'll know soon. Remember, this is a small town. If you are willing to reveal your artistic talents to the world after all these years, you have to accept your name."

Sealy felt a warmth and a sadness with Paul's words. She squeezed his hand and laughed. "With Louise as the gossip chain at the post office and Elly at the inn, I'm sure after the funeral the word is out about me. Funny how I've lost my anonymity, a cover I've wanted to discard for so long, but now I feel naked."

Paul cleared his throat. "Let's not go there. I'd tell you not to worry, but I have a sick feeling that Diane still scares her brothers. Danny believes she also harassed his wife. Charmaine had been diagnosed with deep depression and often appeared paranoid. The week before her death, she confided that Diane would follow her, make unkind remarks about her parenting skills. Danny thinks Diane is fixated on ruining our lives, with you as the next target."

Sealy put the cookies in the oven, washed the countertop down. Her easy smile gone, her voice deeper, she responded, "I'm not one to cower. I wish you had told me before. I guess I have no choice…"

Before Sealy finished her sentence, in came Roxie with Reese following close behind. "I knew it. You're baking. I could smell something sweet. Guess what our word is. Daddy thought it was perfect."

Paul picked up Reese, gave her a kiss, and went for Roxie. "Grandpa, wait a minute. This is important."

Sealy felt the spell of doom dissolve. She took two spatulas and scooped out leftover batter. "Do you have time for a lick before you reveal the word?"

Giggles filled the room. After the last lick, Roxie blurted out, "Popcorn! Get it, as soon as you say the word, the badness goes away. Oh, PopCorn!! Or Pop Corn!!"

Sealy chimed in, repeating the word over and over. "Do you ever just say *corn*, or does *pop* have to be with it?"

"Sealy, you're so silly. If you just say corn, then you can say corn dog or corn fritters. Nope, it has to be popcorn."

Paul moved in toward Roxie. "I'm so glad we got that settled. Now for my kiss."

Sealy let the seriousness of Paul's information recede into the background. She marched Reese over to wash her hands and face and whispered, "I bet Roxie will leave a cookie dough kiss on your grandfather's cheek. Take this wet towel to him, okay?"

As the girls and Paul headed to the dining room, Danny entered the kitchen. Despite his clean-shaven face and neat attire, he lacked his natural bounce. Since the girls seemed okay, Sealy wondered why he was forlorn. "If you're looking for Roxie and Reese, they've headed to the dining room with your dad. They might be a little hyper after some cookie dough batter."

"I came to talk with you privately."

"Oh popcorn! What have I done?"

Her joke had the appropriate effect. Danny relaxed his stiff stance and leaned on the counter. "Oh, I don't believe you could do anything wrong in the eyes of the kids and my dad."

"And you, have I offended you? I thought you realized my intentions coming here were pure. What happened?"

Danny bent his head and mumbled, "It's just the opposite. I came in to warn you. When the girls and I had dinner at the burger place, I overheard the gossip. The word is that you're here for revenge. Apparently, Diane has told her friends that you feel cheated from some inheritance."

"Your dad and I were just discussing that my identity as a Morris would be common knowledge by now. He mentioned your worries about Diane's fixation on ruining the family. Being a target isn't new to me." Sealy sighed as she opened the hot oven. "It's a leap that I'd want money or an inheritance that isn't mine for the taking. Besides, I don't need anyone's fortune."

Danny snagged one of the hot cookies. "I think Diane is the one seeking revenge, not you. She's bad-mouthing her brothers as well. Some conspiracy theory that they are here to take back the farm."

Sealy sat down at the kitchen counter with a fresh cup of coffee. "Danny, thanks for the warning. I think we should work on this together. Find out as much as you can about the rumors. I'm known to be a great investigator in the real estate world. It's time to find out what happened to create this mess. I only wish my mother had been forthcoming."

Something told Sealy that the key to the mystery was Chuck's stares.

Paul drummed his fingers on his desk. After searching the internet, he finally located a reference to the agency where Mr. Jewels worked. He held the phone number up to the light as if it contained answers to his father's promise to Sealy's mother. The area code indicated the state of Maryland. Paul punched in the numbers. After five rings he slammed the phone down. Annoyed with himself, he took a deep breath. He still believed in his father. He didn't want any information to ruin that. Sealy's decision to confront Diane's attempt at character assassination, forced him to confront his father's loyalties.

Calmly, he plugged in the phone number again.

On the first ring an older woman answered, "Hello, hello. Is anyone there?"

Afraid he had the wrong number, Paul summoned his patience. "Hi, I'm calling for Mr. Jewels, one of the adoption agency's employees. Is he in the office?"

"Yes—well, no. There isn't an office anymore. The agency closed a while back. Mr. Jewels is retired. Can I give him a message?"

"Please tell him that Paul Morris called. He knew my father."

Before he could give out his number, he heard a click. Tempted to call back, Paul wondered if the woman would pass on the message. His father would call his waffling prudent vacillation. Paul decided to wait a day or two and try again.

For the rest of the morning, Paul worked on shoreline issues, flood recovery applications, and the new budget proposals. Important distractions kept him grounded. He finally raised his head from town issues when his stomach growled. He grabbed his jacket and headed out.

Whiffs of fried onions and potatoes drew him down to the wharf. Paul slipped into his favorite diner and ordered a crab cake sandwich and their specialty potato salad. Tom, the owner, brought out his food. "Haven't seen you in a while. How are you doing since your dad passed?"

"I've been busy, Tom. Thanks for asking. Between the town's needs and going through my dad's paperwork, I can't see an end in sight."

"Tough times. When my dad passed, I had to deal with the paperwork of the restaurant, old debts, and a pile of weird history. Wish you luck. Don't let the gossip get to you. My father thought the world of Richard and your mom."

Paul ignored Tom's comment on gossip and took a bite of the sandwich. "You make the best crab cakes. Did your dad leave you all his recipes?"

"Yep, and that's where he left so many other photos and notes. Hard to reconcile the man I knew to the one before I was born. I even found photos of Richard's brother, Barry."

The mention of Sealy's father caused him to pause. Paul took a drink of water, before he responded. "I'd be curious to see the photos sometime. Might be an idea to gather these from all the old-timers to commemorate history."

Paul finished eating and returned to his office. Meetings, phone calls, and paperwork filled the rest of the day. He closed the last file and stared out at the wharf where Tom stood outside of his restaurant. This was his break time between lunch and the dinner hour. Tom's discovery of his father's life intermingled with the recipes reminded Paul of his mother's sewing kit's secret compartment. What else might be hidden in his father's belongings?

As Paul walked out the door his secretary stopped him. "Sorry I didn't get this to you earlier. I just checked the phone messages from my lunch break. You had a phone call from Ocean City, Maryland, while you were gone. An elderly woman said she was returning your call. She didn't say why."

"Thanks, I'll take the note and get back to her. See you bright and early tomorrow."

"I hope not, it's Saturday."

Sealy walked along the gallery alley with a sense of purpose. Since her talks with Paul and Danny, she'd made progress with her connections throughout the real estate world. Her expertise was on the West Coast, but many of her colleagues had ties to the Atlantic states. Going back to the deeds of ownership revealed the priorities and pulls on towns and communities.

The ownership of most of the stores and restaurants downtown had been passed on to family members through the centuries. The supermarket and inn, however, were owned by a shell corporation that had ties to development firms. The previous owners still held partial ownership, but the other names weren't available. Based on the rumors, Sealy expected to find Geordie's and Chuck's names on some deeds. What she found was that Diane was partners with the owners of a few bars and fancy restaurants and that the escrow companies had thick files on Diane's various transactions. Her brothers' names appeared as partners on only one property outside their ownership of their land: the Golden Goose Gallery.

Surprised where the address led, Sealy opened the door to hear the melodic *do, re, mi…* A thin young man, dressed in black pants and a red vest, stepped forward and introduced himself. "I'm Joseph, here to help you."

"Pleased to meet you. It's been a few weeks since my last visit. The gallery looks different. The artwork is modern, edgy. Is the owner here?"

Joseph smiled. "I'm the manager. I've been away for my quarterly retreat. You must be referring to Jessica, my great-aunt. When I'm away she fills in and replaces my displays based on her own artistic or mystical whims. What can I do for you?"

"I'll look around a bit if you don't mind. I'm new in town and I had no idea of how the gallery worked. I came to talk with your great-aunt. Jessica and I had an arrangement."

"Jessica is full of surprises. To tell you the truth, the store suffers and thrives when she is here. Jessica has no concept of money, only art. Loyal patrons often prefer her arrangements. She really believes in the name of the gallery, Golden Goose."

Sealy laughed. "I feel awkward about the arrangement. Jessica commissioned a painting from me, in payment for one I purchased."

"You'll have to take that up with her. If she made that arrangement, she wouldn't have written down the sale. Most likely it was one of the paintings from her collection. She owns another gallery in Maryland."

"Oh, do you know when she'll be back? Or could you give me her contact information?"

"Jessica is funny that way, private. She never gives out her phone number or address. And as far as her return—that's the million-dollar question. She comes when I take my breaks. She really is dependable."

Sealy studied Joseph's serious demeanor. She recognized the distant look of hollowed eyes, his closely cropped hair, and the careful use of the word *breaks*. From his thin and dapper appearance, Sealy realized he had cancer. His great-aunt filled in when he had treatments. "Here's my card. If you talk to your aunt, please let her know I stopped by. Can I ask you a question? What is your favorite piece on display?"

Joseph's face lit up. "How nice of you to ask." He walked over to a small wire sculpture of a child holding a kite. "This one, it makes me smile."

Sealy held it in her hand. "Is it for sale?"

"Yes, but I'll miss it."

Sealy looked at the price. "I'll buy it and you take it home. I have one that is similar, one my mother gave me."

"Oh my, you're too kind. Jessica made this."

By the time Sealy arrived at the post office, Louise had already put up the closed sign for the day. Sealy rushed down the street and called out to get her attention. "Louise, wait up. I'd like to talk with you."

Louise turned. "My goodness, this must be important. You're huffing and puffing. Catch your breath and spit it out."

Sealy realized she hadn't run for over a decade. "Don't make me laugh. The last time I ran was when I fooled myself into believing I could compete in a 5K race for charity. Turns out I'm better at donating money. Give me a minute."

"There's a bench on the corner."

"Thanks. I wanted to talk to you about my artwork and some rumors floating around town."

"I'm the right person. You make a great subject. Since the funeral reception, Diane's been busy inferring all kinds of stuff."

Sealy raised her eyebrow. "Good. Danny warned me. That's why I wanted to talk with you. I thought you might help me with my plan."

"Oh my, a covert operation. How can I help?"

"I don't have it all worked out yet. Feeling my way in the town with all the various allegiances. I've run into bullies before. They show their fears and project it on others. From what I understand, Diane has targeted me. I'm researching, doing my groundwork on her weaknesses. Once I know what she fears, then I can balance the playing field."

Louise sat back on the bench. "Most people stay clear of Diane. She has her fingers in everything. Be careful."

Sealy nodded. "I'm not telling you anything new. You also warned me at the reception. Danny blames Diane for his wife's breakdown and death. He claims Diane harassed his wife, made her more paranoid, and will do the same to me. I'm not looking for trouble, but I don't back down. My mother, even with all her secrets, dealt with issues."

Louise looked out in the distance. "The Morrises have had their share of grief. Your mom lit up the world while she lived here. Mary protected everyone."

"I wish I could have been a fly on the wall. What can you tell me about the owner of the Golden Goose Gallery?"

"My, my, you have been doing research. Jessica owns the place. She's one of my favorite characters. I can't say much as she keeps to herself when she is here. She ages well, like I do. I have a vague recollection of her from when your mom lived here. If I recall correctly, Jessica attended Richard's art academy but disappeared after her fiancé was killed in a car accident. It's been about ten years since she opened the Golden Goose. Some relative runs it most of the year. He isn't as colorful as Jessica. What's this have to do with Diane?"

"I'm not sure. I met Jessica—or I think I did—the other day. She sold me one of her paintings only after I told her what I saw in it. She insisted I purchase it with either spare change or bartering my own work. Odd isn't it? The painting wasn't for sale. Maybe I'm seeing connections where there aren't any. I just find it odd that she owns the building but doesn't live here."

"You surprise me, Sealy. Sounds just a bit *woo-woo* to me. Diane would never be involved with the likes of Jessica. Diane's style is more devious. You're right to look for Diane's weakness. Hubris and greed—no different than most people. Only problem is, Diane doesn't have any other redeeming qualities to balance her out."

Sealy feigned shock. "Sounds like you've tangled with her before."

Louise narrowed her eyes. "I'm not going to spill my personal beans, if that's what you mean. Just leave it as a scorned woman seeks her revenge. Diane is always on the fence. I think the loss of her dog as a child started her down of path of obsession. Died because she fed him too much. Her brother's dogs didn't die. Simple as that."

Looking at her watch, Sealy stood up. "I've got to catch my ride back to the Hawk House. You've been helpful."

"What did I say?"

"Simple. Diane suffers from the closed heart syndrome."

As Sealy walked away, Louise asked. "That's it, that is your plan. You better have more than that. I refuse to do anything illegal…"

"Good, me too. I have a working theory about buying land and buildings. Apparently, Diane is an entrepreneur with a twist. Like you said, she has her fingers in everything."

"Okay, keep me posted—no pun intended."

"One more thing before I go. Who have you told about me being a 'famous painter'?"

Louise stifled her laugh. "No one directly. Just the truck driver who loaded the paintings you mailed. And one of the guests at the funeral reception. He was coming in from the garden when you were talking to the press. Now that you ask, I thought it strange that he was at the reception without a connection. Real cordial. Talked as if he was raised in the army or worked for the government. You know how all the firemen say 'yes ma'am.'"

"Well, if you think of anyone else that you might have mentioned me to, let me know. Someone is researching my entire existence."

Louise chuckled. "The question is, Will you bring the town fame or shame?"

Sealy waved Louise off. "And I consider you an ally?"

As he walked into his father's old art studio, the smell of aged paint and turpentine caught Paul off guard. He hadn't ventured in since he was a little boy. Hours would pass as he mimicked his father's seriousness, painting on his own easel. What else would a lonely boy do without a mother or siblings?

Paul stood in the middle of the room, surrounded by canvases stacked against the walls. Most had never seen a frame or an audience of viewers. During the past years, his father only painted outside even though the studio with vaulted ceilings, skylights, and large windows offered him a perfect environment. Paul thought it was the stairs that stopped his father from coming inside, but now he knew the memories had held him off.

Gingerly he approached the shelves. The supply section had its own order. One shelf for the oils—tubes and tinctures of ground compounds—gradations of each color on the spectrum, all mixed by hand. Another shelf held tools, brushes varied by handle size and curvature, shape of the bristles and hair type. His father had labeled each tray holding spatulas, sprayers, and scrapers by size and flexibility.

Paul must have stood in one spot for over ten minutes when he heard Sealy's voice.

"Paul to earth, come back, wherever you are. Are you okay? I've been standing here watching you."

Paul shrugged. "I'm overwhelmed. I don't know where to begin. I'm glad I asked for your assistance. Tom's discovery in his father's recipe box reminded me of the letters you discovered in my mom's sewing kit. It could be a fool's mission."

Sealy walked over to the window. "First off, we need fresh air and light." She raised the shades and opened the double-wide window. A cool breeze flowed in, and the natural light spread on the floor creating a rainbow. Dust particles floated in the air.

"This is exactly why I invited you to help me. Already I feel better."

"Do you have a plan on tackling your search for clues?"

"My dad was meticulous in everything he did. I thought I'd go one shelf at a time."

Sealy smiled slyly. "Yes, the prudent way. I have a feeling your father used his emotions too. Why don't we let the sunrays dictate where we begin?"

Paul laughed. "The rainbow will disappear."

"I brought tape and pens. We can mark our order and take our time. Let's do it."

Paul settled into a rhythm. He chose the cooler tones of the color wheel as Sealy went for the reds and warmth. The angles of light spread the two of them far apart and then met in the center. At the tip of the prism, on the upper shelf, Paul thought he had found the pot of gold. His hands shook as he brought the flat metal box over to his father's palette table.

Sealy approached the table. "Are you going to open it?"

"Just a little nervous." After taking a deep breath, Paul continued, "Here goes." Paul jiggled the clasp free with the help of his army knife. He found a stack of 8"x11" typed paper with the formulas for each of the colors his father used. Below that he found a notebook listing all his paintings, named and numbered, as well as the colors used on each painting. Paul gave a nervous laugh. "I was hoping for more. My father left details but no message."

"Can I take a look?" Sealy studied the lists and smiled. "This may be just details to you, but it's an artist's history. The numbered paintings go back in time. I'd bet my life that Richard's paintings from the 1960s would show all that was going on."

"You're saying that we can travel back in time and answer the mystery of your existence through the paintings?"

Sealy sat down on a bench by the window. "Here, take the box—it was just a whim. I caught the name Jessica on one of the lists. It might be significant. It doesn't matter."

Frustrated, Paul found himself pacing. "It does matter. Are you getting cold feet?"

"Me? No, I'm on a mission. I keep seeing connections. I just wonder if it is my imagination or intense desire getting in the way."

Paul sat down straddling the bench. "Desire for what?" Paul studied Sealy's face. Her eyes sparkled behind the half moons of tears. He knew his question was unfair. "You don't have to answer that. You came looking and now I'm looking too. No matter what, we're linked."

A tear finally reached Sealy's cheek. "Yes, we're linked. I'm thankful for that."

"I sense a *but* coming. This question is going to sound like you: What is worrying your heart?"

Sealy caught another of her tears with her tongue. "Good choice of words. My head worries that I've brought the world into your quiet town. My heart worries that the answers to the past might fray our relationship."

Paul had the same worry, and he knew he wanted more. "Let's call it a morning and tackle the rest later. I look forward to seeing my father's earlier paintings. Besides, I might have more information about our Mr. Jewels."

Sealy had divided her days between sorting through Richard's earlier paintings and researching in the library records, examining articles from the period her father ran the winery to the present to see if she could find information with Diane's name attached. What she found left her leerier of Diane. Sealy wanted to make sure her findings weren't coincidences or something more sinister.

Sealy waited at the dining table for Danny and the girls to appear. Like clockwork they arrived from school and ballet lessons famished. Sealy smiled as she listened to their chitchat on the way in.

Roxie looked up at her father. "Daddy, that's the fourth time you said *popcorn* today. Good thing we invented the word. Otherwise, you'd be in debt to us for a dollar apiece."

Laughing, Danny hustled them through the house toward the dining area. "Since when did the price go up?"

Just before they entered, Sealy called out, "Reese and Roxie, I'm in the dining room with cookies and juice. Danny, I have treats for you too."

After a flurry of show-and-tell from school, the girls disappeared, and Danny remained. As he took his second cookie, he queried Sealy. "The treats for me were a dead giveaway. Dad said you were on a mission to unravel the past. What did you find out that you need to lure me in?"

Sealy feigned surprise by covering her eyes with her hand. "In less than three months, you've both learned my tricks. I'll either have to leave or be more interesting."

Danny put up his hand in denial. "No one is insinuating you should leave. Seriously, what have you found?"

"I found alarming coincidences. Hear me out. In the 1960s there was a horrible accident. Diane was the first on the scene, as the accident was on one of the curves near here. Your wife died almost at the same spot. Diane reported the accident."

Danny remained silent, staring beyond Sealy. When he finally answered, Sealy could barely hear his voice. "Diane has always popped up out of nowhere, a spook, always with a reason, always with an ulterior motive. Who was in the first accident?"

"A young man who left a pregnant wife. They claim he was drunk, took the turn too quickly. He was close to the same age as Diane and her brothers—early twenties. All this is kind of sketchy. The man worked at Richard's art school, and when it closed, he was hired at the winery. His fiancée was an artist.

Apparently, Diane didn't like her. No one could find her after the accident." Sealy paused in contemplation, twirled her hair. "According to the papers, her name was Jessica. I wonder if she is the owner of the Golden Goose Gallery."

"Have you told this to my dad? How does it connect?"

"I haven't told him yet, but I will tonight. As best as I can figure it, my father was out with Diane's brothers that night. Geordie and Chuck had been drinking with Jessica's fiancé. My father vouched for Geordie and Chuck's whereabouts, even though they couldn't remember the evening. Apparently blitzed. It became another stain on the Morris name." Sealy stood up and walked over to the window. "I don't know why, but my father seemed to take all the flack back then. Haunted, maybe even hunted. He left here knowing something was wrong all those years back. I believe Charmaine knew something was off too. Her paranoia was real."

As Danny banged his hand on the table, Paul appeared. "Danny, no need for that. Sealy was just delivering information. I overheard the conversation. Remember, it was your warnings that triggered digging into Charmaine's death."

"I apologize, Sealy."

Sealy returned to the dining table. She softened her voice. "Have you ever really looked out at the view? Something about the lighting at this hour casts a spell. The trees change just before the sun descends in the afternoon. The sky fades to a light gray, almost like a storm but not as ominous. I should be the one to apologize. But really all our digging means we're letting the light in. Powerful."

Paul pulled Danny close and gave him a bear hug. "We promised ourselves to be strong. None of it will bring back Charmaine or, for that matter, change history."

While Paul reassured Danny, Sealy occupied her hands with the napkins on the table. She folded and refolded until she had six doves ready to take flight. After Danny disappeared to check on the girls, Paul picked up one of her doves. She tried to smile, but her cheeks resisted, and her lips drooped. "I'm glad you overheard the conversation. I don't think I could repeat it again. It's too sinister."

"I love your napkin doves. We'll figure this out." Paul pulled her up from the chair and cupped her face in his hands. "Has anyone ever told you that your eyes and smile give you away? You could never play poker. You're brave, see the best in people. Don't change."

Sealy picked up all the doves. "I won't let Diane's energy become mine. I'm not that kind of a person. Louise, our local gossiper, verified Diane's hold on the town. Funny, if we all let go, she'll drift away. I always wondered at my mother's rules. She never gave power away. Maybe that got confused with love."

Paul shook his head. "I doubt that. She gave you love. That's been clear since the day you arrived. But you're right, Diane has no power over us unless we give it to her. Let's stick with our plan. Laying out the pieces of the puzzle."

Sealy sighed. "I'm drained. Sleuthing takes emotional energy. Do you mind if I retreat for a bit?"

"I have the perfect antidote to the blues and lack of energy. Would you like to take a walk to my old stump house?"

"That depends. Do I need to walk far?"

"Up a hill and over. You can see the gazebo from there. I'll bring the wine and snacks."

Paul hoped this distraction would soothe Sealy's frayed nerves. He understood heartache, but he never felt an uncertainty about his origins or the sense that he didn't quite fit in. Not sure how she would take in his new discovery concerning Mr. Jewels, he hoped being out in nature would put them both at ease.

Paul waited by the front door ready with the picnic basket when he heard Sealy call from outside.

"Heh, slow poke, I've been ready for at least ten minutes."

As he stepped out, Paul glanced at his watch. "How did you do that, totally change your clothes and slip by me in the kitchen?"

"Practice. I put on my sneakers—just like I used to do with Jeannie when we would slip out from my mother's and grandmother's watchful eye. I even brought binoculars."

Paul admired Sealy's quick change in attitude. "Yes, and you put your hair in a bouncy ponytail, like Reese and Roxie. Very becoming."

"I'm ready for an adventure."

Once past the trail to the gazebo, Paul took the lead. An almost invisible path had been carved out of the woods. He smiled, remembering making the tunnel under the gnarly branches of the trees and the ivy vines he used to create a hidden doorway. "Watch your footing as the path hasn't been maintained."

Sealy stepped past Paul. "Looks to me someone has been out and about. Maybe the girls or Danny. Whoever was here used a rake or cane to move the leaves out of the way."

Paul bent down and studied the markings. "Danny wouldn't do that. He's a little superstitious with keeping the stump house hidden. I doubt he's been up here since Charmaine passed away five years ago. He'd never bring the girls here, at least not yet. Later he'll fix it up for them."

Sealy kneeled beside Paul and snapped a photo of the path and then the view. "Who knows what this means. I might as well take notice. Are you worried?"

"Not really, but I'm tired of all these mysteries. Let's go. We're on an adventure, right?" Paul took the lead again, humming an old tune from the movie *The Sound of Music*. Seeing Sealy's grin was worth his off-key rendition.

Humming along, Sealy laughed. "I love that song. It reminds me to listen to the birds and what surrounds me. My mom sang it to me whenever I was sad."

Paul continued walking on the path, made a few switchbacks, and stopped as they crested the hill. "Okay, now comes the fun part, finding the old stump house. It should be to our right in between the pine trees. Be careful not to touch poison ivy."

Paul and Sealy set to work moving the ivy and fallen branches. After a short while the hidden doorway appeared. Sealy bent her body in half and ventured in. Paul followed.

Still crouched over, Sealy looked for a spot to sit. "You must have been shorter when you made this. I barely fit."

"That's part of the charm. The inside is divided in two." Paul waved Sealy on. "Just step over that big root and you can stand up. I made benches in an L shape."

"Oh, you're so clever, even the sun shines through on this side."

Paul pushed away debris that had filtered in and made space for them to sit. He brushed off the cobwebs along the trunk's walls.

Sealy focused on the baby spiders as they scurried away. "I think we just disturbed another generation."

Paul pulled out a makeshift table made of a thin slab of wood fixed with twine to crisscrossed branches. "The wind and rain vibrate the webs. I wouldn't worry about the babies, by now they've found their safety spots. Time for our wine and snacks."

Sealy took her time settling in, staring at the walls, and looking upward. "Is there a way to peak out from the top? I'm curious imagining you coming here long ago."

"I was a nerd back then, still am. I'd bring a sketch pad and climb up a ladder. That's gone now. I always came alone, until after Danny was born. Even my wife never came in—she had a fear of spiders. I'm sure she'd be less worried about the babies."

"I had a special spot in the attic at my house where I'd sit on the windowsill and open the window to dangle my feet. I'd draw what I saw. My mom accused me of peeping on others. It's amazing what one can see from above." Sealy rose. "I'm feeling closed in. Do you mind if I climb to the top to peer out?"

"Sorry, I didn't think this through. Two tall adults don't quite fit the same. So much for my adventure. Let me put the food away. Then I'll give you a boost up. There should still be metal rungs to rest your feet on."

The top of the stump house was only a few feet above them. Paul cupped his hand together, accepting Sealy's sneaker.

"Paul, are you sure you can hold my weight?"

"No problem. On the count of one, ready, go." Paul felt Sealy's strength, and despite her strong appearance she was surprisingly light. "How is it up there? Is there enough room for two?" Silence. "Are you okay?" When he didn't get a reply, he stepped on the makeshift table and hoisted himself onto a small platform.

Sealy stood facing the road, binoculars glued to her eyes. Paul didn't dare speak. He walked up to her side and peered out. To his naked eye, all appeared normal. A road, cars, tree limbs cascading close to the power lines, and a slice of light between the leaves on the far side. He waited, holding his breath, as he noticed a person standing near a metal railing.

Sealy put down her binoculars, her face flushed and her breath coming too quickly. "I don't know if you could see. According to the maps I studied, that's the corner where the accidents occurred. Guess who popped out of the brush?"

Before answering, Paul took the binoculars from Sealy. "No denying it, Diane has staked herself out at the corner turn." Paul ignored the gnawing tingles along his arms. "She must have a reason."

Sealy shook her head. Paul noted the firmness of her gaze, the stiffness in shoulders, the lack of smile.

He took her hand. "Let's not jump to conclusions."

"I'm all for that, but we can't be naïve. Whatever motivates Diane, your family, our ties appear to be the center of her concern. I thought I had a plan, but I may have to double the risk factor. Emotions plus danger."

Paul interrupted, "I have more information on Mr. Jewels, which will either complicate our plans or make them riskier."

Sealy squeezed Paul's hand. "Don't think I didn't notice your use of *our* in this. I do need support. Go ahead, tell me."

Paul's words rushed out. "Mr. Jewels came on a personal mission to see my father. He's been retired for years. He's connected to Jessica, the owner of the gallery where you purchased that painting. I talked to Jessica in Ocean City, Maryland."

Paul watched the wheels turn in Sealy's head as she made the connections and responded. "How do you know this Jessica is the same person? What did she say?"

"I remembered your conversation at the gallery. Didn't Jessica's nephew say his great-aunt had a gallery in Ocean City? I doubt if I'm wrong." Paul sighed. "When Jessica returned my call, she didn't say much, only that she would make sure to tell Mr. Jewels to call me back."

With his answer, Sealy nodded. "Okay, some pieces are falling into place. Let's head back. Thank you."

Paul didn't ask what pieces and where they fell. Sometimes explanations weren't needed.

Sealy found herself back at the library for more research. This and sorting through Richard's paintings kept her distracted from worry. When Sealy's phone rang, she jumped.

"Jeannie, what's up?"

"You're whispering, are you okay?"

"I'm in the library, trying to find photos of two people who were in an accident in the 1960s."

"Call me back when you can talk."

With the abrupt click, Sealy packed her bags and brought the newspaper files up to the checkout counter. Once outside she crossed the street, slipped into a small café, and headed toward the back where she found an empty booth.

On the first ring Jeannie answered: "That was quick."

"Remember, I'm in a small town. The library is walking distance to this old coffee spot where they serve drip coffee with no extras. Only the old-timers come here, so it's rowdy enough that no one can overhear our conversation." Sealy took a deep breath. "I know it's too soon, but have the results come back from your DNA?"

"I'm not calling about our DNA. For goodness sakes. Take your own test if you're so riled up about this. I'm angry now. You've been gone almost three months and I feel like I've lost you to another family. What was wrong with your life here?"

Sealy let her sister rant until her steam petered out. "What happened? I've been gone this long before on business and vacations and it never bothered you. Are your kids and grandchildren okay?"

"You're incorrigible. I'm worried this time. Another person came asking for you. He was young, super polite, and in his thirties. He could have been one of my kids."

"What did he want?"

"That's what got me. He said he had tracked down your name because of your artwork. A lady who worked at the post office told him that a famous artist was shipping out her work. He'd come all the way from Maryland. The odd thing was he kept asking about our parents. It spooked me."

Sealy remembered Louise's confession at their meeting outside of the post office. Louise had mentioned her paintings to a polite guest at the funeral. She made a mental note to check the guest registry. "What did he look like?"

"Handsome, recent haircut, but he left some waves on top. He had eyes that reminded me of you."

"Oh, Jeannie, are you making fun of me or is that what you saw?"

"Both. I knew you'd ask. You are exasperating. This guy had the serious look you get. He's focused and wants to find out something. The journalists didn't scare me, but his gentle, polite manner gave me the heebie-jeebies."

The hair on Sealy's arms rose in salute of an unspecific inkling. "I think the same person was snooping at Richard's funeral. I never intended my coming here to open a can of worms in your life. I'm sorry."

"Sealy, you're too focused on solving this like a puzzle. Don't you see me in the picture, anyone else? We are in the same life! What happened to nurture and nature? All this about DNA. Whatever went before our existence, does that define us? Mom raised us to be good people. That counts."

Sealy stared at the customers. One elderly gentleman was eating apple pie and sharing it with a lady friend. Another was eating alone at the counter, smiling at her. "I agree, but it isn't us I'm worried about. My existence affected other people. I may appear to have been the catalyst by coming to Maine with Mom's photo, but another two generations are looking for me. Not just Richard or the Morris family. Odd, isn't it? What am I key to?"

The silence at the other end of the conversation made Sealy nervous. "Jeannie, are you still there?"

"Yeah, something the polite guy said. He told me that time was important. I didn't ask why."

The word *time* stuck in Sealy's mind. She felt her own urgency, as if time was running out. "Well, that makes sense. Mom died with a secret, Richard is gone, and that generation is fast disappearing. Maybe he thinks I'm needed."

"Needed for what? Your blood?"

"Exactly. Jeannie, I've got to go."

Part Three
Stepping In

Paul glanced over at Sealy in the passenger seat. Lying in the most reclined setting, she looked like an adolescent, exhausted from playing sports too hard. He'd been driving for over eight hours and for the most part Sealy had slept.

The decision to travel at night was his. Sealy had been calm putting her fears into words. He could still hear her question: *What if this is about a genetic need? Not my need to know who I am. I keep thinking about Jessica's nephew and her dedication to him with his cancer. Some cancers need a genetic match for a stem transplant. And Mr. Jewels bullying your dying dad, almost threatening consequences…*

Paul thought Sealy's fear was a giant leap of assumptions but not implausible. He worried that her sense of urgency might cause her to be reckless. After their talk at his office, he cleared his calendar for a few days.

The night sky slowly faded from its rich black to a gray with blue tints trailing off as the sun made its rotation. Sealy stirred and unraveled her body. "Where are we?"

"Good morning, Miss Sleepyhead, we just crossed into Maryland. By driving at night, I avoided all the traffic from Boston, New York, and Philly. How'd you sleep?"

"Dreamed of popsicles. Root beer and grape—the only ones that would work. My mom wouldn't take ice cubes at the end of her life."

"That would explain your murmurings. You learn a lot watching people sleep."

Sealy feigned embarrassment. "Oh my, now I'll have to hide from you. You've seen my real self."

Although Sealy joked, Paul envisioned a more intimate scene. His words gave him away. "I haven't watched anyone sleep for years. Good thing I had to keep my eyes on the road."

This time Sealy blushed. "I guess that's what happens when you go on an adventure. Thanks for driving through the night, especially after a full day of work. I wasn't the best of company, talking in my sleep. My dreams aren't usually so vivid. I thought my mom wanted to tell me something, but her mouth was too parched to talk." The sun continued its slow rise in the sky where the dominant gray subsided. Sealy stretched her arms upward. "I wish I had my paints with me. The cerulean sky glistens with a glaze of the morning dewdrops. I never tire of how nature inspires." She reached over to touch Paul's hand on the steering wheel. "I'd love to get something to eat before the next steps."

Paul kept his eyes on the road. "Can you use your cell phone's GPS to find a café open early in Ocean City? We'll be there in about forty-five minutes if that is soon enough for you. My brain is frazzled at this point."

As Paul drove, Sealy concentrated on searching the internet. She was all smiles when she straightened up to look at the road. "I found the perfect spot. According to this, there's a diner that has homemade English muffins and baby potatoes sautéed crispy with all the offerings. Its right on the boardwalk. Opens at 7:00 a.m."

Paul's stomach rumbled. "Now I'm starved. My brain and belly will appreciate the fueling."

Paul pulled into Ocean City just as the hour hit seven. "Okay, keep your eye out for the diner. What was its name?"

Sealy chuckled. "Morning Glory. The logo looks just like the painting of Jessica's gallery, the Golden Goose. The illustration has the same playful feel."

At the mention of Jessica's name, reality hit Paul. "I'd almost forgotten why we came. I wish we had called her first. This might be a wild-goose chase."

Sealy's smile faded. "I didn't want to risk messing this up. I don't believe Jessica would respond to words alone. She must look into your eyes—she reads people. At least that is what she did when I purchased her painting."

Paul found a parking spot on a narrow side road, perpendicular to the shore. All the shops were small local businesses that faced the boardwalk and the ocean. Only a few people were walking the beach with their dogs or jogging. "I agree with you. Ocean City folk and Jessica aren't much different from us. Our town isn't as touristy, but our sense of privacy and eye contact with the residents is important. When I called looking for Mr. Jewels, I felt her distance. She couldn't read me."

Sealy interrupted, "There's the Morning Glory, right between a gallery and a dress shop. Looks like the tables are filling up."

As they approached, two older women left smiling, arms looped by the elbows. Paul wondered if they were old friends or sisters or a married couple. Another elderly gentleman rushed out still holding his billfold open. Paul assumed he had paid for the women, but the gentleman walked in the opposite direction down the boardwalk. Paul and Sealy entered and found two empty tables. A sign stated, "Seat Yourself, leave the rest to us."

Paul sat down in the booth and Sealy hesitated, eyeing the spot next to him. "Good choice of places to eat. Did you want to sit here or facing me?" he asked.

Sealy scooted in next to Paul. "I hope you don't mind that I'm next to you. Old habits die hard. I usually face the patrons, but then again, I eat alone. That's my favorite way to find character features to paint. Those who rise early have lines of wisdom on their faces. You see the beginners of the day, so different from those who stay up late to close a town. I shouldn't really say that, considering we both haven't slept with the drive, and our clothes are rumpled."

The waitress arrived and placed two menus on the table. "I couldn't help but overhear your conversation. You two don't look that bad. I'd say you're chipper. This visit must be important for two strangers to be here this early. I take it you're not here on vacation."

Paul waited for Sealy to answer.

"We're here to talk with Jessica, the owner of the gallery. Do you know her? She commissioned a painting from me, and I wanted to follow up with her."

Even though the waitress smiled, Paul felt her laser gaze determining what to say next. Sealy had told a truth, but not the whole truth. He wanted to warn Sealy to be careful with what she revealed. He reached for her hand just as Sealy tapped on his thigh. Message delivered.

"Well, you two came to the right place. Jessica owns this diner, and it's attached to her gallery next door and her dress shop on the other side. She's a bigwig in the town, but you'll rarely see her. We love her ways—present but always absent."

"I can see why you love her. She has a way of knowing things and trusting. That's exactly why we came in person all the way from Maine. I met her only once at her other gallery. She's not the kind of person you forget. When does her gallery open?"

The waitress looked at her watch. "That always depends. If she's painting, then she'll wait until the light isn't good. If she's volunteering, then when she's done. I've got the keys to the gallery, and the door between the diner is always open when the store is open. That way I can help. The dress shop and the diner each have their own managers."

Paul lifted his menu toward Sealy. "How about ordering now? The smell of potatoes reminded me that I'm depleted."

"Oh, I'm sorry, I should let you two place your orders."

Once the order had been placed, Paul sighed. "Did you catch our waitress's name? She seemed helpful but I sensed her probing. You're wearing off on me, Sealy."

Sealy took a minute to answer. "Take a look at the paintings on the wall. The diner is an extension of the gallery. I had no idea when I met Jessica that she was so successful and powerful. If I'm wearing off on you, then I'll need your insights. Doesn't that painting on the left back wall look familiar?"

Paul scanned the wall and found what appeared to be a small unframed canvas in the style of his father. He slipped out of his seat to get a closer look. He returned to the table shaken. "The painting is one of my dad's smaller canvases. It has his signature. I've never seen it."

"Yes, and it's the exact scene minus the little girl and woman that Jessica painted. What do you think it means?"

As the waitress approached with their food, Paul thanked her and faced Sealy with a sheepish look. "Let me think about it. I can't analyze on an empty stomach, especially when everything looks so good."

They ate in silence. Paul noted that Sealy only ate her muffin. "You aren't hungry?"

"Just thinking about Danny and the B&B. I bet he would love these homemade English muffins. Maybe we can convince the waitress to give us the recipe."

Paul pushed his plate toward the center of the table and laughed. "Are you saying you want the recipe and will be around to share it with us? Or are you wondering about the painting hanging in the diner? I think it means that my father knew Jessica. We figured that she attended the art school he ran."

Sealy wiped her mouth with the cloth napkin and set it on top of her unfinished breakfast. "The place is emptying out. I guess we can talk a bit here, or do you want to walk along the board-walk?"

"I'm all for walking. I need to stretch my legs. Besides, you're twirling your hair, which means you're nervous."

Paul paid for both of their meals. As they walked out the door, their waitress came up to them. "Here's a brochure of the paint-ings on the diner's walls with a list of artists and something said about each painting."

Sealy took the brochure. "Thanks, we'll be by later when the gallery opens."

As soon as they walked out of the diner, Sealy took off her shoes and rolled up her pant legs. "I can't help myself. The sandy beach calls. Meet you down by the water's edge."

Out of breath and exhilarated, Sealy waited until Paul had caught up. Together they strolled, dangling their shoes. She watched Paul's feet sink deeper into the wet sand. The solidness of his presence felt right, but she wondered if his imprint would dissolve slowly, fade into a less intimate place. She let the salty air and moist breeze settle along her skin. She could almost taste the ocean. "Have you noticed the color change from oatmeal white to pale orange? I love how the sand filters through my toes, sifting even though the fine grains are wet. I'll have to paint a scene like this. I wish my brain filtered the important facts out. There are too many coincidences that don't make sense."

"You're staring at my feet, Sealy; will they, too, be in the painting? I think you're trying too hard. Finding my dad's painting at the diner is testament to a connection of artists. I've never seen his work outside of his studio. I guess he endures." Paul took her hand. "I'm not worried about what we find out here with Jessica. Your instincts are sound. But I don't want us to stop being close, whatever that means."

Sealy looked into Paul's eyes. "I may have been looking at your feet, but it was your solidness that I was appreciating. There are ghosts in our closets, but you aren't one. Tell me, what does worry you?"

"I feel like a sleuth. Not quite trusting what people say. The waitress was protecting Jessica. I wonder why. Don't you think it odd that Jessica owns three thriving businesses?"

"Yes, artists' brains are wired differently, and few have a mother like mine pushing the financial aspects."

Paul continued, "My point exactly. From what you've told me of your encounter with her, Jessica wasn't concerned with money. I didn't imagine her an entrepreneur."

"Me either. I wonder where she got her seed money. Only someone with real passion could gather enough people to work for her and prosper." Sealy sighed. "What does the brochure say about your father's painting?"

Paul opened the brochure and read, "Richard Morris's painting, called *Remaining*, evokes a serene path, undisturbed by those who pass through time. Note the small figures off in the distance—they almost disappear."

"There's our clue. We didn't find a painting in your father's studio because it's here hanging in the diner. Jessica's painting *Crossroads* goes with this one."

Paul studied the brochure. "I can't see the figures. I guess we'll have to wait until we go back and see the actual painting. What shocks me is that my father has never sold one of his paintings. I can't remember him gifting them either."

Sealy walked closer to the water. The tide had changed. The waves covered her ankles, and then before she realized it, they'd crept up to her calves. The world seemed to slip away; a cold chill passed over her body. She turned back to face Paul. "I just had the strangest sensation, an image of my mom and I strolling down that very path. My mother was squeezing my hand as if to hurry me along."

"Let's get to a place where you can get dry. You're soaking wet. I have a towel in the car." Paul wrapped his arm in the crook of her elbow and walked back to the car. "Sealy, are you sure you're up for this? It's like you've seen a ghost."

Sealy tried to smile but she knew that her eyes gave her away. "Thanks, once I dry off I'll be okay. I remembered when you told me about the lost baby years ago and the horrible car accident where Jessica's fiancé died. I wonder if that history travels through time. I mean, I know trauma stays in one's cells."

Paul shook his head. "Is that your real question? I don't want to discourage you, but please remain in the present with me. I'll race you to the car."

Sealy's eyes popped open in surprise. "Thanks. Not even my sister can pull me back like that."

As Paul took off, he yelled, "Well, you're a force to contend with, part of your charm. Let's get to the B&B we booked and shower. The gallery won't be open for a few hours."

Sealy left Paul to deal with the confusion of the booking. Somehow, they had given them one room instead of the two Paul had requested. Ever the diplomat, Paul had handed her the keys to the room as he remained at the front desk to sort the matter out.

She chuckled thinking of the poor boy's look and comment. He tried to act the part of a seasoned receptionist, but she suspected he was the owner's teenage son helping out. "I'm so sorry for the error. With the same name, I made the mistake. You both look tired. While I see if anyone cancels, I'll let you wash up at no charge."

Refreshed from her shower, Sealy walked down to the B&B living room. Paul lay sprawled across the sofa, eyes shut, feet dangling off the edge. This had to mean that there wasn't another room available. She took a deep breath and exhaled, emitting a soft whistle.

Paul's eyes popped open. "No one has whistled at me ever."

"Not intended. I exhaled not realizing my lips were puckered." Sealy smiled. "I can't say you're at your best at this moment."

Paul sat up. "There won't be another room available tonight. A group from New York is down for a wedding. Should we look for another hotel or B&B?"

"There's only one bed. What do you think?"

"I think we have a dilemma."

Sealy nodded. "Why don't you take your bag upstairs, shower, and take a nap? I'll scout around for another hotel. If I can't find a place, I can sleep in the oversized chair." Sealy handed Paul his bag and didn't wait for his answer. "I'll check back in a couple of hours."

Still early in the day, Sealy enjoyed the absence of foot traffic as she headed out to find another place to sleep. The bed-and-break-fast was two blocks off the main road. She walked slowly taking in the picket fences, manicured lawns, and Victorian houses. Away from the tourist shops, the neighborhood emitted the air of aristocracy, formal and gentrified. She wondered if the newly refurbished homes carried with them the old virtues or more of an openness to present lives. As a realtor, she thought of the land-scaping, the outside painting, and presentation of home as not only a truth about the owners but a sign of how they wanted to be perceived. Something about the rows of homes reminded her of Diane's brothers, Chuck and Geordie. They seemed old with their set ways of dressing and patterns, yet they exposed a check-ered history, still maintaining an air of conventionality.

Sealy pictured Ogunquit's storefronts and the pages of her real estate search. The revelation that Diane owned partnership in so many buildings and Chuck and Geordie only the one storefront, Jessica's gallery, suddenly made sense. The brothers had invested elsewhere for different reasons. Jessica's apparent entrepreneur-ship rested on what appeared unlikely benefactors. Sealy shook her head. Maybe there was another benefactor. Did this even mat-ter? What story was she trying to unravel?

The breeze from the ocean passed through to the side roads. Sealy heard the clang of a sign against a store post. She looked up to find the Ocean Breeze B&B with a vacancy sign in the window. A bell rang as she entered, and a young man neatly dressed in a dark shirt and freshly pressed jeans walked out to greet her. "Wel-come to the Ocean Breeze. I'm Dean. What can I do for you today? Are you here to visit a guest or to rent a room?"

Sealy noted Dean's hair, wavy in the front but closely cropped along the sides. His eyes followed her as she got her bearings. She couldn't help but stare back. "I'm sorry, I don't mean to be rude, but something about you looks familiar. Have you ever been to Ogunquit?"

"No, but my great-aunt has a gallery there. One of my brothers runs it for her. Maybe you have me confused with him."

Nothing about him looked like the young man he called his brother. It was the haircut that appeared familiar—Jeannie's teasing description of the man who had come to her door with inquiries. "That could be it. To answer your question, I'm looking for two rooms, for tonight and tomorrow. The sign says you have vacancies. I hope that includes the next two nights."

Dean sifted through his reservations and smiled. "You're in luck. The wedding in town had some guests cancel at the last minute. If you'd like, I can make sure they're clean by noon. It was a family of four, so the rooms are adjoining."

Sealy sighed in relief. "That's perfect. You can put the two rooms under my name, Sealy Morris. Here is my cell phone number and credit card to hold the rooms."

Dean's hand shook ever so slightly as he took the credit card. He cleared his throat. "Excuse me, are you the artist, the one who goes by another name?"

The question wasn't expected, but it made sense. Dean could have gone to her sister's house. By sharing her talents with the press, Sealy had provided him with the crumbs. She extended her hand. "Yes, in fact I am that artist. Do you know my work?"

"No, not really, but my aunt had me do some research."

"And let me guess: you attended the funeral of Richard Morris, and then traveled to the West Coast to find out more."

Dean turned the color of a beet. He had difficulty swallowing. "Is that why you're here?"

Sealy shook her head. "I researched another matter, which brought me to your aunt. It would save me time if you could let her know I'm here with Richard's son, Paul. We intended to pay her a visit when her gallery opened."

"I can do that. If she wants to get a hold of you, may I give her your cell phone number? Otherwise, I'll call you. Do you have anything else I can relay to her?"

"No, I think not. You'll make a great investigative reporter. See you later."

Paul paced outside of the bed-and-breakfast as he waited for Sealy's return. His quick shower and nap had revived him, but a missed phone call from Danny left him on edge. No message meant it wasn't an emergency, but he sensed something was wrong.

He couldn't help himself from chuckling when he saw Sealy jogging down the street. Her head tilted toward him, her arms pushed the air, and her legs seemed to lift off the pavement. He waved and she raised her hand, giving a thumbs-up. Although it might have been awkward to share a bedroom, he wouldn't have minded. "Looks like you had success in finding us a new place to rest our weary souls."

Catching her breath, Sealy rested her hand on her chest. "Yes, yes, a double yes. I just had the weirdest interaction. I swear a spell has been cast over this trip. Is there a bench nearby? I need to sit down."

Paul motioned toward the front porch where a bench swing large enough for the two of them sat idle. Happy to have a diversion, his concern about Danny could wait until Sealy had told him the news. "Let's sit here. I don't think we're in a hurry to leave quite yet. We only have to collect our bags."

"Ocean Spray—I mean Ocean *Breeze* is owned by Jessica. Don't you see, the B&B has room for us, but she owns it!"

"Calm down, you're talking half thoughts, and I can't make the leap. You found a new place for us to stay, and Jessica owns it. Okay, why is that so important?"

Taking a few breaths, Sealy shook her head. Her hair tumbled out of its bun and fell softly on her shoulders. She smiled and twirled one end with her right hand. "Remember when I told you about someone coming to my sister's house asking questions about me? Jeannie always makes fun of me when I ask what the person looks like. She painstakingly described him. The young man at the counter was him. He recognized my name and asked if I was the painter with another name. I called him out and countered by asking if he had been to my sister's house. Guess what?"

Paul ran his fingers through his hair and realized why Sealy twirled hers. The sensual touch of the hair didn't just calm her; it was an entry to thoughts. His scalp tingled. "I'm not good at guessing. Besides, I can't tell if this is good or bad news as you're bouncing around."

"The young man at the Ocean Breeze is the brother of the manager who runs Jessica's gallery in Ogunquit. She knows everything about me. Before she gave me her painting, I had never heard of her before. I don't think you knew about her either. Don't look at me like that. Please stay with me as I connect these dots. Whatever my mom didn't want to tell me, or your dad didn't want to say, they left clues."

Paul tried to calm Sealy. "Maybe you are the clue. At least your existence holds this all together. This isn't new information. All it tells us it that Jessica is looking for you. You already felt you were needed. The real question is why. Now we'll find out. But you're sensing something else—otherwise you'd be calmer."

Sealy nodded, held herself in a tight hug. "I keep thinking about Chuck and Geordie. If I had time, I could research if they were the initial benefactors to Jessica."

"You could ask her directly, without having to resort to records. Although we are here on your intuition, Jessica has been looking for you. It's no coincidence that Mr. Jewels came to visit my father. I think it would be a fair question, and it might help us understand why both parents kept secrets. I think Jessica needs to share." Paul unwrapped Sealy's arms and held on to her hand. "You don't want to hear anything bad about your parents. Neither do I."

Before Sealy could answer, Paul's cell phone rang. "Danny, what's up?" As Paul listened, he gripped Sealy's hand tighter. "Are Reese and Roxie hurt or upset? Good. Nothing was taken from the house or the winery? Okay. We'll be home in a couple of days. If you need me, I'll return sooner. Yes, check in on Chuck and Geordie."

Sealy placed her other hand on top of Paul's. "What's going on?"

Paul took a deep breath. "Seems there was a break-in at the house and one at the winery. Also, Chuck and Geordie were driving on that corner, where we spotted Diane, where Jessica's fiancé was hit and where Danny's wife died. Danny and the kiddos were in the car and witnessed their car swerving. Danny was lucky they weren't hit. He stayed with Chuck and Geordie until they felt okay to drive away."

Sealy sighed and closed her eyes. "Earlier you said I was the glue that held all this together. I'm worried that another story is behind all this and will pull us apart. Diane is out for vengeance. Her nature is to take what others love. Maybe you should go home. I can manage on my own."

Paul shook his head. "I think we need to talk to Jessica together. Remember, she was in the first accident at that spot. Besides, I don't want to return home without you."

Sealy looked at the sun as it cast a pale purple shadow on the boardwalk. Nothing dramatic, but the brightness of the morning had dissolved. The Morning Glory had a line of hungry customers waiting to enter for lunch. Sealy watched patrons leave their names and wander over to the gallery.

"Should we go inside the gallery?" she asked. "See if Jessica is there?"

Paul looked at his watch. "Do you think it wise to talk to Jessica with the gallery full of people?"

"Don't worry, they'll filter out soon. If Jessica is there, I'm sure she'll recognize me and come over. I've been rehearsing in my mind what to say."

Paul opened the door, bowed, and motioned Sealy to go through. "You must be nervous. Usually, you just blurt out your thoughts."

Paul meant his words as a tease, but Sealy felt a slight twinge of hurt. "I suppose I never felt this vulnerable. I've my ways to cope." She entered the gallery with the purple shadow of the morning's sun. Not waiting for Paul, she stood in the center of the room.

Sealy sensed Paul's approach. He came to her side and whispered, "I'm with you. I apologize for my insensitivity. If you look to your left, you'll find my father's painting. They moved it from the diner to the gallery."

Sealy felt the warmth of Paul's breath on her cheek, and a chill ran up her arm. She turned to face him. "I'm the insensitive one. I assumed you'd realized I'm confident for others but not when it involves me. How could you know this in such a short time? Besides, your world has been shaken as well." Sealy reached for Paul's hand as he guided her across the room to Richard's painting. After a quick look she spoke. "Can you make out the small figures we saw before?"

Paul walked in closer. "No, the two people aren't there. I'm not sure if this is the same painting."

Sealy took out a magnifying glass to examine the paint. "Hmm, this painting is almost identical, but the colors are muted. The dark used in the negative spaces pushed the distance away, as if the path remains suspended. Either the people have vanished or they never existed. I think—"

Before Sealy finished her thought, she heard Jessica's excited voice by her side. "You nailed it. It wasn't painted at the same time as Richard's other painting."

Not sure if she imagined the voice, Sealy stepped back and turned to face Jessica. She wore a long flowing navy skirt that folded within itself, exposing yellow daisies. A white blouse topped off the ensemble. "Jessica, you're here. Do you remember me? "

"Of course I do. I look forward to hanging the painting you're doing for me. Paul, I haven't met you yet, but Richard used to talk about you. I'm glad you and Sealy found me. It makes it all simpler to explain."

Paul gave Jessica an easy smile. "I'm afraid I don't remember if my father talked about you. Sealy has told me about your unusual request for payment on one of your paintings. That's all I know."

"Yes, my world works in strange ways. I think yours does too, Sealy."

Sealy removed her sweater and undid the first button of her shirt. "Can we go sit down? I'm a little overwhelmed."

Jessica looked at Sealy. "I know just the place. Behind the café, I have my private spot under a magnolia tree. Follow me, I have a table prepared with lemonade and our famous sand dollar cookies."

Once settled, Sealy relaxed. "Thanks. I had rehearsed a mini speech to reintroduce myself, but I needn't have bothered. Seems you know way more than I had imagined."

Jessica passed around the cookies. "Fill your own glasses if you don't mind. My hands shake, not so much that I can't paint, but I spill lots. Where to begin?"

"I'm curious and I'm sure Paul wonders why you have two of his father's paintings. As far as I know Richard preferred to keep his art private. Paul and I cleaned up Richard's studio, and I even saw some of Paul's earlier paintings."

Jessica beamed. "Artists express themselves in a universal language. I'm glad to hear, Paul, that you still consider yourself a painter. I suspect that your work as the town manager keeps you too busy. That's what happened to Richard." Shaking her head, Jessica continued, "That was so long ago. I assume you know about Richard's art academy. I was a student there. One of Richard's assignments was to have us paint a scene over and over, each time with a different story behind it. The two he painted were examples. He gave them to me. Many years later I used his painting in a different way."

Sealy thought of the painting she had purchased. She realized that Jessica had priced it based on her connections and vision.

"Yes, and I purchased one of them. Would you have given it to someone else or only to a woman about my age?"

Jessica's eyes welled up. "I can't say. Only I had a sense about you. I had hoped for a buyer who would feel empathy and wonder what wasn't portrayed in the scene. Hope is eternal, if that answers your question. But I doubt that it does. Have another cookie. I think we'll be here awhile."

Paul jumped in, "I don't believe in coincidences. No need to shy away from issues. Both of us have questions."

Sealy reached out and touched Jessica's hand. "I'm sorry. Tell me about your grandnephew who runs the gallery. What kind of cancer does he have?"

The tears in Jessica's eyes slide gently down her cheeks. "So, you guessed. Joseph has leukemia. He needs a stem cell transplant from an almost perfect genetic match. His brother has diabetes and a weak heart, so he isn't eligible. The waiting list is too long for Joseph. I'm afraid he might die without a donor." Jessica held on to Sealy's hand and looked into her eyes. "You see, I've been searching for the baby I gave up when my fiancé was killed. I relinquished all rights to know about her parents or her future. My brother, Jake Jewels, tried to help me."

The world seemed to swirl around Sealy. She stared into Jessica's eyes, traveled through time to when she was an infant. "So you are my mother?"

Jessica turned her palms upward as if the heavens would shower down an answer. Her voice quivered with her plea. "I hope so, for Joseph's sake. You'll have to take a specific test, not the normal DNA test. My brother couldn't be sure of the records as there were some problems that he thought Richard could solve. But would you take the test, and be a stem cell donor, if it is true?"

Sealy knew another person's life rested with her decision. It didn't matter what she felt.

Paul woke with a start. So much for trying to rest at the new B&B. He had a midafternoon nightmare, with Diane holding Danny hostage, Roxie and Reese running along the road alone. Unsettled, he called Danny to verify his dream wasn't real.

Danny picked up after the second ring. "Dad, is that you? Your voice sounds muffled."

"I just woke up. I'm worried after your last phone call. What's the news?"

"Wow—sleeping in the middle of the day. Are you okay?"

"I'm giving Sealy some space after our meeting with Jessica. I'll fill you in later. Did you find anything stolen in the house or winery? Are the girls okay?"

Paul heard the kids laughing in the background and instantly relaxed. His worst fears were just that.

"Reese and Roxie have some friends over from school. I realized living out here could be isolating for them. You're okay with that, aren't you?"

"Sure, good call. Now tell me about the house"

"The only place touched was Granddad's art studio. I can't tell if anything was taken, but it is a mess. I thought I should wait to let you see it. Especially because you and Sealy had worked so hard up there. Your office studio seems okay, but you need to check for yourself. The winery appears untouched. I've tested all the barrels. Nothing is amiss there. Someone tried to get into the main office. The only thing I found out of sorts was a file cabinet of old ledgers."

Paul paced around the room, circled the bed, and peered out the window. He thought of his dad's secrets, the anomalies from the old ledgers that caused Sealy's father to leave. Paul had taken photos of all his father's paintings as well as the old ledgers. "Have you reported this to the authorities?"

"Yes, but nothing with any monetary value was taken. They're going to keep surveillance around our properties and where the accident happened. It's the best I could do."

"I should be home in a couple of days or sooner. Are you sure you can handle everything with the businesses and the girls?"

"I'm good with the B&B, only one new visitor for overnight. The winery is in more of a rest state. I do miss Sealy's special touch with the kids. I hope she's coming back with you."

Paul's heart skipped a beat at the thought of Sealy. They still hadn't talked after Jessica's conversation. "That's the plan. We have a few more loose ends to figure out."

After Paul hung up, he knocked on Sealy's door.

Sealy called out, "Hold on a second." She opened the door and waved him in. "Jeannie, Paul's at the door. I'll call you back later."

Sealy stood barefoot by the window. Her hair was pulled up high and spilled out like waves of a waterfall. She wore a loose-fitting sleeveless shift. Viewing her this way, Paul realized how much he didn't know about Sealy's private moments. "Are you sure you feel comfortable with me in your space?"

"I didn't think about it. I mean, if this is awkward, we can go downstairs."

"No, it's just that we haven't talked about you not being related by blood. It makes a difference."

"Yes, we will have that conversation. But I can't quite go there yet. I'm wrestling with my feelings toward Jessica and Joseph's illness. My gut says I'm not related to you. I'll take the test to see if we share the same family markers.

"I just got off the phone with Jeannie. Something is up with her DNA test. Based on my grandmother's and mother's stories, she thought she'd have a Celtic background. Seems her ancestry test shows a hundred percent Mediterranean. Jeannie thinks she's been lied to all her life. The DNA test she took wouldn't have helped us figure this out. It only tells ancestral breakdowns, not the specifics. Who knows anymore?"

"Can I at least hug you?"

Sealy reached out to accept his embrace. The hug was more than he anticipated. He felt all of her as she held on tight. Paul closed his eyes, breathed her in, and then stepped back. "We should get ready to meet Mr. Jewels. Jessica left us hanging on that one. Another mystery."

"Hmm. Yes, what was I thinking? Your arms are dangerous. I'll get dressed and meet you downstairs in a half hour."

"I'll recover from the hug by then. See you in the living room."

The walk over to Jessica's home took less than fifteen minutes. Jessica answered the door with her brother, Jake. After directing them to the living room, she quickly disappeared. Mr. Jewels sat stiffly on Jessica's overstuffed chair. Sealy didn't know what to make of him. Dressed in a white shirt and thin blue tie, he acted as if he was there in an official capacity, not like he was at home with his sister.

Sealy sat by Paul's side and watched him nervously pick at the platter of fresh vegetables and dip that Jessica had left. She took pity on Mr. Jewels. "Jake, are we waiting for your sister to return? She's been gone for a while."

Mr. Jewels cleared his throat twice as he picked up his pad of paper. "I'd prefer you called me by my full name. Waiting for Jessica, no, I think not. We should sort this out privately. It really isn't Jessica's concern. I tried to talk to Mr. Richard Morris before he passed. All of this could have been avoided." He sighed. "Now I'm forced to right an error and break confidentiality. It has to do with adoption papers that were forged or misrepresented. It came to light in my search for Jessica's baby's parents."

Paul pushed the appetizers to the center of the coffee table. "Go ahead, tell us. What do the papers say? I need to know what my father did."

Sealy felt removed, as if the conversation wasn't about her but Richard Morris. Mr. Jewels tapped his pen on a document, stared at her as if she were an aberration. Then he faced Paul with raised eyebrows and pursed lips.

"To tell you the truth, it is all confusing. Jessica's baby was adopted by your father and mother. But you see, that's not possible. Your mother was already gone, and obviously you are an only child. I checked the dates and signatures. Your father's signature matches but not your mother's. Oddities, you must look at oddities. Don't you agree?"

The room came into focus as Sealy remembered her sister's surprise at finding her mother's notary stamp with her maiden name, not her married name. Jeannie had been riled by that. "Mr. Jewels, how were the adoption papers signed? Full names or just the last name?"

"Hmm, let me check. You're right, it doesn't say Lorraine Morris. Just Mrs. L. Morris, not a complete name. But it does say Richard Morris. The notary stamp is for a Ms. Leigh Mary Jones."

Sealy gasped and bowed her head. "I'm so sorry, so sorry."

Paul turned toward Sealy. "Shh, you have nothing to be sorry about. Who is Leigh Mary Jones?"

"Leigh Mary Jones is my mother's maiden name. She notarized her own signature—it was all a lie."

Mr. Jewels ruffled the documents in his hand. "If you could please let me finish. This happened so long ago. I'm in my eighties. Bear with me. Technically the papers would stand as Lorraine Morris. Legally it would be Leigh Mary Morris. I dug deeper to find that Barry Morris and Mary Morris were denied any adoptions due to Barry's character. I assume, Sealy, your mother committed fraud because of her overwhelming desire to adopt you. I'm the one who is sorry. I signed off on the papers originally. I was new at my job, overworked, and desperate to prove myself. I think this would appear as a conflict of interest on my part as they adopted my sister's child. I assure you I didn't know—once the future parents are cleared to adopt, I wouldn't have been privy to who they adopted. "

"Mr. Jewels, why don't you and I sort this out and let Sealy find Jessica?"

Grateful for an excuse to collect her thoughts, Sealy mouthed the words *thank you* to Paul and headed for the kitchen. Knowing how sensitive the situation was, she turned and offered her hand to Mr. Jewels. "I apologize for what we couldn't have known."

Paul stood up from the sofa and walked to the opposite side of the living room. The room was overcrowded with beautiful artwork, pottery, jewelry, blown glass. Nothing matched. The blue antique urns sat next to earthen ceramics. The finery, polished and fragile, made the other seem clumsy. Paintings worthy of Norman Rockwell's realistic renderings hung next to expressionistic works more like that of Jackson Pollock. Native totem pole miniature carvings rested on a redwood dresser most likely made by the Amish. Compared to the gallery where Jessica carefully themed her exhibits, her home felt like a sanctuary of memories. Paul had a hard time organizing his thoughts with the disarray.

"Mr. Jewels, I can see now why you wanted to talk with my father, but what did you expect him to say? He was dying."

Waving the documents, Mr. Jewels countered, "This is a legal document, done illegally. Your father misrepresented himself."

Paul pointed to the papers. "I'm with you about upholding the law. Adoptions are sacred, just like parenthood. I'm sure he was considered a fit person to be a father, as was Mrs. L. Morris. Shouldn't you be more worried about Sealy, the child who is now an adult?"

Undoing his tie, Mr. Jewels steadied himself as he rose from the chair. "You sound like Jessica. She's annoyed with me. I'm detail oriented; she's freer in her outlook on life. I must protect her. Don't you see?"

The urgency in Mr. Jewels's voice startled Paul. He immediately thought of Diane and then her brothers. "Who are you protecting Jessica from? Certainly not me or Sealy."

"Did you know that Jessica is rather wealthy?"

Disgusted, Paul swallowed the bad taste in his mouth. Mr. Jewels, with all his professionalism, shriveled before his eyes. "So this is about money, not love or rescuing Jessica's nephew? How could you even…"

"Mr. Morris, calm down. Once again you jump to conclusions. Money is involved but not the fear that Sealy would be involved. I wanted to talk with your father about money anonymously sent monthly to Jessica. Jessica claims she doesn't know who sent the money for the last sixty years."

"Why would my father send her money? If the adoption was blind, he wouldn't have known whose child they adopted. Your conclusions don't make sense."

"Jessica said the same thing to me. She thought the money was a settlement for the accident that robbed her of her fiancé. I sense something else."

Paul's investigation of the winery books didn't show any huge sums going out. Only discrepancies when his brother was there, and now with Danny in charge, all inventory issues. His father's personal checking account was modest and only dealt with household expenses. "How big are the sums deposited? If it isn't a settlement, what do you suspect?"

"Large enough to invest in local businesses. You'll think I'm paranoid. As Jessica's brother, I suspected foul play years ago with the accident. Recently Jessica has been getting hang-up phone calls."

"Can you trace the calls? House lines still have that ability?"

"No, Jessica refused. She thought it might be her long-lost daughter trying to make contact."

Paul barely listened to Mr. Jewels's answer. "When did the calls start?"

Mr. Jewels rifled through his papers. "I wrote everything down. Time of day too. According to this, they started about three months ago. Only one or two a week and then when I was away, trying to get ahold of your father, Jessica said she changed the ringer on the phone. She claimed that it only rang four times, not enough for her to get there to answer. Now the phone rings eight times. No matter who answers, there is a click and then a dial tone."

"Three months ago. What changed?"

"Jessica did. She's obsessed with our nephew's health. She stopped painting. Said that only dark scenes came to her. She refuses to paint darkness."

Paul stared out the window as a cloud covered the sun. Not usually superstitious, he sensed that Jessica's darkness wasn't imagined. Sealy's visit had triggered events years in the making. She had arrived as their first guest at the B&B and soon afterward one of the last of that generation, his father, had died. He had so many secrets.

Paul counted the names of those left from his father's famous art school: Diane, Geordie, Chuck, and who else? There were those in the town who might remember.

"The real question, Mr. Jewels, is what do you propose to do about the legality of the adoption? I don't think anyone cares."

"I care." Mr. Jewels waved his arms toward the window. "My concern isn't about my reputation, if that is what you think. It's about another story. Help me find out what happened back then. Jessica was in shock. I believe the accident that killed Jessica's fiancé, Peter, was intentional. If you help me with this, then I'll let the legal issues rest."

Paul revised his opinion of Mr. Jewels. "A bargain that doesn't make sense. Just ask Sealy and me outright to help you. You're an honest man who made a mistake. The other people involved are dead. Unless you believe there is a scandal within the adoption system, let the whole issue rest. I promise that Sealy and I will help. Remember, her mother and my uncle Barry suffered too." Paul paused, not sure if he should mention the break-ins and the near-miss accident along the same road Jessica's fiancé had been killed. He compromised. "I promise to investigate any connections I find with those who were alive during that time. Do you have ideas where we should begin?"

"No, I'm not good at this. Personal stuff isn't my style. Besides, I'm too old. I need help. I just wish Jessica would be more careful. She trusts everybody."

"Mr. Jewels, we're talking in circles. If Jessica is anything like Sealy, she's stronger than you imagine." Frustrated, Paul ended the conversation. "If you think of anything else or if Jessica does, let me know. Which way to the kitchen?"

Paul shook Mr. Jewels's hand and went to find Sealy.

Sealy felt a sense of familiarity in the kitchen. An old refrigerator with its rounded top stood in the corner, with a more modern gas stove at the end of the black Formica counters. Unlike Jessica's living room, the kitchen was a clean mixture of old and new, with the brightness of the outdoors. Jessica had placed fresh flowers on either side of the counters and a bouquet of lavender in the center of the table. The back door to the yard was open to view the edible garden. Sealy hadn't anticipated bursting into tears. Jessica handed Sealy a handkerchief. Sealy dabbed her eyes and continued their conversation: "I apologize. I'm not sure if these are tears of joy or sadness."

Jessica half hardily patted her hand. "Your eyes tear like a leaky faucet. I've trained myself to hold back the tears by shutting out the light. Best not to show too much emotion."

Sealy felt Jessica's discomfort. "I used to think that, but not so much anymore. I know this is awkward, me being here. I can't change that, but I'm nervous too. I can't help myself, like twirling my hair when I'm thinking."

"No need to sit on your hands to keep them still. I can get you some snap peas to shell." Jessica popped up and placed two bowls of snap peas and a receptacle for the compost on the table.

"Thanks, this is better. If you don't mind, tell me something about your time at Richard's art school."

Jessica looked up from her bowl of shelled peas. "Funny you should ask that and not more about your real father, my fiancé, Peter. I guess I'm coming into your life too late."

"Not at all, but I confess a photo of my mother…I mean, a photo of my adopted mother with Richard was what brought me to this part of the world. I wondered if he was my father."

"You mean you're worried that the mother who raised and loved you, your entire life, had an affair. I can't speak to that. She certainly wasn't involved with Richard when I met him. He was loyal to his wife. It was the problems of his brother, Barry, that upset him."

"Could you tell me about that?" Sealy noted Jessica's pale face, a slight frown, and her quick turn to see if anyone was by the kitchen door.

"It has haunted me since my accident. Something Peter said before the crash. My brother thinks that is why I'm getting hang-up calls now. Odd, isn't it?"

"Jessica, this could be serious. What did Peter say?"

"It was about the brawl with Diane's brothers. Barry was upset about the wine. He accused them of tampering. Everyone was drunk."

A knock interrupted Jessica's response. "It's me, Paul. Can I come in?"

"Just a minute, Paul, Jessica and I are almost done."

All business, Jessica stood up. "I'll call you about the genetic tests. I think we can do them in Ogunquit. There's a cancer center not too far away."

By the time Paul walked in, Jessica had cleared the kitchen table. Sealy noted a return of color to Jessica's face and an upturn to her lips, an attempt at a smile. She hadn't noticed Jessica's hair yesterday. Today a stream of light filtered through familiar tight ringlets reminiscent of Sealy's hair as a child. As she hugged Jessica, she felt a tug in her heart, like a comb moving through years of curls.

Even the air outside of Jessica's home felt heavy. Sealy sighed and looked at the sky. "Can we walk a bit? I need to clear my mind."

"Yes, I take it your talk with Jessica didn't end well. Mine with Mr. Jewels left me at odds with the situation. He is a strange man. Hard to imagine him as Jessica's brother."

"Be careful now, they are both my family. I'll be calling him Jake." Sealy meant it as a joke, but the words caught in her throat. "I didn't realize the deep effect of knowing for sure that my father isn't Barry or Richard. Peter is my father's name. A man I never met—a ghost of sorts."

Sealy let her feet do what her mind couldn't. One foot before the other, each step moving forward, missing the cracks. She concentrated on letting her mind roam. Paul's hand slipped into hers.

"Thanks, I needed to feel someone solid. I thought I'd be relieved knowing the true story of my origins. I was a stranger in my own home. But with you, Richard, Danny, and the girls, I'm comfortable. I'm still not so sure about Jessica."

Paul gave Sealy's hand a squeeze. "At least the part about me and the rest won't change. If it does, I hope it will be for the better."

Sealy looked at Paul quizzically. "Do you mean for better or worse?" She held up a hand as if to stop Paul from talking. "Don't answer that. All I'm seeing is that it's going to get stickier. Finding another mother wasn't what I sought. Damn that photo with Richard and my mom. Now I have two mothers, a father with a tainted reputation who isn't my real father, and a mystery about why my real father, Peter, died. And I can't leave out a nephew who might need my stem cells to live."

Paul pulled Sealy closer, moved her loose hair out of her eyes. His lips found hers. The kiss came softly, both a statement and a promise.

Sealy suddenly felt shy, vulnerable. "I don't want to assume anything. I didn't expect this either. Whatever this is."

"By *this*, do you mean a kiss, feelings, a closeness, a sense of well-being?" Paul resumed walking but now his arm had slipped around Sealy's waist.

Sealy's steps fell in line with Paul's. "Yes, but let's not label the feeling, okay? I'm thinking of Danny and how the girls will react. And there is my sister, Jeannie. I think she should come out here. Would you mind?"

"I didn't know there were rules. Got it, no labeling what we feel toward one another. Go slowly so we don't upset the apple-cart with Danny and the girls, and invite your best friend and sister to stay with us." Paul drew Sealy in closer. "I have a few requirements too, but I'll discuss those later."

Sealy laughed. "Hmm I haven't considered any of this new terrain. I guess I'm staying longer than my three-month reserva-tion." She felt her cheeks redden. "That is, if I'm a match for Joseph's DNA, who knows how long the stem cell transfer will take. Then there is the business of my biological father and his death." The thought made her shiver. "I never asked his last name. I'm sure it's in that article I found."

Paul feigned surprise at her explanations. "One step at a time. Let's get back home to Ogunquit. I see it now: Sealy Sleuth, pri-vate investigator."

"I suppose you're right. My poking around feels like that. Let's hope I'm not putting anyone in harm's way."

Paul and Sealy pulled up to the Hawk House just as the sun dipped below the trees. Their route followed the coastal sunset as it reflected off the water. The home view of the sun's disappearance suited his muted mood.

The drive had been easier in the daytime with Sealy spotting him periodically. On the very last leg of the trip, a quiet had settled in the car. Paul's mind had switched back to the town and Danny's last phone call about the burglaries. Sealy sat with pen and paper detailing clues and ideas on future searches about the accident with her father, Peter.

The front door opened and out poured Danny, Roxie, and Reese carrying a huge banner painted in bright green lettering and pink flowers: *Welcome Home, Grandpa and Sealy. We missed you.* Even before they got out of the car, Paul heard Roxie and Reese squeal, "We have a surprise for Sealy."

Paul hugged each of the girls. "What a great welcome committee. But no surprises for me?"

Danny stepped forward with a huge grin. "It's a surprise for all of us. You'll see when you get inside. Bring in your bags later."

Reese and Roxie each took one of Sealy's hands. Reese grabbed Paul. "I'll hold your hand too."

Roxie chimed in, "Sealy, you don't have to close your eyes because…because it's love."

Paul squeezed Reese's hand. "Yes, I feel the love."

"No, silly, you have to see it."

Once inside the entranceway, Danny called out, "You can come out now, they're back."

Sealy gasped. "Oh my goodness, Jeannie, it's you!"

Paul watched Sealy as her sister stepped forward. The physical contrast was palpable. Sealy, with her fluid body, hugged fully. Jeannie, all smiles, shorter and more tentative, closed her eyes. When they broke apart Paul noted Jeannie's wider face, blue eyes that seemed half closed to Sealy's expressive hazel ones. Both had tearstained cheeks.

"Jeannie, how did you know I needed you here?"

"You left me no choice. I can't keep up with you." Jeannie wiped her tears with an embroidered handkerchief. "Besides, I have the Morris markings on my chin, so I came to meet the rest of *my* family."

Paul heard an edge in Jeannie's voice, one he'd never heard from Sealy. "Sealy talks about you all the time. Just the other day she told me it was time you came to visit. You must be able to read each other's minds. I'm sure Danny and the girls made you feel welcome."

If Sealy sensed any tension from Jeannie, she didn't show it. She twirled Jeannie around. "Yes, looks like we have more people in our lives. When did you get in?"

"Danny met me in town early this morning. I flew in on a night flight. He put me in the room next to yours. Staying here is very intimate. I mean cozy and quaint, not like a hotel."

Sealy's smile evaporated. Paul watched her adjust to the tone of voice as she guided her sister upstairs. "I think this is the first time you've been to a small town. We lived our whole life in the city. Everyone here is genuinely friendly. Come up with me while I shower so I can fill you in on what's been happening. I'm so glad you're here."

Paul held the girls back as Sealy and Jeannie disappeared. He remembered Sealy's words after they left Jessica's house—*and there is my sister, Jeannie.* Sealy already fit into his life with his son and grandkids. It might not be as easy with her sister.

Sealy stayed in the shower until the hot water almost burned her skin. The heat penetrated the sudden stiffness she felt in her chest. The old sense of conflict with her sister had returned. Jeannie at her best was full of love, but when twinges of jealousy or insecurity took over, her tone of voice smarted. Switching to freezing-cold water, Sealy waited to step out until her internal temperature reached an equilibrium to the new dynamic.

She called, "Jeannie, are you still here?"

"Yes, although that was a long shower. It gave me time to snoop around. Neat drawers, and plenty of space in the closets. Are you sure you left enough water for the rest of the family? In hotels you never have to worry about that stuff."

Sealy walked out of the bathroom with a towel around her head and a terry cloth robe. "I expect you're wondering about my robe too. They provide it and change the sheets when I let them, just like any other B&B or hotel. What's bothering you? I need *you*, my loving sister, not someone who is picking a fight."

Jeannie stood in front the mirror by the dressing table as she watched Sealy's every move. "Tell me, are you leaving me out of your life? I mean, goodness, you find our relatives who aren't your relatives and then leave me to pick up the pieces. My husband thinks I'm crazy and my kids could care less. Where am I in this?"

Sealy felt like a hive of bees had attacked her. She counted the years between their ages as if this could explain the sting. "The least you could do is turn around and face me. Instead of staring at me through the mirror."

Jeannie moved away from the dresser and stared. "I see you brought Mom's old hairbrush."

"Yes, I've been using it since she passed. Look, I'm thankful you're here. This isn't my doing or yours. It isn't about us. It's about our parents, yours by blood and mine because they raised me. It's about a young man who might die without my stem cells."

The towel around Sealy's head fell to the floor. As Sealy scooped it up, she wiped the tears that coated her face. She silently pleaded with her sister to soften.

Jeannie remained quiet for what seemed a century, and when she answered Sealy her voice came out in a whisper: "You always have a different view. I guess it makes sense to you. But why do I feel so bad, as if Mom didn't care about me enough to share?"

"That's the wrong question. You sound like our grandmother, looking to pick things apart. Let's try to pull their histories together. Besides, we need to clear this up so your kids don't find a mess when we pass."

Jeannie's shoulders relaxed and her eyes softened. "This isn't easy for me. I get your point, and I'll try. What do you need?"

Sealy opened her arms. "First off, a real hug, not the kind that makes me wonder if you're mad. Then I need you to put your science background to work. Not about our DNA. This is more about chemical compounds and alcohol. All the mystery and problems started before we were born. I think Dad's problems began here and continue today. It's all connected to the winery."

Jeannie smiled. "You have a vivid imagination and live a life way more interesting than mine."

"Guilty as charged about my imagination. Why do you think I paint? My life is no more interesting than yours. Please don't negate your years as a wife, mother, and your career at the lab."

"Okay—no lectures. I'm here to help and curious about Mom and Dad's past. Set me to work."

"Agreed. Let me get dressed. We can talk later."

Sealy purposefully didn't tell Jeannie about her feelings for Paul. It would be obvious soon enough. No need to add to her angst.

After Paul cleaned up from the trip home, he met Danny outside at the gazebo. "Thanks for taking care of everything. You deserve a raise for dealing with Jeannie. When did you find out she was coming?"

Danny gave his father a questioning look. "Why not meet in the house? Are you worried about something?"

"I wanted to talk to you first without the kids around and catch up."

Danny picked up the games the girls had left on the table and rearranged the chairs to face the tree line. "Jeannie isn't at all like Sealy. She called the day before her arrival. Not that we can't take guests at any time. But she refused to listen to my instructions about the airport and connections. I met her at the airport instead of in town. I did it for Sealy's sake." Danny looked back at the house. "I try not to judge, but you asked."

"Again, thanks." Paul cleared his throat.

"Dad, what is it? You're acting like there's a secret."

"No, I don't want any secrets. That's how all this started." Angling himself so he could watch the house, Paul continued, "You should know that Sealy and I are more than friends. It's complicated. We're not blood related, but we found her real mother, which creates another layer of intrigue. Also, your grandfather might have had an affair with Sealy's mother, but not until your grandma had passed away and Sealy already existed. Not our business. Sealy and I don't know the whole story, but it all connects to the winery and the shenanigans of Diane. I'm sure of it."

"I guess that's good news and bad news. You're lucky Sealy found us."

Danny's grin reassured Paul and he couldn't help but grin in return. "I hoped you'd feel that way. We're taking our relationship slow, or trying to."

"Slow or fast, we're good. I'm more worried about the winery. I did some snooping on the road near the accident. I noticed a weird smell and that the normal upkeep of the brush hadn't been done. I thought you could check with the highway maintenance engineer."

Paul took out a pad of paper from his back pocket. "I'll put that on my list. When I get back to my office tomorrow, I'll contact them. I'll also check with the safety records for other accidents or complaints." Paul heard voices coming from the garden deck. "I can hear Roxie and Reese laughing with Sealy. They'll be looking for us. Should I know anything else before we go in?"

Danny turned to see Roxie running circles around Sealy. He waved. "Only that Diane's brothers have left four messages while you were gone. They seem agitated. I see them walking in town on my taxi runs. Louise and her gossip tree say they're talking about their future foundation. Diane is spreading rumors about her brothers being born-again alcoholics. Their bad blood is leaving a nasty taste in the town."

"We've only been gone less than a week. Not that my absence had anything to do with this."

"Dad, here's my advice. Don't let Diane's energy get to you. She's tried to destroy the Morrises in the past."

Paul gave Danny a hug. "Wise words from my son, who must have learned that somewhere. With Sealy's insights, I think we can nail down Diane's shenanigans." As he listened to Sealy's laughter, Paul wondered at the emotional toll. "Sealy is determined to understand what happened. There's more to this now, with her real mother, Jessica, involved. Let's go in and get some of the love Roxie and Reese are doling out."

Sealy ran up the stairs and knocked on Jeannie's bedroom door. "Hurry up, Jeannie, Danny's got to leave for his run into town. It's our only way in."

Jeannie opened the door a crack. Dressed and bleary eyed, she shook her head. "Hold your horses, Sealy. You know I'm not good in the mornings. What time did you get up?"

Sealy felt like a mother clucking. "Jeannie, you're harder to corral than Roxie and Reese. I've been up since dawn. My normal routine hasn't changed since we were kids."

"I haven't had my coffee."

"I know. Breakfast is served until 9:00 a.m. for the guests. I boxed up fresh-from-the-oven biscuits, blueberries, and homemade yogurt, with a cup of black coffee. You're lucky that there isn't school in the summer or Danny would have left already. Hurry up, I'll meet you downstairs." At the toot of Danny's car, Sealy ran outside. "Come on, Jeannie, I'm out the door. You can ride shotgun. I'll go in the back."

While they waited for Jeannie, Sealy slipped into the back seat of the taxi. Danny's eyes widened at her choice of seating. He glanced at her through the front mirror. "Thanks for making your special cookies yesterday. The kids missed your great snacks. What's with this, you're getting in the back seat?"

"Thought you could bond with Jeannie up front, woo her with your great descriptions."

"I've already done that. She prefers the back seat."

Sure enough, Jeannie slid in next to Sealy.

"Jeannie, here's your goodie bag and coffee. If you need something else, we can get a snack in town. I'm heading up front. I don't want Danny to feel like our chauffeur."

Jeannie looked horrified. "Sorry, I didn't mean anything by it. I'm not used to this."

Danny shrugged. "Suit yourself. I'm not offended. Guests choose what they want, and I guess family does that too. I'm glad the girls are too young to sit up front—fewer battles to deal with."

"Yes, that's so true. Jeannie always pulled rank being oldest."

"Hey, no fun picking on me. You've got the advantage now. Besides, I was up late last night researching wine, distillation processes, bootlegging, and toxic by-products. Can we head to the library?" Jeannie paused. "That is, if it's on your route."

Danny answered, "That's Sealy's second home. But if you need information on chemicals and science stuff, I'd head over to my old professor's home. He's retired now, but he knows his stuff."

Sealy nudged Danny's arm. "You continue to surprise me."

Danny viewed Jeannie in the back seat. "You and your sister are dogged in your pursuits." He glanced over at Sealy. "I'm not sure if you meant the surprise part as a compliment. But with you two working together, I'm sure life will be interesting. It's decided. I'll let you off at Dr. Schul's house. Just tell him I sent you. Call if you need a ride back to the town pickup point. But I suspect you'll walk."

Sealy waved Danny off and encircled her arm in Jeannie's. "Your eyes have cleared and you look human again. I'm so glad you're here. Small towns are awkward. The town and even Danny might seem standoffish, but behind their protective façade, everyone is nice. After almost three months here, I'm no longer considered a guest and you don't have to be. I shouldn't have given you a hard time this morning."

"Oh, that. Well, I can be stuffy, especially when I'm jealous. You always make people feel comfortable, but I do too. Just differently."

"Yeah, I know, when you're focused on a science puzzle the outside world disappears. I remember you at school, forgetting to eat or shower. For me it's different, I'm not working my left brain with my real estate clients." Sealy paused. "I'm also with Danny's kids each day and with Paul. They ground me. You've never seen me with kids besides your grown ones. Shocking, isn't it? No need to be jealous."

"Enough chitter-chatter. Let's go find Danny's professor. You can lead and I can talk science, okay?"

Sealy checked her watch as she and Jeannie left Dr. Schul's house. Moments after they descended the porch steps, Dr. Schul poked his bald head out the front door. "This is my advice: don't go too deep into the science of winemaking. Trouble is easy to spot when formulas go awry. Same in life."

Sealy waited until he disappeared before she spoke. "Let's get something to eat. I think our brains will burst if we don't get on another wavelength. You have that glazed look as if you just swallowed an encyclopedia."

"Sure, you lead. I'm overwhelmed."

Sealy took the books Dr. Schul had lent them from Jeannie's arms and guided her down the main street to the OQT Inn. Just as on the first day Sealy had arrived, Elly commanded the front desk. Her recently permed hair and smile greeted the line of tourists and business folk. As they passed, Elly gave Sealy a salute of recognition.

Sealy paused in front of the mural of the inn's opening celebration with her mother, Mary, and Richard, prominently featured. "I thought you should see this with your own eyes."

Jeannie gasped and covered her mouth to hide her surprised murmurings. "I believed you, but wow, I don't remember mom ever looking so happy. Incredible. Love memorialized. She was such a different person with us."

Jeannie's comment hung in the air as Sealy continued to the restaurant. Briefly her thoughts went to Paul. She couldn't fault her mother for finding love. The restaurant buzzed with customers. Sealy looked around for a place to sit when a waitress caught her eye. "I'm surprised that the restaurant is still so full this late after the lunch hour."

The waitress smiled wearily. "The crowd surprised us too. Three fishing yachts appeared at the harbor this morning. We're swamped. I remember you, you're Ms. Morris, staying with Paul, Danny, and the girls."

Sealy's cheeks reddened. "Yes, I'm Sealy. I've eaten here with Paul before. Do you think you can find me and my sister a spot?"

"Hmm, I do have a small booth way in the corner we save for special clients. Come, follow me."

Jeannie poked Sealy with her elbow and whispered, "'Special client,' no wonder you want to stay."

Sealy seated herself facing the dining room and piled the science books by her side. "I'm not that special but the name Morris is. You get used to it. I suppose once they find out I'm not really a Morris, things might change."

Jeannie picked up the menu. "Nothing changes unless you change your last name. You're not going to do that, are you?"

"No, of course not. Let's order, I'm starving."

"Me too. What can we get quickly?"

"My favorite catch-of-the-day fish chowder and their home-made breadsticks."

By the time the food arrived, Sealy's hunger had taken over. She dove right in. Jeannie followed suit, smiling as she dipped the breadsticks into the chowder. When Jeannie finished her food, her mind took over. Sealy listened to Jeannie go on and on about the makings of wine: the tannins, sulfur, yeast, tartaric acid, and chalk to remove excess acid. When she finally took a breath, Sealy interjected. "I'm sure Danny and Paul know all this. We're looking for an additive that isn't customary and dangerous."

Jeannie paused and cocked her head. "You're right. I got it. Sorry for spouting my knowledge of winemaking, it's a bad habit. It isn't what I or any legit winemaker knows. It's what we don't know that counts. Dr. Schul marked spots in each book that may be of importance."

Finished with her chowder, Sealy pushed her bowl to the side of the table and thumbed through one of the books. Various pages contained faint pencil marks in the margins. "I wonder who made these notes. I doubt if Dr. Schul would deface a book, especially after he made us sign our names and put down a deposit before he lent them to us. He even put our names and date on the back page." Sealy stared at the last page. "This book had been shared with his students all the way back to the fifties. Dad's name is here. Oh my, Diane's name is here too."

Jeannie grabbed the book. "I guess this is where I begin tonight, reading pages that have pencil marks in the margin."

"Good idea. Let's go. My stomach is queasy."

"From the food?"

"No, seeing Diane's name in the book confirmed my worst suspicions."

The town had survived without Paul's guidance, but his desk loomed like a volcano with files flowing from mounds into valleys. He attacked the most pressing issue, flood control and reimbursement. After much talk between the state and the federal government, Ogunquit had finally received FEMA money for property loss. Next, he'd have to find monies for restoration and prevention.

It was close to noon before Paul followed up on Danny's concerns about safety of the roads where Diane's brother nearly collided with him and the girls. Paul promised he'd inquire about the smells emanating below the bluff where Sealy and he had climbed. His assistant brought him a list of accidents and incidents at the same location.

Paul read and reread the statistics. The data only included the last twenty years, but a pattern of monthly incidents for odors emerged. The most recent occurrences of both smell and car accidents happened this past weekend. Complaints from neighbors described the stench as both sulfurous and pungent, which caused some to feel nauseous, dizzy, and blurry eyed. They also talked about a flash of light. Since Paul was in contact with the district Department of Natural Resources and Environmental Protection Agency about the recent floods, he put in calls for an investigation of the site.

Paul rubbed his temples, hoping to stave off the headaches he feared would be coming once the departments reported back. A ray of sun fell across his desk. He smiled thinking of Sealy and her urgent request to meet at the café near Jessica's gallery.

Sealy paused outside of the Golden Goose Gallery. After lunch she sent Jeannie off to fend for herself and find Danny's taxi for a ride home. Jessica had called with the results of the DNA tests. Nervous and sensing urgency, Sealy had called Paul to meet with her afterward. Her hands shook as she gripped the doorknob. Tinkling bells announced her arrival.

Once again, the gallery had transformed. Instead of the desert scenes, only seascapes lined the side walls. Most were watercolor and ink, wharf and fishing boats interspersed with realistic scenes of distant waves meeting the land. One oversized oil painting hung along the back wall, real enough to imagine you were inside a bedroom looking into the kitchen.

"Sealy, we're over here at the back of the store," Jessica called.

Somehow, Jessica had created an illusion with a mirror across the way. Sealy might have enjoyed the playfulness at another time, but today she felt tricked.

"Clever." Sealy walked toward the painting where Jessica and Joseph sat.

"From the frown on your face, I can tell you're not amused. Joseph said it would make customers uncomfortable, but I tend to do that. Part of my charm or a cover for my own discomfort. Who knows? I don't care what people think as much as he does."

Sealy turned toward Joseph, who had deferred to his great-aunt. "Joseph, I agree with you. The illusion only works when someone is in a good humor, not worried. How are you feeling?"

"Hopeful. Thanks for getting the blood test so quickly. The lab put a rush on the order. I appreciate you letting us see the results first. I'm told donors get upset if they can't help. Even though I only met you once, can I hug you? Your DNA is almost a perfect match."

Sealy covered her face as the tears clung to her cheeks. "Hug me at the risk of being showered with teardrops." Joseph embraced her with surprising strength. Sealy felt each skeletal bone of his frail torso. The intensity of his need to live went straight to her heart. "Is there an extra seat for me? I'm overwhelmed. Does this mean I can give you my stem cells?"

Jessica pulled up another chair for Sealy and poured her a lemonade. "This is serious business. Joseph and you have to face a battery of exams before they decide if you're a good donor and if Joseph is strong enough for the procedure. You'll be hospitalized for a bit."

Sealy sat on her hands with her back against the chair, her feet planted firmly on the ground. She listened with the attention of an eager but naïve student.

Jessica glanced at Joseph, then continued, "By the time they're finished with testing your heart, checking all your vital organs, mouth, eyes, and who knows what else, then you begin."

Joseph stood up and put his hand on his great-aunt's shoulder. "You can stop now. I think Sealy understands enough. No need to scare her away."

Sealy noticed Joseph's firm but insistent redirections of Jessica. They had a bond, more like one of mother and son, than a great-aunt and nephew. She wondered how different her life would have been if Jessica had raised her instead of Mary. *No use thinking of what-ifs.*

"No worries, I'm not easily scared. I'll do what it takes."

Joseph smiled. "I'll get the numbers you'll need to set up appointments."

When Joseph had disappeared from hearing range, Jessica grabbed Sealy's hand. "Not a word of this to anyone but your immediate family and Paul. I don't want the town to be awash with gossip." After her outburst, Jessica's smile returned. "I'm a nobody in the community. No one knows who I am in terms of the past. Just like you."

"Good job trying to deflect. You have that in common with my adopted mom. She hid all past secrets."

"I'm sorry, Sealy. I've disappointed you. Did you expect me to be kinder, motherly?"

Sealy shook her head, but inside she wondered about their relationship and the effect of secrets. So much of everyone's behavior stemmed from love and fear. She wasn't about to question her feelings on love and refused to be afraid.

Joseph reappeared with the list. "You two are whispering, which tells me it's time for me to listen in. I'm good at that. People tend to think I'm invisible. They talk in hushed voices and reveal secrets. Even you two do, just because I'm ill." He faced Sealy and sat back down. "I know more than Jessica about the town. She comes and goes and doesn't live here. I'm considered a non-entity, even though I've been at the gallery for five years. Locals always gossip but not chitchat of complaints like at the post office. Here customers have money and show off. They want something."

Jessica stared at her nephew and kept her chin up as if to realign the situation. The tension in the air drifted upward, a cloud ready to burst at any time. Not sure if the stress of the stem cell transplant had everyone nerved up or if Joseph knew something about the past, Sealy held her breath as Joseph made his observations.

"A few new customers recently appeared. Old-timers by the looks of them, not really the artsy type. A woman named Diane came in twice. I only know her name because she had her cell phone on speaker and she nearly twisted her neck looking over the counter. I kept my eye on her. The second time she wanted to know if we had old paintings of the area, a specific road. Claimed she wanted to decorate her home with the works of artists from an art school that used to be in the area.

"Then there were two men who had seen the painting you bought here, Sealy. I think they were brothers. The painting reminded them of someone they knew. They were anxious to buy some more of her work. Hats off to you, Jessica.

"I may be teetering on the edge with cancer, but I don't want to live in the shadows. So please stop whispering. Ask me what I know, tell me what is going on."

Paul sat in a back booth at the restaurant. As soon as he saw Sealy enter, he jumped up to meet her halfway. "I was worried. Your meeting took longer than I expected." Before she could answer, he gave her a quick hug and whispered in her ear, "I found Louise frantic to talk with you. She's sitting at our booth."

Sealy raised her eyebrow and slid into the booth. "Louise, I had you on my list to visit. What have you found?"

Louise's words came out in a rush. "While you've been gone, our favorite Diane and her brothers are at it. Something's brewing. Paul said Danny called you about the near-miss accident with Chuck and Geordie. It triggered a memory in the artistic community, at least for the old-timers. They say the area is haunted and that they used to party there. You know the spot is just outside Diane's property line. She's telling everyone that her brothers are senile and alcoholics. It's the same rumor spread about Barry, your father. The whole town figured out your connection to the Morrises. They want to blame you."

Sealy reached out to hold Louise's hand. "Blame me for what? You lived through it. What secret has everyone spooked?"

"Well, I'm not proud of this. You know I like women. I think the new term nowadays is that I'm gay. When your father lived here, he took care to help everyone, no matter the circumstance. One night I drank with the artist gang—a special brew that Diane brought. Chuck and Geordie were there, and I lost control. I don't know if Diane came onto me or if I read the signals wrong. I made a fool of myself with Diane. She egged me on. I don't remember much, but Jessica and her fiancé were there too. Everyone split and I had to call Barry as Diane suddenly turned on me, like a witch. I think that is what she wanted, for Barry to come to see her at the party."

Paul admired Sealy's calm demeanor, complete absorption into Louise's telling. Paul interrupted, "Can I ask you a question?"

Sealy nudged his foot under the table. Louise appeared not to have heard him and she continued, "It was that night—the night Jessica's fiancé had the accident. Jessica wasn't drinking because of the pregnancy. She had to pry her fiancé away from the group. The town has been hushed about the whole thing. Diane told everyone a different story. Said the brandy came from Barry, a gift. She's been rewriting our memories ever since."

The waitress stopped by for the order and the three let the conversation drift off. Once she was gone, Paul whispered his question: "Why are you just now telling the truth? What kind of a hold does Diane have on you? The whole town loves and respects you, their opinion won't change. Or is there something else?"

Louise shook her head. "It's a small town. Lots of reputations to protect."

Sealy sighed. "I understand your caution."

Paul blushed. "Oh, you're protecting your relationship, keeping someone you love safe because she is still in the closet."

"Something like that. Isn't that always what one does for a loved one? Look at what Mary did for Barry and what Barry did for the townspeople. All the while, Diane pulled everyone along to her wishes. If you want to find Diane's weak spot, or keep the town whole, you have your work cut out."

Sealy turned her head toward Paul. "Are you ready for this? I may just ruin your reputation and put the town in a tailspin."

Paul smiled remembering the last night they were together in Ocean City. "What are you proposing?"

Louise looked from Sealy to Paul. "Oh my, what happened on your trip away? You two are love birds."

Sealy's eyes twinkled as she landed a sloppy kiss on Paul's lips. "We'll be the first to expose our own secrets. Diane will be like the Wicked Witch in Oz with water thrown on her fun. She'll melt away."

Louise laughed. "Now we're talking. Bring it on."

Sealy had set up a makeshift office adjacent to Paul's home office. After meeting with Louise, Jessica, and Joseph, her research into the past had taken over the bedroom.

The house rhythm had changed slightly, with more guests arriving for the B&B. The only meal prepared for the guests was breakfast. Usually, Sealy ate with Roxie and Reese in the kitchen and Jeannie ate later with the guests. Dinners remained the same, with the household gathered in the dining room.

Sealy spread out her instructions for stem cell retrieval. The battery of tests at the regional cancer center showed her as healthy with no foreseeable problems for the procedure. Joseph had to gain weight and rest more, but they had set a date for the transfer the following week. Sealy took a daily concoction of drugs to stimulate her stem cells that left her achy and tired.

Jeannie barged into Sealy's office without knocking. "I know what happened. I figured out what Diane did and is doing."

"Wow. That's great. Can you hold your horses a sec while I finish laying out my instructions?"

"I thought this was priority?"

"It is, but I don't want to mess up for Joseph's transplant."

Jeannie glanced at the calendar and instructions and then over at Sealy's whiteboard. "Do you want to hear what I found or is that empty whiteboard titled *Secrets* your plan? Looks like I'll have to wait until I starve."

Sealy placed the last of the instructions on the table. "Very funny. Go ahead, tell me. Hopefully your discovery will convince the town to accept what happened years ago. Whatever you figured out with Diane is just the beginning. We have to prove it and make sure this doesn't destroy people's lives."

"Diane's making brandy from wine. Distilling. Wine wouldn't cause the symptoms of fumes, nausea. I bet she has a distillery hidden. A leak in a still's column could allow explosive alcohol vapor to escape. The vapors are highly volatile and toxic. They can cause hallucinations."

Although Sealy had suspected something like this, her insides twisted. "Jeannie, can you prove this? What do we need to do?"

Jeannie paces around Sealy's desk. "Isn't that where your beau, Paul, comes in? He must know the procedure. Ask him. Once there's access to the property, I can test the air quality and the soil, even the plants. Or the EPA can do this if they have jurisdiction."

Chills ran up and down Sealy's spine. Her hands curled in anger. "Louise mentioned drinking something on the night of the accident that killed Jessica's fiancé. If this is true, Diane's shenanigans killed two people, ruined lives. The death of Danny's wife might have been on purpose. She ruined our father."

Jeannie took hold of Sealy. "You already knew this. Don't freak out. Besides, you have a plan. Your whiteboard awaits." Hugging Sealy tightly, she continued, "Oh, how I have missed you."

Sealy felt a wet tear along her cheek. Knowing her sister watched, she made a show of catching it with her tongue. "Got it. Now, no more sappy stuff. I can't get too riled up in case it affects my stem cells."

Jeannie shook her head. "That isn't how science works. Stick with what you're good at—painting and solving problems. I'm the scientist in the family."

Sealy smiled. "Yes, you are the scientist, my wonderful sister, and the best of best friends."

Even though Paul was beyond tired, his heart soared to see Sealy at the dinner table. Three months ago, his life held a settled rhythm that satisfied his needs. Her presence added accents, colors to an otherwise dull picture. He watched as Roxie and Reese circled Sealy with new drawings they had made. He caught the tail end of their conversation.

"Oh, thank you for the wonderful drawings. Is this me in bed?"

Roxie laughed. "Yes and no. Daddy said you were going to the hospital but don't have to stay over. I put you in a big chair that goes up and down."

"Ah, I see, a recliner. What's this with my hair?"

"That was Reese's special touch."

Reese pointed to the ponytail and curls. "I know everything has to be tidy at the hospital. But your hair doesn't always listen. Sometimes your curls escape."

Paul walked over and peered over Sealy's shoulder. Visualizing Sealy waking up in Ocean City, he mused, "Let me see that. I agree, this is you!"

Once the girls' giggles subsided, Paul sat down. "Does anyone know where Danny is?"

Sealy shrugged. "After he dropped the girls off for the day, he headed out again. Usually, he says where he's going when he leaves me with Roxie and Reese."

Paul had a sick feeling inside. Danny always ate dinner with the girls. "No worries, I'm sure he'll be here soon. He can always warm up the leftovers."

Reese whispered back and forth to Roxie. "Shh, don't tell. Daddy might get mad."

Paul pretended not to hear their whispers and filled his plate. He noticed that Sealy's plate remained empty. "Am I the only one going to eat?"

"I wanted to wait for Jeannie. She said she was going for a walk. Besides, I'm not hungry. The medications affect my stomach."

"Sorry, I forgot about Jeannie. You're worried about her?" Paul stood up. "Change of plans. Everyone, pile into my car. Girls, if you need a snack, grab some bread and cheese from the kitchen. We can eat when we get back."

Sealy rose slowly. "I think I know where Jeannie is. Off to do some tests by the road. Knowing Jeannie, she couldn't wait for you and the EPA. Sorry, I can't control Jeannie when she is on a mission."

Paul cupped his hands along Sealy's downturned face. He wanted to scoop her up and whisk her away from the drama. Instead, he kissed her eyelids and held her hand. "No sorry needed. Hopefully we'll find her on the road heading back here."

Once they had settled in the car, Sealy silently thanked Paul for his decision to hunt for Jeannie. He headed down the driveway and onto the road where the girls and Danny had their accident. If Paul hadn't recognized the urgency of the situation, she would have gone on foot by herself. The only thing stopping her had been the girls. Whenever Danny took off unexpectedly, she had become Roxie and Reese's mainstay. She felt like a friend, comforter, and sitter. The joy Reese and Roxie brought to her outweighed any sense of obligation.

Sealy could still feel the gentle pressure of Paul's lips on her eyelids. The sudden lurch of the car interrupted her thoughts. "Paul, what is it? I don't see Jeannie."

"Look farther around the edge of the curve. That's Danny's car poking out of the brush. I only noticed it when the sun hit the metal rim of the tire. I'm going to park on the side of the road and walk down. Stay here."

Sealy held up her hand to stop Paul. "Nope, you stay with the girls. I'll walk down. It's more natural to see me on the road than you. I do it daily. I'll call you if something is wrong."

Before Paul could object, she slipped out onto the road. With no shoulders to walk along, Sealy strode beside the grass edge and hugged the bushes. She steadied herself every few yards with the telephone posts that lined the road. Her pace quickened as she approached Danny's car. The doors were locked, and the engine felt cold.

She spotted broken branches and an overgrown path. Sealy texted Paul. *I found a trail. Going to take a quick look.* A wave of nausea hit Sealy. She kneeled quickly so as not to fall. A dark cloud covered her vision. From a distance, she heard her name. "Sealy, Sealy, let me help you stand."

Two arms pulled her up. She felt like her body was splitting in two. One side floated in the air and the other rested on a soft pillow. Sealy waited for her mind to close the gap. Words surrounded her, but none entered her ears. A spray of salty breeze enveloped her.

Paul held Sealy in his arms. His voice cracked with fright and anger as Jeannie placed the vial under Sealy's nose. "Do you always carry smelling salt in your backpack?"

Jeannie shrugged off the question and attended to her sister. "Her eyes are fluttering. It worked. Let's get Sealy into the car."

Jeannie ran up the hillside to where Danny waited with the girls. "Okay, everybody. We can breathe a sigh of relief. Sealy's waking up. Danny, I'll stay here with Roxie and Reese. Be careful how you lift her. She'll be dead weight."

Roxie cried out. "Oh no, Daddy, is Sealy dead?"

"No, sweety, Sealy will be okay. Jeannie meant that she'll be heavy to carry, like when I pick you up when you've fallen asleep. Don't worry."

"Oh, you mean like when you carry Reese back into her bed and she doesn't hold on?"

"Yes, exactly."

Jeannie mouthed *I'm sorry* to Danny as he headed off.

Paul looked relieved as Danny came back down the trail. "Danny, come around to her legs. I'll cradle her head as we lift her up. Be careful, the first steps are steep."

"Got it. Good thing Sealy didn't hit her head. No lumps or blood."

"Thank goodness you found her so quickly. She texted me minutes before."

"Jeannie warned me that Sealy would come looking for her. I couldn't help myself. I had to go with Jeannie to investigate. Hopefully we have enough to shut Diane down."

Paul only half listened. Sealy squirmed and tried to pull away. "Gentle now, Sealy. It's me, Paul, and Danny's got your legs."

As they walked up the path, Paul felt as if he was being watched. Sealy began muttering. Paul bent his head down to hear her.

"Did you see the flash of light?"

Not sure he heard her, Paul asked, "Sealy, are you awake, your eyes are shut?"

"I'm awake. I felt the light through my eyelids. Wait till you come to the next telephone pole. I bet there will be another flash."

When Paul arrived at the next pole, as if on cue, a stream of light hit the pole's metal tag. "Danny, slow down a minute. I think the light flash is someone watching us."

Sealy struggled to sit up. "Let me stand. I'm fine. The light's coming from above."

"Danny and I have you. Relax, we'll be back at the car soon."

Danny kept walking, as did Paul. When they reached the car, Sealy tried to stand up on her own but collapsed into the front seat. Reese and Roxie smothered her with kisses. Danny pulled the girls off. "Give Sealy some space. I know you were worried."

Paul scanned the upper hill. "Sealy, describe where to look.

"Near the old stump house."

Paul pulled his binoculars out of the glove compartment and walked behind a tree. Sure enough, he spotted a figure standing above them. Another flash of light bounced off a pole. A flash of recognition came over Danny's face. Just as Danny started talking, Paul jumped back in the car. "Time to head back for dinner. We can talk afterward."

Jeannie gave Sealy a hug. Clinging to her samples, she got into Danny's vehicle.

Exhausted, Sealy sat outside on a lounge chair. Danny had left to put the girls down to sleep and Jeannie had disappeared into the kitchen. They'd soon be back. With Paul by her side on another lounge chair, she savored their alone time. "Thanks for bringing out a blanket. I'm chilled on the inside and out."

"I knew you would be. Can you explain what happened this afternoon?"

"I'm not sure if I stumbled because of the medications I'm taking or the light flash or a smell. Spooky, but I know there's a scientific explanation. Let's wait until Jeannie and you get the sample results."

Paul smiled. "Knowing your sister, she'll find a way to get results in our kitchen." He paused. "Something else is on your mind."

Sealy's words came slowly. "Diane has been waiting a long time to seek revenge. I think she's narcissistic and vindictive. You can't let a person like Diane into your mind. If you reveal anything to a narcissist, they'll use it against you. They hate being ignored."

Paul shivered as if a wave of cold air hit him. "Exactly. Her revenge has tainted the old stump house. I felt violated. It's creepy that someone invaded the private place I made and shared with Danny and you."

Sealy's slid off the rubber band holding her hair. The curls slipped through her fingers at a pace that mimicked her words. "I need to warn everyone to be careful. Danny senses this too. He and the kids are at risk." She kept her face calm even though her tearful eyes gave her away.

Paul studied Sealy's face. "You are beyond tired. We can't do much tonight. Let's talk with Danny and Jeannie and plan out our strategy."

"Either I'm so tired that I'm hearing things or they're coming back and whispering."

Paul lowered his voice. "Why don't you sleep with me tonight? I'd feel better having you next to me."

Sealy sighed. "I'll toss and turn, maybe pace the floors. When I get this way with a problem, I'm insufferable."

"Here they come. I'll take that as a yes."

Sealy closed her eyes listening to Jeannie and Danny chat about the path leading to a brick building overgrown with ivy, the doors locked and windows covered. Nothing seemed incriminating except for the vented exhaust pipe from a back wall and the burn pile with charcoal, oil paint crystals, and bonemeal. All the ingredients Richard used in making his tinctures of paint. This wasn't a coincidence.

Sealy sat up. "Paul, did you check Richard's studio after the break-in?"

Paul's face paled. "Yes and no. I just looked to see if the paintings were there and the easels and brushes. Nothing was gone."

Danny added, "Same with the winery. Nothing was taken that I could see."

"Exactly." Jeannie looked at Sealy. "Mom always knew when I raided the kitchen. I never took food, or utensils, but she'd find the baking soda half full or the vinegar bottle almost empty. I had made my presence known without realizing it."

Thoughts raced through Sealy's mind. "Intentional. Diane wants her presence known but wants to be invisible. That's her power. Okay, I've got a real plan now. We must gain the trust of the townspeople who are beholden in some way to Diane. First on my list is to look at the business owners who sold their property to Diane and find out why. The records I collected will help. I bet Louise knows more. The trick will be to have them reveal why they are afraid on their own."

Danny smiled. "We were looking for the wrong things. Just like your mom did with Jeannie. Clever, stealing stuff for your chemical experiments from everyday baking supplies. Jeannie, would anything we found today be toxic if ingested?"

It took Jeannie a moment to respond. "That depends on what it is combined with. Could be Diane stole that stuff just to be a pest. I'm more worried about how we prove anything. I hope you have good chemists in this town."

Sealy shot her sister a warning look, but Paul didn't seem to notice her innuendo. He turned to face Jeannie. "Let's give them a try with you there. I think I can arrange that. Say you are a former research chemist looking for work?"

Jeannie made a face. "Very funny. My other concern is how we will get anyone to expose their secrets so Diane can't use it against them."

Danny interjected, "If it helps, I can probe my local fares about old gossip."

Sealy moved her blankets off her lap and stood. She placed her hand on Paul's shoulder. "Paul, can I ask a favor of you? I know, as the town manager, you can't get involved. But maybe you can convince Chuck and Geordie to tell you what they have been hiding."

"Hmm, and the reason they would after all these years. It can't be for revenge toward Diane. Things could get nasty."

Sealy imagined the winery blowing up or another car accident with Roxie and Reese affected. She pulled at the tangles from underneath her hair until the silky strands ran freely through her fingers. "I agree, but each person who says their truth out loud, like Louise and maybe her lover, even myself and you, well…we become powerful again. We don't have to tell the world, only be willing to stand our ground."

Paul paced the hospital hallways making an ellipse through the apheresis section of the cancer ward. He'd left Sealy under the watchful eye of Jeannie as they harvested Sealy's stem cells for Joseph's bone marrow transplant. Somehow Sealy's bone marrow had been primed to create extra stem cells to replace the ones removed from Joseph earlier in the week. With the three of them in the curtained-off cubical, Paul felt anxious. The more Jeannie talked about percentages needed for the extraction to be successful, the more agitated Sealy became. He couldn't watch the sisterly dynamic.

What really bothered him was Sealy hooked up to a machine. Common sense and the doctor's words contradicted the tug in his heart. Sealy had reassured the girls about the safety of the procedure earlier in the morning and they had promised not to worry. He'd do the same. The fact that they were two hours from Ogunquit didn't help his mental state. Privacy was important, but the distance kept him close by, as he didn't want to leave her for the just-in-case scenario.

As he passed the nurses' station, the head nurse stopped him. "Sealy's sister stepped out for a coffee. She asked me to tell you."

Paul thanked the nurse and hurried back to Sealy. He found her with a pad of paper staring out into some distant thought. He whispered not to startle her. "Are you okay?"

Sealy's lips turned upward at his voice and her eyes followed. "I'm glad you're back. My sister means well, but sometimes she can't tell when I'm saturated. All this talk of stem cells has me thinking about my own story of adoption and of my parents and what they went through to have a second child. The back side of Jessica's story of how she had to give me up. It isn't the DNA that worries me, but the stories lined up together."

Paul sat down by Sealy's recliner and took hold of the arm not connected to the apheresis machine. "Sometimes you amaze me. Here you are saving someone's life by this procedure and at the same time solving a mystery."

"I'm glad that at least *sometimes* I amaze you." Sealy's smile flattened into a line and the twinkle left her eyes. "Seriously, all these years you have lived here and knew nothing of your father's brother. I wonder if my parents knew I was Jessica's baby. Your dad knew Jessica too. He knew everything and even allowed my mother to use his name on the adoption papers. Who else knew about the adoption?"

Paul peered over Sealy's shoulder at her pad of paper. She had divided it into three columns. One heading read, *Mysterious Accidents*, the next *Diane's Holdings and Secrets*, and the final one was marked in all capital letters, *JESSICA, ADOPTION, THREATS, MONEY PAYMENTS*. Paul squeezed Sealy's hand. "I can't wait until we're out of here. I'll give you a proper hug. I wonder if it matters who knew what. I mean, unless it's a threat now, does that information get us any closer to finding out why Jessica is fearful, or why Diane haunts us all?"

Sealy contemplated her answer. "No, but Diane could have used that information or might still. I'll have to be careful that none of this hurts Jessica or her nephew Joseph."

Paul thought of Chuck and Geordie. They had to have known something was up. "I've changed my mind."

Sealy sat up straighter. "What do you mean?"

Paul rose from the chair and leaned forward. "I'll hug you now even with your disheveled hair and being attached to machines." He closed his eyes as Sealy leaned into his arms. "Thanks, I needed that. I just thought of something. Chuck and Geordie seem to be avoiding me. Each time I suggest meeting for lunch, they can't make it. Seems odd, since they came to me with their foundation idea."

Sealy raised her arm, which triggered a sudden beeping. "Oh my, I forgot I was attached."

Two nurses came rushing in as well as Jeannie, flushed and out of breath. The nurses turned off the beeper and resituated Sealy's arm. They left with a wordless nod.

Jeannie stood back until they were gone. "Wow, you certainly caused a commotion. I bet it happens all the time. I just happened to be on my way to tell you who I saw in the cafeteria."

Paul waited for Jeannie to continue. Her pause lasted past his patience. "I don't mean to be rude, but I don't think we are in the mood to guess."

Jeannie looked at Sealy. "Sorry, old habits. I saw Diane and her brothers in deep conversation. I tried to listen, but I didn't want them to see me. Not that either of them knows who I am. I don't think Diane saw me snooping the other day on the road."

No one spoke. Only the swirl of the apheresis machine filled the air. Paul watched as Sealy's eyes widened and then closed. She finally said, "No one comes to a cancer center unless they have cancer or are accompanying someone. Jessica wouldn't have told Diane or the brothers about this."

Paul looked at the time left on Sealy's machine. "I think you'll be done within the hour. I'm going to slip down the cafeteria and see if I bump into them. It could be why Chuck and Geordie aren't answering my calls. If I remember correctly, one of their parents died of cancer."

"I don't think it matters if they know I'm here. If they ask you, you can tell them I'm getting tests. I'm not going to hide, but I wouldn't say anything else about Jessica and her nephew." Sealy sighed. "Paul, let's be normal people for a bit. We're all guilty of something. Even though I'm hell bent on figuring everything out…we're human. So are they."

"I agree. I'll be back soon."

A week had passed since Sealy sat at the cancer center. She'd heard nothing directly from Jessica or Joseph. Only an email with the doctor's release note. It was as if she had become invisible in the process. The concept of donors laid itself bare. How silly of her to expect something. *Donor* means you gave and expected nothing in return. Still, Sealy wondered if Joseph would have a new chance to live and if Jessica would reappear in her life.

Sealy surveyed her makeshift art studio. After her last shipment of work to the gallery her goal of one painting per week had barely been met. As she packed up her latest painting to send off, she felt a gnawing sensation, first in her stomach and then in her heart. Her mother called it a premonition, but Sealy saw it as a sign of change. At least she hoped what was to come would be kind and positive for all concerned.

Her agent had called to let her know that the latest showing had been successful, and the gallery wanted more of her works. Sealy almost permitted her agent to reveal her identity as Sealy Morris, not her pseudonym, but realized that would be jumping the gun. Many artists had pseudonyms for privacy, but her reason had been to hide her art ability from her mother. Once Sealy learned of the illegal adoption, all her mother's distaste for her painting made sense. Still cautious, Sealy would wait to announce her real name to the world once the issues with Jessica were resolved and Diane became less of a threat.

With the painting under her arm, she negotiated the stairs. Thank goodness for the railing as Reese and Roxie appeared out of nowhere. "Girls, slow down. What's up?"

Roxie stopped to answer. "It's Jeannie. Dad saw her on the road, running back to the house. Have you seen her?"

Swallowing down panic, Sealy said, "Let me put this down and we'll go look for her. Could be that she was just out for a run."

Roxie shook her head. "You and Jeannie are too old to run. You walk fast. Besides, Daddy is looking for her on the road. He thought she might have fallen."

Sealy hoped this had nothing to do with the gnawing feeling. She already felt guilty for cajoling Jeannie out here. "Come with me. I don't want to leave you alone in the house, and your grandfather won't be back until later."

They headed down the driveway holding hands, Reese singing, "Mister Moon, Mister Moon, you're out too soon, the sun is still in the sky." Leave it to the girls to make her smile despite the circumstances."

As they arrived where the road met the driveway, a car approached. Jeannie sat in the back seat waving and Louise drove through with another woman on the passenger side. Louise rolled down the window. "I was coming out this way for a visit with Betty and I found your sister on the road. Thought I best bring her back here."

Jeannie rolled down the back window. "I'm okay, just hobbling after I slipped on a rock. I got distracted."

Sealy noticed the tightness around Jeannie's eyes. "We'll meet you back at the house. Hurry and go through. I see Danny's car headed this way. And if I'm not mistaken, Paul's not far behind. He must have left work early."

The girls ran ahead. Sealy waved Danny through and paused to fill Paul in on the situation. She walked back to the house slowly, letting the adrenaline pass through. Paul greeted her at the door with a hug and said, "Danny found an ice pack for Jeannie's ankle. She's okay."

Sealy sighed. "I was afraid Diane had done something to her. I don't like this type of tension. It isn't good for any of us to think the worst. I've got to change my attitude."

"Nothing's wrong with your attitude. We'll get through this."

Sealy walked with Paul toward the living room. Louise and her friend sat beside each other laughing with Roxie and Reese. Jeannie sat with her foot propped up, eyes closed. Before they entered, Sealy paused. "Will you promise me something?"

Paul pulled Sealy close. "This sounds important. Before I ask you what I'm promising, I'll answer yes."

Sealy squeezed his hand. "Never mind. I'll ask you later when we don't have a gaggle of people staring at us."

Louise called out, "Come on in, we won't bite. Jeannie says she's going to complain about the roads to the town manager."

Jeannie sat with her leg propped up with pillows "I said no such thing, Louise is just showing off."

Sealy took a seat on the ottoman by Jeannie and facing Louise. "Does anyone want to tell me what happened?"

Jeannie raised her hand. "It's my story to tell. I took a walk, fiddled with my phone, and stumbled. Louise found me sitting on my butt. Satisfied?"

By Jeannie's snappy answer, Sealy knew better than to question her. Something more was going on. Louise had placed a finger on her lips in some shared secret. Sealy sighed. "Alright then. I'm glad you're okay and Louise miraculously appeared for a visit." She turned toward Louise and her friend. "Please excuse me, I'm sure everyone knows who you are. Care to introduce me?"

"I can speak for myself. I've been quiet too long. The town knows me as Betty, the former high school principal. In case you're wondering, Louise and I are lovers. Now that my husband passed, I don't have to worry about anyone's reputation but my own. Louise and I both knew your mom. But we weren't together back then."

Jeannie's eyes popped open with talk of their mother. Sealy realized that this was more than a social visit. "Reese and Roxie, I have a favor to ask. Could you tell your dad we're having a meeting and let the cook know there'll be more people for dinner? And the biggest ask of all is, can you two make a get-well card for Jeannie?"

Roxie looked at Reese. "Sure, but I know what you're doing. Dad does this all the time when we shouldn't be listening. I get it, we're kids, and this is grown-up talk."

Paul burst out laughing and so did Betty. Sealy shooed them out with a hug.

Once the girls had left, the festive mood dissipated. Louise began, "I told Betty about the accident years ago that started all this. We talked lots about holding secrets and the power it yields." Louise shrugged. "Secrets are different from gossip. Gossip can harm one's ego, it spreads, and people recover. Secrets can ruin lives even if they're never discovered."

Betty moved to hold Louise's hand. "I've never known Louise to stand down from a bully, so when she told me about Diane's hold on the town, I realized that her inaction was due to me. Well, I can't have that. I don't need protection now for sure. I'm not afraid of gossip and won't be bullied by secrets. Besides, this town needs to relax. No offense, Paul."

"None taken. My role here is personal unless laws have been broken. Louise, what more do you need to tell us about the night of the accident that killed Jessica's fiancé?"

Louise stared at Sealy and then at Paul. "It wasn't just brandy and alcohol that Diane supplied back then. She ran high-stakes poker games with no limits on betting. Lots of people owed her money."

Paul asked, "Who was at the game that night?"

Louise stared at Betty and waited for her nod. "I played, and Betty's future husband was at the table. Lots of the old fishermen came, but most have passed on already. The owner of the lobster restaurant used to come. I'm sure that Barry, your father, wasn't there that night. I was the only woman there besides Diane. I often won, but I think the games were rigged. I don't know if her brothers were involved in the scamming. Whenever I won, I had to pay a percentage to Diane. I stopped going after the night of the accident."

Paul added another question. "How did everyone pay their debts?"

Louise sighed. "My debt was manageable. I sold a few pieces of art. Diane was always nice about it, but when she wanted a favor, she'd stick the hook in. After the night of the accident, Diane made sure no one mentioned her name and whenever Barry Morris's good name was brought up, Diane inferred that he was the culprit for the drinking. Everyone let him take the blame. No one mentioned the high-stakes poker games. Jessica knew about them. She'd watch her fiancé and brother play. That night, the stakes were higher than usual. If I remember correctly, the pot was over a thousand dollars. Jessica's brother was there too. And for sure Diane's brothers, Chuck and Geordie, were at the game. No one said anything to go against Diane."

Sealy reached for the water pitcher Danny had left and filled Louise's glass. "Take a drink, you just drained yourself of a lifetime of holding back. Can you tell me if Jessica has more than one brother?"

Louise shrugged. "I didn't pay attention to that. The one I knew was named Jake—we called them the Jays. If I remember correctly, the man was short and intense. Always looking from side to side, as if the wrath of god was upon us. He left early that night with Jessica and her fiancé, Peter."

Betty moved in closer to Louise and took over the conversation. "Before my husband died, he had nightmares. Diane figured prominently in them. He mumbled about his debt to society."

Sealy zoned out of the conversation and let the two of them ramble on about the past. Again, she felt the gnawing sensation in her belly. She looked back at Jeannie. Eyes closed, she appeared asleep, but Sealy knew better. Her stillness was her cover. Something had happened to distract Jeannie on the road. When Louise's and Betty's voices petered out, replaced by Paul's, Sealy paid attention.

"But the gambling part is disturbing. Do you know if Diane continues with the poker games?" he asked.

"Maybe. I know she doesn't need money as she owns most of the buildings after they went into foreclosure. I suspect that was her hold over everyone. But I doubt that is the reason she continues. Diane still has a hold on most of the town in one way or another. I hope your winery is protected, as Diane supplies you with grapes. She wants power."

Paul nodded in agreement. "Diane could have destroyed my family years ago when we didn't know about her shenanigans. You don't need to worry about us. This new information has veered away from the personal and into the realm of my job as the town manager. I'll figure something out."

Betty stood up. "Louise, it's time to go. Jeannie has nodded off and I can tell your friend Sealy is anxious. Let's give them some space. Nice to meet you all. I hope to see more of you, with or without Louise."

Sealy walked with them to the door. "Thank you both, I appreciate your risking negative comments on my account."

Louise beamed at Betty. "She's the best. Besides, I liked your mother."

With Louise and Betty gone, the room had emptied. Sealy found Jeannie alone, eyes open and alert.

"I knew you weren't dozing. Tight lips are your giveaway. What's going on?"

Jeannie's mouth slowly opened. "It's not Diane, if that is what you're thinking. Well, not directly. I had a phone call from my family. Bob with all our kids on the speakerphone. To sum up, they want me home. The call jolted me to my senses. I've been vicariously living my life through you. I'm going home. I can't abandon them."

Sealy felt the knots in her stomach unravel. "Good. I mean it, you're right. I want you here, but all this directly involves me. Mom and Dad's history didn't change your life. I found myself in a new way. Even ignited old fires in this quiet town."

Jeannie grinned. "And you have a new flame, maybe a permanent one. Paul and you are meant for one another." She paused. "I might be more use to you and Paul away from here. Besides being one less person to feed and worry about, I can check for more clues in Mom's stuff. Oh, Sealy, I have to go to save my marriage and myself. I'm a coward at heart."

The knots tightened again inside her stomach, twisted up through her heart. " Jeannie, you never said. Did you come here to escape into my world because yours was so bad?"

"Just for a little bit. Can you blame me? Searching for our mother's past lover sounded ideal. Then came the intrigue. I wasn't noticed at home. I needed to be needed. What I said about Diane is true. She feels irrelevant and will go to any length to be center stage. Take care of yourself."

Tears trickled along Sealy's cheeks to the outer side of her jaw. After hugging Jeannie, Sealy asked, "When do you leave?"

"I have a flight out tomorrow."

Paul couldn't sit still with his thoughts. He needed fresh air and movement. At the gazebo he sought his father's counsel. He felt the presence of his father in the garden and in his birdwatching wicker seat, but nothing came in terms of advice. His father's steady gaze, the vibrancy in his entire being, had set a course of what? He'd thought his father had believed in honesty, chose right from wrong. But Paul questioned his actions with all that had been exposed about Sealy's adoption, the unfairness laid upon his brother, and now the ongoing fraud in the town.

Diane had run the town on another track—gambling, booze, bribes—all big-city stuff. As the town manager, Paul inherited this even when his father was alive. Paul sighed. Diane had power. What she didn't have was love. Paul had received love. He knew that as a fact.

But what did love have to do with it? Everything. Greedy for attention, Diane's mission seemed to center on robbing others of their pride, family, and money. Whatever Diane was playing at recently, it seemed reckless.

Walking back to the house, he found Sealy waiting for him in the garden. "How long have you been sitting there?"

"After I talked with Jeannie, I saw you head out to the gazebo. I figured you were contemplating your next steps as the town manager. Jeannie is heading home, a crisis of guilt for leaving her husband and kids. She needs to go." Sealy listened to the breeze rustling the leaves. "Listen, even the conifers make sounds; the needles talk differently than the deciduous leaves."

Paul hugged Sealy. "And what do they say?"

"Oh, that they're tired of the mysteries of the past. Even though they stay green all year, their ears burn. Time to let go."

"I guess I heard them as well." Paul looked out past Sealy. "I think we need to talk to Diane directly and see if we can get some answers." Paul turned back to face Sealy. She stood fiddling with her hair and hugging herself. "You're afraid, aren't you?"

Sealy sighed. "Not for myself, but for Danny and the kids. Even Jessica. I don't want to tip our hands. Betty mentioned Jessica's brother—Jake. Our Mr. Jewels. He knows something we don't know about the accident. I think it's time we talk to him, and Geordie and Chuck."

Paul responded in his business voice. "The way forward isn't up to us. I'm obligated to deal with the environmental issues at the site of the accidents and the ongoing gambling."

"I know."

Paul took Sealy's hand. "Let's go back in and talk over a glass of wine. Come back to my room so we have some privacy. That is, if you want to?"

Part Four
Sharing All

It had been almost a week since Jeannie had left. Sealy hadn't realized how much space her sister occupied in her mind and heart. Without her physical presence she felt adrift. Talking with Paul offered comfort, love, and a sense of the future, but…the undefined part in any equation is what rattled Sealy.

As promised, Paul had set in motion various investigations. None were made public. Sealy slept fitfully and wondered if her suppositions about Diane were wrong. Instead of asking her directly, Paul decided to meet with Chuck and Geordie again. Their presence at Richard's funeral had escalated the drama just as much as her own presence at the Morrises' house had set in motion the revelations of past indiscretions.

On her way to join Paul and the brothers, Sealy walked past the Golden Goose Gallery. A Now Hiring sign hung in the window. Her heart sank. With no information on the success or failure of the stem cell transplant, Sealy worried that Joseph was too ill to continue as the manager of the gallery. She'd circle back after lunch to find out more. Jessica's silence triggered a fear that the hang-up calls she'd been receiving had morphed into something more intense.

Sealy hurried across town toward the wharf to join Paul at his favorite fish restaurant. She spotted Geordie and Chuck on the last leg of her walk and greeted them. "Good, you're just arriving too, I thought I was late. Paul swears by this restaurant."

Chuck smiled. "We've been coming here since high school. Best chowders in all of Maine. I worried that the old man would have sold it. His son runs it now that his dad passed."

Geordie opened the door for them both. "I see Paul has a table waiting for us. Good thing as all the local fishermen come here too."

Paul stood up and made space for Sealy to sit next to him. A small peck on the cheek made her blush like a teenager. She ignored Chuck and Geordie's stares and smiled at how they were dressed. They looked like twins, dressed in identical clothes, freshly pressed faded jeans, belted, with a dark polo top. Sealy couldn't help but speculate on this considering their physical differences.

Chuck put his menu down and gave her a puzzled look. "Sealy, aren't you two cousins? Be careful, this town is ripe for rumors."

Sealy didn't miss a beat. "That's exactly why Paul and I invited you two for lunch. First to give you our good news, and second to find out about old rumors."

Paul rested his hand on Sealy's knee. "In case you're wondering, we found out that Sealy is adopted and is no relation to my family. We fell in love."

Geordie took a sip of his water. "Why tell us? That is such a personal story."

Paul patted Sealy's knee. He paused as if searching for the correct words. "I realized that you both are interested in a nonprofit for wayward mothers and children in trouble. I thought that you would find some joy in Sealy's story."

Sealy took a deep breath and continued, "Yes, it's connected to someone you two know. I just found out since my arrival here four months ago. I wasn't completely honest with you. According to the world, Barry and Mary were my parents, but when I found a picture of my mother with Richard, I wondered about the past I didn't know. At first I thought Richard and my mom had an affair. Since my father had died and I knew nothing about the Morrises, I was suspicious. Come to find out, not any of them were my natural parents."

Geordie drummed his fingers on the table. "Did you find your birth parents?"

"My birth mother found me. You know her—she's your partner in the building that houses the Golden Goose Gallery."

"How do you know we own part of the building?"

Sealy tried to smooth out the tension in Geordie's voice. It was clear that they didn't want to mention Jessica's name. "I'm a realtor. I know how to hunt down all kinds of real estate transactions. I find it interesting that you had invested in Jessica's building and not others in town."

Chuck nodded. "Yes, that would have been done through our trust. Blind instructions for the arts."

Paul called the waiter over. "Please let Tom know we are here. He wants to make a special dish for us. We'd like some wine, too, with glasses for everyone. If you still have any of the Hawk House Ruha, we'd like that. If not, one of your drier blends will do."

Geordie sat back in his seat. "Paul, you're like your dad, smart and one to follow up on inconsistencies. I guess Chuck and I should relax and enjoy our conversation. I see you have ulterior motives for this lunch, not just incidental questions about our nonprofit foundation."

Chuck followed Geordie's lead and relaxed back into his seat.

Sealy eased into the next conversation. "I wanted you both to know I'll be doing an exhibition at the Golden Goose Gallery. I verified the artist of the painting I showed you. I'm sure you recognized the style. The artist is the owner of the gallery and my birth mother. Funny how serendipitous all this is."

"Great news about your future show. Chuck and I remembered someone from the old days with a similar style. Even though we are part owners of the property, we only visited the gallery for the first time a few weeks ago. Like I said, the purchase of the property years ago was bought through our trust. I look forward to seeing your artwork."

Geordie had again deflected the conversation away from any discussion of Jessica. Sealy knew better than to press. She and Paul had agreed that they should let the web unravel on its own.

Paul waived at Tom as he made his way toward their table. The waiter followed with a pot of chowder, biscuits, and crab cakes. "Tom, thanks for doing this and taking time to sit with us. I saved you a spot next to me. I don't know if you know Chuck and Geordie."

Tom made himself comfortable and Paul poured generous amounts of wine.

Paul raised his glass. "Enjoy."

Tom laughed. "Here's to the old and new customers. I remember you both. I know all the locals, even if they don't live here now. I was just a young kid helping my dad out, but I remember you. My father told me stories about escapades in his youth. Your names were mentioned. Seems everyone comes back to their roots."

Geordie smiled. "I guess we stick out like sore thumbs. Now we are considered city folk."

Tom laughed again. "Yeah, you both look a little too tidy."

Chuck joined in. "I always liked your dad. We weren't close but we knew each other."

Tom looked over at Paul. "I guess that's why Paul asked me to prepare your lunch today. Paul thought if we sat down together it might help clear up some issues. When my dad was in hospice, he referred to that time as fun gone wrong. Too much gambling and drinking. He often talked about an accident after one of the gambling nights and the death of a friend named Peter. It haunted him. He apologized to me over and over for having lost ownership of this building. I inherited the restaurant, but not the land.

I think others in the area had the same problem. Don't get me wrong, I'm content, as he left me all his recipes and journals."

The din of the restaurant covered their conversations. Sealy wondered what else the patrons were oblivious to. She watched as Geordie fiddled with the utensils by his plate, and Chuck held on to his wineglass as if it were his best friend.

She broke the silence. "I think my father, Barry, got mixed up in the gambling as well or at least knew about it. Isn't that when he bailed you two out of scrapes? And he was accused of something at the winery. Can I ask you to tell me more? I think it's important."

Chuck overrode his brother's worried frown. "You've been digging into the past. What does it matter now? We already told you about how we felt that Barry always came to our rescue. Can't we all live in the present with our better selves? That's why we want to create a foundation."

Paul raised his glass as if to make a toast. "That's a worthy cause, but one thing I learned about making wine is to look for clarity. Right now, everything about your proposal is murky. I wanted to have lunch with you two, Sealy, and Tom to figure out how the past continues to haunt the present. If I don't try now, Ogunquit will never be free. Your ideas on helping others in the future is great, but the town still has problems stemming from that time."

Sealy caught Chuck staring at her. His face had turned chalky white. "Chuck, are you okay? You look like you've seen a ghost."

After another sip of the wine, Chuck raised his glass, mimicking Paul. "To be clear, I've been haunted all these years by that time. I feel responsible for Jessica's loss of her fiancé, Peter. Not directly, but I showed Diane how to distill the wine into brandy. I brought some of the grapes Diane had skimmed off her deliveries to Richard's winery. I brought the brandy to a poker game. Peter was losing by lots. Drank too much. The accident happened because of me." Chuck faced his brother. "Geordie, no matter what you think, I want to get this out. So don't stop me."

Geordie waved his hands in the air but remained silent.

Chuck continued, " I was a coward. Diane warned me against saying anything and I listened."

The table went silent. Tom nodded as if Chuck's confession verified something. Sealy whispered, "Why did you listen to your sister? What else are you hiding? What power does Diane still hold over you?"

Chuck bent his head. "Something I'd rather not say."

Geordie spoke up. "Our family life involved abuse. All three of us were adopted. Maybe that is why. I don't think we need to get into that or anything else."

Sealy reached for Chuck's hand. She held it between hers. After a moment, she asked, "Were you in love with Jessica? Is that why you feel guilty, and you stared at me? I must resemble her in some way."

Chuck squeezed her hand. "Not in your looks, but in her ways. Something about how you look at people and your defiance. I apologize if I've made you feel uncomfortable."

Before Sealy could respond, she glanced out the window. Diane stood outside staring in.

Abruptly, Tom stood up. "I have to get back to the kitchen. I suggest we find a private place to meet next time."

Sealy walked slowly from the wharf over to the Golden Goose Gallery. She felt a chill go through her body when she envisioned

Diane's reaction to seeing Sealy, Paul, and her brothers in the restaurant. The woman's eyes threw daggers.

Sealy hoped Chuck and Geordie had escaped the restaurant without a confrontation. Brothers and a sister adopted from separate families. That explained Chuck's sensitivity and the brothers' present desire to create a foundation for children and mothers in need. Sealy had been lucky with her adoption and being raised in a loving family, but apparently not so for their blended family.

She made a quick detour and popped into the post office.

Louise had her back to the door but greeted Sealy as the bell announced her entry. "If it isn't the famous artist." Louise turned to face her. "I saw you in the mirror as you entered. I hoped you would stop in as the gossipers were wagging their tongues. Your lunch at the wharf may have appeared innocent, but everyone noted Diane peering inside. If your strategy is to melt the ice queen, you'll fail. Her anger is worse than her greed."

Sealy grinned. "I knew I could count on you to set me straight. According to you, my choices are a hot Diane or a frozen Diane. Perhaps we can make her irrelevant by not engaging. They say being ignored is like death."

"You know she's sick. Not just mentally. I've seen her mail. Not the inside messages, but I sort and see return addresses. Lots of bills from doctors and clinics. You didn't hear that from me."

"Not to burst your bubble, Louise. I appreciate the slip in protocol, but my sister saw Diane at the cancer clinic in the next town over. Diane's brothers were there too. Seeing them today, I can tell they aren't ill. I suspected Diane has cancer unless they were visiting someone."

Louise gave a belly laugh. "You're finding your place in the gossip mill and using it as well." Her tone became more serious.

"I can't speculate how being ill will affect Diane. Some soften when faced with their mortality, others harden."

Sealy paused as her thoughts cleared. "True, but if we find out who else shares these secrets and quell their fears, Diane is left with herself. I don't want to hurt her or anyone, but I have questions that center on her hold over the town." Taking a deep breath, Sealy continued, "Tell me about Jake Jewels. He's Jessica's brother and was at the poker games. I always thought he lived somewhere else."

"Jake Jewels is a funny duck. At least he was back then. He didn't live with Jessica and the family. He went to a boarding school but visited on holidays and summertime. I'm not sure he wanted to be a loner. He drank lots at the parties and gambled as well."

"Would Diane have a hold over him?"

Louise's shoulders sagged. "Most likely. As much as I admired your mother, Mary, the one who raised you, she knew when to leave well enough alone. I'm sure that's why she left town. I don't want to offend you, but small towns are funny. Old people are funnier. Your theory about exposing Diane's secrets is hogwash. She won't melt away like the Wicked Witch. Ask Jake yourself."

Sealy noted the tears in Louise's eyes. "I'm leaving now, but not before I give you a hug. Thanks for your honesty, I'll be on my way."

Paul picked up his pace when he saw Sealy leave the post office. Out of breath, he caught up. "You're upset. I could see that a block away."

Sealy raised her hand, warning him off. "Louise set me straight with the workings of a small town. I can't force people to see what they don't want to."

Paul took Sealy in his arms. "Shh. You know that's not unique to small towns. What else is bothering you?"

"Jessica, her brother, Jake, and us."

"Whoa. How did you take that leap from their situation to ours?"

Sealy turned her head. "I don't like being in the public eye, and neither do you. If I decide to stay, that changes."

Paul studied Sealy's eyes, which had lost their sparkle. "My life isn't private. I'm the town manager; everyone watches me. The more transparent we are, the less people need to speculate. You're more than special to me and so many others. You fit in." Paul curled his fingers through the tips of Sealy's hair. He calmed his voice to sound steadier than he felt. "We can do this. Besides, the whole town is ready for change. I'll tell you later what happened once you left the restaurant. Where are you going?"

"I was heading to the Golden Goose."

Paul took Sealy's hand. "Perfect. We'll walk together."

As they arrived, a group of people poured out of the gallery. Paul waited till the last one had disappeared to comment. "Something unusual is going on. I wonder if this is a good time to pay a visit."

Sealy stared at the door where the Now Hiring sign was still posted. "No time is a good time considering what Jessica and Joseph are dealing with. Let's find out."

Paul followed Sealy's lead as she slowly walked through the gallery. In the corner, a few people congregated around a display of miniature watercolor paintings. Each seemed to tell a story of a person, a family, or an event from old photos. The table sign read, *Memories of Life's Losses*, with the subtext, *If you have a photo, I'll honor the image.*

Sealy strode through the maze of new displays to the opposite side of the room where Jessica, Joseph, Jake, and Diane drank tea. Paul signaled to Sealy to veer off. They moved quietly back to the paintings of memories and out the door.

Paul had been holding his breath as they left and now inhaled the fresh air. He grabbed Sealy's hand. "That wasn't an innocent meeting. Did you see Diane's face?"

"I didn't. I was looking at Jessica and Joseph. It was like they had put a shield up to deflect Diane's power. You seem more afraid than they did."

Paul glanced behind him. "I'm more wary than before. I wonder if Jessica anticipated Diane's appearance. I don't put it past Diane to use Jessica's goodwill to make herself relevant and spook the town."

"Paul, maybe Diane wants to reinvent the past and literally paint a picture of herself as a better person. Rewriting history seems to be what bullies do. I bet Jessica is stronger than you think. Each time I come here when Jessica is present, the gallery seems bewitched. I don't know if she is aware of her own powers."

"Maybe so. But I don't want to take any chances."

"What do you propose?"

Paul thought of the customers at the restaurant and smiled. "I bet most of those we ate with this afternoon have photos of their own they'd want painted."

"Well then, Jessica is going to need help with her art."

Sealy woke from a nap and smiled to see her phone light up with a message from Jeannie. Instead of texting back, she called. "I'm glad you texted. I miss you."

Jeannie sounded rushed. "I've got to go to meet the family for dinner. Can't talk for long. Did you read what I wrote?"

"No, you know how I hate texting. What's up?"

"I found a box of Dad's old journals and paintings. He wrote everything down about the accident. He even mentions Diane and how she terrorized her brothers. I'm going to ship them to you. He has a journal with recipes for dry wines and special breeds for grapes. I had no idea about Mom and Dad's life before. They hid so much."

Sealy couldn't imagine anything worse than what they had already discovered. Wasn't the bad press of embezzlement, her dad's drinking, and Chuck and Geordie's confession of how they took advantage of his kindness to protect their shenanigans bad enough?

She imagined her sister getting ready for dinner with her kids, grandkids, and husband. Nothing from the past would change her situation. "Have you told the family about all this?"

"Of course I did. They have a right to know. Like you said, secrets fester. Besides, all this will bring us closer, allow us to talk."

Sealy whispered another question: "Before you hang up, is there anything illegal?"

"Do you mean about your adoption?"

Sealy paused. "I conveniently forgot about that. I was thinking more about the illegal brandy making and Diane's gambling."

"Plenty here to make everyone squirm, but I'm not sure. Remember, I'm a scientist not a lawyer. The whole story is sad."

"Are you crying, Jeannie? What's up?"

"The truth sucks. Poor Dad."

"I promise, I'll make this right, even with all the wrongs. Do me a favor: snap a photo on your phone of the most important parts of what Dad wrote, then ship the other stuff off."

Paul stood in the middle of his home office where he had set a table for Sealy and himself to view Jeannie's find. To keep them focused, he opened the windows. The breeze scattered the neat piles. He was on his hands and knees gathering the stray papers as Sealy walked in with two glasses of wine.

Sealy teased, "Is this your way of shuffling the chronological order of Barry's journals and paintings?"

"I thought I'd use one of your techniques where you scramble everything to find new revelation."

Sealy laughed and kneeled to help him. "I bet you didn't realize the wind had picked up. Let's work together to gather this mess."

Paul stood up with his stack. "A quick hug before we begin." He closed his eyes and felt a wave of déjà vu sorting out his mother's and Sealy's mother's correspondence. "This might be more intimate and painful than our mom's letters. Are you sure you want to do this?"

"I'm stronger than you think. Besides, Jeannie's already read this. We owe it to her and the town."

As they sat silently reading Barry's journal, Paul noted the tears on Sealy's cheeks, her fingers entwined in a knot of hair.

"I have an idea," he said. "I know Jeannie sent the highlights of the journal, and we can read the whole thing later. Maybe we should just skip to the last entries."

"Only if you read it out loud. I don't trust myself not to skip around and miss key points. Your voice would help."

Paul placed the last pages on the table between them and began to read.

I know my apologies are too late. I see now that I protected the wrong people. I was weak thinking I was strong. Mary stood by me, but I failed her too. My actions caused so much family pain, caused others to hide and lie, even if I never did anything wrong. I wanted to be a hero, but I'm a coward. If you are reading this, you are my children, Jeannie by birth, Sealy by love. For you two, I mourn. Selfish of me to think others would change and that I would be the changer.

That fateful night of Peter's death was the last straw. I don't know if you can call what happened an accident. Some might—at least that is what the town and I did. But anticipated consequence, a roll of the dice, and eventually the statistics change.

So many evenings I bailed Geordie and Chuck out. Left the winery wide open. They'd call drunk, bruised, or with no money. It was intentional, no accident. Their unloving sister set me up, along with all who gambled. While I was gone, she would steal or damage the wine, leaving no trace of her comings and goings. I know because later I caught her, but by then I was shackled to complicity. Diane took revenge on everyone who loved others deeply. She twisted her lack of connection into a chain of control. That night Chuck called, said Diane had doctored the wine, made a potent brandy that made everyone sick. When some of the guys had passed out, Diane closed the card game down. It didn't matter who went where or if they could drive. No one dared go against her.

This last straw, the one that took Peter's life, altered my own. I had no choice but to protect Diane's brothers from her wrath. She not only abused them physically but schemed to kill them. Someone else died instead. There are other truths that aren't mine.

My loves…

I left in shame, not because of the rumors but because I lied. I am weak, I am sorry. Mary held the family together. I made her swear not to tell… Even my brother, Richard, didn't know all that went on that night. He and Mary became accomplices in cleaning up my mistakes. My behavior compromised so many people. I left this as a record in case the worst continues. Maybe the threats to the town will stop, maybe Diane will change or pass into her own sunset, inflamed. I believe in love, but truth is more powerful as lies erode everything.

I wish I could say more. I'm a painter and created wonderful wine and brandy. I've left my paintings and my best recipes, proof of who I could have been. My talents remain even as I leave you. Maybe you'll be braver than I was. If so, find out more. Maybe I have left you enough to be stronger. Pained, I have drunk my life away and damaged others. Forgive me for taking the coward's way out.

Paul's voice faded. He put the paper down, spent. Neither spoke as Sealy's silent tears fell. He turned to face Sealy's bent head and self-embrace. He unwrapped her arms and encircled her in a bear hug and felt the heaves of her muted sobs.

Sealy tried to speak, but no words came.

Paul held Sealy's face in his hands and gently moved the curls that covered her cheeks. He planted a soft kiss along her tears. "Sealy, this is worse than I expected. Barry was a good man who made mistakes. He was riddled with so much guilt he couldn't live his life."

"I haven't cried like this ever." Sealy sighed. "Must mean I feel safe with you. My dad wanted us to be brave, I guess Jeannie and I will be."

Paul put his finger to his lips. He whispered, "The little munchkins are coming."

"Perfect timing to change our mood." Sealy turned toward the hallway. "Here comes the giggles of Reese and Roxie, and barks?"

Within seconds came a knock at the door and in burst the girls each carrying a caramel-colored puppy. Roxie lifted the puppy up for them to see. "Guess what Daddy found on the side of the road!"

Paul offered, "Two sheep?"

Sealy laughed. "Your granddad is silly; I know, he found two soft pillows that bark?"

Reese and Roxie exchanged looks and shook their heads. Danny came into the room holding another puppy. "I can explain. We visited all of Mommy's favorite spots. On our way home we passed where the accident occurred. All the bushes are down, and the county is cleaning up the area. The girls spotted the pups in a box. Since Charmaine loved dogs, we thought it was a sign."

Paul saw the puppies and the reference to Charmaine as progress. He squeezed Danny's shoulder. "I know where we store the dog beds from our last litter and the indoor kennel in the garage. I'll help you set them up. But first I need to hold one of the pups."

Danny made the exchange. Paul led the way out while the puppy licked his face.

Sealy quickly dressed as she wanted to catch Danny on his first run into town. She and Paul had been up all night, trying to piece together the blanks left by her father. Not much new to go on, but at least it validated what they had surmised.

Sealy took out the photo of her mother and Richard. It gave no hint of the nightmare of their past lives, only a sense of well-being. She had thought it was an affair. Dang, she remembered her words back then when she packed up the house. *It's for the best.* Maybe it had been for her mom. Somehow, she and Richard had found peace and maybe one another. Now, it was her turn to make peace with the past.

Danny sat in his taxi with one of the pups in his arms. "Don't tell me you're going to drive around with the puppies."

"No, I just wanted to feel this one's licks. It's the runt of the three and I thought I'd give it some extra love. The other two puppies slept with Roxie and Reese."

Sealy watched as Danny accepted wet licks over his entire face. "Do you have names for them yet?"

"The girls are waiting for you to help them. I left them last night while they made a list."

Sealy took the puppy in her arms and snuggled. "I'll run it back in the house and put it with the other puppies and the girls."

By the time she returned, Danny had loaded his deliveries into the taxi's trunk. They drove to town in comfortable silence, listening to the radio and the local weather. An announcer interrupted with breaking news: "Outside the post office a group of residents staged a protest parade, moving along the main street to the town manager's office. Their signs vary, but all allude to speaking out on injustice and bullies. Most of the people in the protest are business owners and retired elderly people. When questioned, they smiled and told us to speak out if we knew of an injustice."

Sealy suspected who was behind the protest. "Danny, can you drop me off at the post office? I want to speak to Louise."

"Sure, but if I was you, I'd stop off at the Golden Goose Gallery and Tom's diner, and you might want to check out Elly at the inn."

Sealy turned to watch Danny. "What are you keeping from me?"

"I heard through the taxi grapevine that Jessica and Louise are preparing for a reveal at the gallery. Today is just the beginning, more like a marketing of the event."

"Should I be worried, or more importantly, should your dad be worried?"

Danny shrugged. "Where were you heading before you heard the news on the radio?"

Sealy smiled. "All of those places. And you?"

"I'm delivering wine to the inn and other clients. If you want a ride back, meet me at the inn about one, a little later than normal. I have a lunch date."

At the word *date*, Sealy raised her eyebrow. "Not an appointment, hmm. Have you met someone?"

Danny's look of embarrassment told her it was true. "Yes, I think so. I mean, I've run into her a few times, and we get along."

"Good for you. Let me know when you want to reveal your friend's name. I'd love to hear more."

Danny dropped Sealy off in front of the post office. "Don't say anything to the kids."

"Of course not. That's your job."

The street walks in front of the post office were empty but the doors were wide open. Louise stood behind the counter sorting mail. Sealy called out to avoid startling her. "Louise, I heard there was some sort of a parade this morning."

"You just missed them. A bunch of old folks making a stir. I'd be with them, but I'm still employed, and I'd hate to lose my job even though I'm way beyond retirement age. Got to pay the bills."

"Do you know who's behind it?"

Louise gave Sealy a Cheshire grin. "I think Betty talked to Tom, and Tom talked to Jessica, and Jessica talked to her brother, who talked to Chuck and Geordie, and I don't know why the old lady swallowed a fly. Perhaps she'll die."

Sealy burst into laughter. "You answered all my questions. Thanks."

"No, don't go yet. That was too easy. These folks are riled up, not knowing what to do about the accidents in the past or their own behavior. They've had enough of Diane."

Sealy put her hands on the counter. "So they're protesting themselves?"

"I guess so. Maybe they're waiting for some legal action or a big reveal. Who knows? I'm proud of Betty. What are you going to do?"

"I'm going to find out why the old lady swallowed the fly. I don't know if too much time has passed to take legal action against Diane. I found old journals from my father. He details the drinking, the illicit toxic brandy from Diane, and the illegal poker games. The past might not count. Paul is working on cleaning up the site of the accident. Maybe that will reveal more problems for Diane. Off to talk with Jessica, as she holds the key that might unlock this."

Louise waved goodbye as a mother with two toddlers entered the post office.

Even with all this drama, Sealy felt at home in Ogunquit. The only traffic lights in the town were near the wharf and Main Street where everyone entered. The wharf and boardwalk led you to the fishermen, their boats, and eateries. She imagined the parade of protestors turning off to the courthouse as Sealy veered from the post office to the Golden Goose Gallery. The street's peaceful quiet caused Sealy to smile knowing that Jessica sat inside after the protestors and protectors had been unleashed onto the town.

The bell rang, announcing Sealy's entry. Jessica leaped from her post behind the counter. "I expected you, but not so soon."

Despite the extra makeup, Sealy noticed Jessica's puffy eyes and the strain in her voice. "I would have been here marching with the others if you had told me what you were up to. You can tell me now."

Jessica made a motion with her hand, signaling Sealy to follow her behind the counter. Five easels stood in line, ready to use, along with snapshots from long ago and the present. "You can start painting anytime. We have our work cut out for us. I realized that the past won't leave me in peace."

Sealy took a seat next to Jessica's post behind the counter. "Before you tell me what's up with Diane, I need to know why you haven't called about Joseph. I have a right to know."

Jessica turned her face away. "I don't have an excuse. I almost called but I felt awkward. I sent you the doctor's release. I've given so much of my heart to Joseph that I don't know if I have enough for my own daughter. Even Joseph is annoyed with me. I figured you'd understand. It's not like you had a bad life without me."

Sealy closed her eyes, shut out the light, but the tears fell anyway. "Well, if you keep that up, you'll push me away forever. I don't need you to mother me, but I need you in my life."

When Jessica faced Sealy again, her cheeks were moist. "I hear you, and I'll try to share more. Now about Diane. You saw her here the other day. I watched you and Paul come through. Thanks for being persnickety and coming back in. You have one of my better and worst traits." Jessica's eyes twinkled. "I'm hell bent on pushing myself beyond fear. I may be old in years and have secrets, but seeing you in Ocean City, well, I'm tired of waiting."

Sealy wondered if Jessica referred to their mother-daughter connection or if the meeting gave her a sense of closure. "Did you remember something about the accident or about my adoption? Both were secret."

"Are you asking me if I knew who adopted you or if I regretted letting you go? Either way, that doesn't change reality."

Sealy felt a deep sadness as she watched her birth mother flounder around the truth. "No, don't worry about me and reality. My mom had her own secrets. Either way, that part of the past has been established. The why of it and how you feel now is what is important. Something besides love for an unknown child brought you to this moment."

Jessica sighed. "You're astute too. Yes, when Tom came to talk with me after your lunch at his restaurant, I realized that I had hidden one painful truth about the accident. I felt guilty because I was angry with Peter, your father. We argued."

Sealy closed her eyes, envisioning Jessica with her pregnant belly, Peter driving drunk, maybe too fast. Sealy suspected all along that the truth was more layered. "Were you angry that he was drunk or something else?"

"You already know the answer. Chuck never was good at hiding his feelings. He was in love with me, and well, I made a few mistakes. Peter was jealous and suspected it all."

Seeing Jessica's lip quiver, Sealy automatically reached for her hand. "We all make mistakes. Why were you so afraid?"

"Diane, of course. She was and is fixated on destroying her brothers."

Sealy waited for Jessica to say more. When the silence lingered, Sealy gently shifted her hand as she made a move to leave.

Jessica tightened her grip on Sealy's hand. "Don't go. I'm ready to paint the stories of the past, even the car crash. I have so many people in town wanting to have documentation of what went on before. But to confess to you the why is impossible. Diane hated me, because of my talent, Chuck's devotion, and Peter's love. She hunted me down at the hospital after the accident and spread rumors about me to social services. All I know is that behind Diane's back, Chuck and Geordie made sure that my baby, which was you, met with no harm. I suspect they got advice from my brother, Jake."

Sealy wiped her eyes. "Your parents didn't help?"

Jessica shook her head. "My father was long gone, and my mother had her own issues."

The pieces of her past fell into place. A bump in Jessica's belly, saved by two men who owed so much to Barry for his sacrifices and found a way for him to be a father. Sealy's existence became a secret of many loves. Her adoptive parents, Mary and Barry Morris, committed a crime without knowing the deeper truth. Good gone bad, made good.

Jessica handed Sealy a tissue and gave her a cavernous hug. "Joseph has a miniature latte machine here, and I have cookies from my Ocean City café. Shall we indulge?"

They ate and drank, looking at the photos they would paint. After a time, Sealy rose to leave. "I'm not ready to paint quite yet. Can I come back with some ideas of how to pull this together?"

The twinkle had returned to Jessica's eyes. "I'll count on it. Louise and some of the other artists in the old group will be here every evening. Here is a set of keys. Come whenever you want, even if I'm not here."

"One more question. Are you fearful of Diane now?"

"I'm too old to be afraid. But she should be. Her danger comes from holding power over everyone and their fear. She lost that, and who knows what cancer will do?"

Paul read the EPA report for the second time. One line caught his attention: *Toxic and hazardous chemicals were found past the five-foot mark in the soil.* Just the thought of this parched his throat. He drank a full glass of water to wash away the imagined residue. Further, the report cited the residue was consistent with that of a distillery using wood alcohol and high in pectin, fermenting fruits. The scientific term for the result is methanol, which causes optic nerve poisoning.

More damning information made Paul shudder: *Evidence of high intensity fires showed ethanol, a source of central nervous system impairment like anesthesia, which creates dullness or fatal suppression. Ethanol is more dangerous than methanol. The vapors alter perception, even cause hallucinations.*

The only silver lining in the report, if he could call it that, was the top layer of soil. Apparently, the soil held a mixture of compost and an absorbent sheet of mushroom spores. A person with chemical knowledge and land restoration skills had tried to cover the mess up. Perhaps the agency could trace this.

Paul looked up to see his secretary. "The representative from the EPA, Ms. Sittert, is here. Are you available to see her?"

"She's early, but I can see her now."

Paul stood up as Ms. Sittert entered. He had expected someone older, stuffier. Instead, a young woman dressed in what appeared to be her best khaki pants and recently polished work boots walked in. She looked at him questioningly.

"Have a seat. I won't bite. I just finished rereading the report."

As she sat down, Ms. Sittert said, "You caught me off guard. You look familiar. Do you have a son named Danny?"

Paul chuckled. "This is the first time I've smiled since reading about the cleanup. The answer is yes, but I won't ask you why. That should be for another conversation. How can I help you with the cleanup plans?"

"You can call me Amy. I was originally sent here for shoreline restoration issues, but I also have degrees in hazardous cleanups and spillage into water systems. I won't keep you long." She took a deep breath, looked away, and faced Paul straight on. "The EPA holds the town responsible unless you can find the owner of this property and the culprit for the damage. We can help with the investigation and ultimate enforcement."

Not surprised, Paul smiled. "Ms. Sittert—Amy, you delivered the bad news eloquently. I assumed as much. The town and I have our suspicions of the culprit, but we'll need your help proving it. The property is part of an old dispute. There are stories of illicit behavior and fatal car accidents in that area. Your expertise is welcomed."

Amy visually relaxed as she leaned into Paul's desk. "Here is what I propose. First, you must dig until you find unpolluted soil, remove this, and then replant the area with local vegetation to hold the bank and separate it from the road." Enthused, she continued, "Our forensic staff dates and analyzes debris found close by. It's a blend of archeology and crime scene investigations."

Paul hoped they'd find something to tie the toxic waste to Diane. "I assume you and your staff must be present as we remove the dirt."

"We've already taped off the area. Either I or someone else will be taking samples. It won't take too long. It isn't mentioned in the report, but there is a demolished shed in the back. Two sheds in fact. You might find something in there to lead you to the culprits. One of the shacks has been used recently as a storage area. The other was abandoned years ago."

Paul listened and imagined the dismantled poker games. Where did the gamblers go, and what was stored in the shed? He thought of Charmaine, Danny, and the old and recent accidents. "Take care while you're there. The visibility around the curve in the road is problematic. Too many accidents have occurred there. Obviously, this is an ongoing investigation. Someone in our small town will feel threatened."

"Your son gave me the same advice."

After Amy left, Paul pushed himself away from the problems on his desk. He'd let the EPA carry out their investigation and he'd send the gambling and liquor authorities to look at the remains in the sheds. Also, some of the town's police would be sent to oversee the road traffic and to look out for intruders. No matter what, he'd be responsible and protect the investigators and the townspeople.

Sealy sat in the gazebo admiring the gardens still filled with greenery and blooms. Instead of fall, a second summer had slipped in. According to Paul, this meant good fortune. Nervous but happy, Sealy waited for Paul to join her. Jeannie and her entourage had arrived the night before and she assumed they were still asleep. Roxie and Reese had spent the night at a campout with Danny and Amy. Sealy smiled at the thought of Danny with his girlfriend.

Paul came up behind her and placed his hand gently in the crook of her back. "You look like a goddess philosopher deep in thought dressed in subdued colors of the sky. I'm lucky to have you here with me forever. Are you ready for today?"

Sealy had refused to let nerves get the best of her, and the question pried open doubts. How would the town receive the artists' renditions of photos? Hopefully Jessica's faith in old friends would pay off. Even Elly from the inn had submitted photos from the archives, like the ones on the mural. Some included Barry and Richard together before Richard was the town manager.

She answered Paul with honesty: "Which part, the grand presentation of Jessica's genius, or this evening's event? Both could cause a larger scandal for the town."

Paul turned to Sealy. "I should hope so! This is good stuff, bringing out all the characters and history of a modern town. I doubt if there will be a ruckus, certainly nothing to cause an upset. And this evening, well, some elders might feel more romance in their souls."

Sealy rested her head on Paul's shoulder. "You know exactly what to say to make me feel better. I've been so busy painting renditions of the cherished photos, I've lost sight of the depth of their meaning to everyone else. We aren't the center of this. Jessica knows that each family beyond ours has their own stories to reveal."

Sealy sighed remembering all the images. "Did you notice that some of the photos show card games at the backs of their homes? There's not one woman in the photos, all are men wearing relaxed ties with their collars unbuttoned. Who knows if the end-of-day poker games were forbidden gambling or something more innocent? I loved the photos of the children."

Paul took Sealy's hand. "Come on, I promised to help set up the display. I'm sure Jessica is fretting, and we don't want her upset. Danny will be back soon with the kids and promised to bring Jeannie and her crew."

The town was barely awake when they arrived at the Golden Goose Gallery. The closed sign remained, but a chair held the door open. Jessica stood in the center of the gallery wearing a flowing pastel flowered skirt, with a pale green-striped silk blouse. She left the impression of a field of wild grass. Sealy watched Jessica place baskets of gold wrapped chocolate eggs by each display and drop gold confetti on the floor, creating a trail in the shape of arrows to indicate flow through the gallery.

Jessica acknowledged their presence without facing them. "It's about time you two arrived. I need your help with the main wall."

Sealy laughed. "Good morning to you too. You must have arrived before dawn. From your greeting, it sounds like you need a break. Paul and I can set up the paintings. I have the quilt background and the tools to tie it together."

"I only just arrived. I left here at dawn, showered, and returned. No use resting when sleep doesn't come, and there's work to do. Did you bring the pastries?"

Sealy handed Jessica a thermos and a container with two pieces of strudel. "This is for you. My sister Jeannie will bring the rest later. The last batch was cooling, and I didn't want to risk them breaking."

Jessica hugged Sealy. "You're a gem. Read my mind. I'll be in the back, come get me if you need me."

Sealy set to work placing the backdrop on the wall. Paul had insisted on painting Ogunquit's waterfront and rolling hills on a burlap cloth, with areas retreating in darker tones to create a sense of windows. He added clips to mount the patchwork of paintings angled toward the center. Each diagonal moved from the past to the present, creating the illusion of depth.

"Paul, the design is exactly as I imagined. The display looks like a handmade quilt."

After placing the smaller paintings angled inward, Paul waited for Sealy to hand him the renderings for the middle spot. "What have you and Jessica decided for the centerpieces?"

"Hold on a second. Jessica needs to weigh in on the next part."

From the back of the store Jessica called out, "Yes, wait a second. I've got a painting fresh off the easel, impressionistic I hope."

Sealy rushed back to help Jessica. "Oh my, I'll have to see it up to get the full effect."

Jessica laughed. "Said like an artist holding back her opinion. While you hang it, I'll bring out the last two canvases I painted."

Paul placed the painting in the center of the quilt backdrop. Sealy stood back to see the effect. When she looked at it straight on, trees shimmered in the light. From one side she noticed a woman peeking out from behind the trees. Somehow, Jessica had created a sense of the trees swallowing creatures between the folds. Layered above the trees a road wound its way around hills lined with upright vines, a tangle of mazes. The sun's angle highlighted the grapes and revealed a small door going nowhere.

Sealy gave the painting one last look and turned to Jessica. "I'm trying to figure out what you want me to feel. Your painting is realistic yet reminiscent of M. C. Escher renderings, a mystery within a mystery."

Jessica handed the other pieces to Paul. "Here you go. Something to balance out the drama."

Still standing on a ladder, Paul mounted the last of the paintings. "I'm coming down to look."

The trio stared at the display. The last two paintings were portraits of community members that mirrored one another. In both, the people sat at a round table. One was all the past leaders of the town, men and women dressed in festive clothing. The other was of children dressed in their finest clothes. Sealy knew immediately Jessica's inference.

"I see you have more faith in the future, children taking life a bit more seriously."

Jessica nodded. "But not totally. Notice the flowers on the kids' table—each one is painting, not writing with a pen. Their faces are turned to the light coming in from the windows, and while their eyes are intent, there's a sparkle. With adults, the eyes are hooded. Their smile lines take over, but their lips are pursed, holding back. I made a mosaic of scenes on the wallpaper in the room. One has the mural at the inn, and the other has a mural of a new school and playground. The old generation and the new."

Paul sighed. "I recognize some of the faces and the clothes. Are you being too harsh?"

"No, not at all. I look at myself in the mirror and I see life's marks. Until now, I held back and kept my mouth shut."

"My father held back. I hope we are a little wiser. Where are your paintings, Sealy? Didn't you create something for the display?"

Sealy turned to Jessica. "You told me you had a plan for them?"

"Yes, I do, but we have to wait for Chuck and Geordie, and my brother."

"Will they be here soon? Or should I put the ladder away?"

Sealy heard a noise at the entrance. "That must be them."

Before Jessica could answer, Diane entered. Uncharacteristically, she wore a black-belted dress with a wild red, orange, and yellow scarf wrapped like a turban on her head. Her presence sucked the air out of the room.

"Can someone help me bring in my painting?" Diane's request was more of a demand. "No need to stare. This isn't a private showing, is it?"

Paul pulled Jessica aside as Sealy walked over to Diane and said, "We aren't open yet and the showing starts in a few hours. All the paintings were juried before today. You took us by surprise. If you'd like, I could help you bring in your painting, and try to find space for it. You do realize this is a fundraiser?"

"I don't care what you think this is. I know you are up to no good. You appear like a fancy artist, a big shot. You don't have me fooled. You hoodwinked Paul and Jessica, but not me."

Sealy didn't let Diane's words enter her psyche. "I'll help you get your painting and give you the agreement every person showing has signed. If we can find space, your name will be displayed by the painting with an opening bid. You won't receive any money for the sale as it will all be donated to the Ogunquit Foundation for Adoptees."

Without a word, Diane stormed out of the store.

Paul caught up to Sealy. "Are you okay?"

"Yes and no. I can defuse this, I hope. We can talk later. I've got to take charge as Diane might explode her poison on this event. No matter what, I've got to end this. She's dressed to impress, but I bet under her turban she's holding back rage." Sealy rushed out to follow Diane to her car. "I wish you had come to us earlier with your entry. If we can't use it today, maybe you can leave it with Jessica on consignment."

"I bet you didn't know I was an artist, just like Richard and Barry, even Jessica. No one took me seriously at Richard's art institute. All that free love spoiled the place. They had to close. Not many have gotten famous. Their weaknesses got in the way."

Sealy lifted Diane's canvas from her trunk. "I'm glad you kept painting on your own. I'm anxious to see what inspires you." Sealy carried the wrapped canvas into the delivery area. "Wait here, I'll get you a cup of coffee."

"No coffee for me. Ruins my taste buds." Diane refused the chair and stared Sealy down. "If you are so anxious to see my work, look at it now."

Not taking the bait, Sealy guided Diane to a chair. "Jessica can look once there is space in the gallery. Before you leave it, we'll need you to sign the contract and waiver." Sealy smiled. "All business formalities."

"It doesn't matter what I sign—I'll be gone soon enough. This gallery will be gone too. I'm tired of every one of you."

"If you want us to display your painting here, you'll have to sign, like the rest of the artists. I won't let you ruin what we have created for this town." Sealy held out the paper and pen. She waited for Diane's next outburst.

Instead, Diane held her head, swooned, and collapsed against the wall.

"Paul, come quick. Diane passed out."

Jessica and Paul came running. Paul held onto Diane. "Sealy, call 911. Tell them she's still breathing but isn't responsive."

Within minutes an ambulance arrived. Sealy, Paul, and Jessica watched as they loaded Diane. Sealy squeezed Paul's hand and looked at Jessica. "We have to get ready for the opening, but I'm worried that Diane has no one to go with her to the hospital. Do you have her brothers' cell numbers?"

"Of course. I'm old but I know how to create contacts on my phone. I'll call them."

Drained, Sealy sat on the closest chair she could find. Paul pulled up a folding chair and held her hands. "Don't let Diane's words get to you. She's just ranting the nonsensical thoughts left in her brain."

"I know that, but that's what rattles me. Having those thoughts in one's brain is painful. It's as if hatred has consumed her."

Paul followed the line from the Golden Goose Gallery as far as the post office. Louise stood outside, dressed in black pants and a matching jacket. Her hair fell softly on her shoulders, held back by a thin headband.

As he approached, Louise called him over. "Look at this crowd. I know they aren't here to see an old lady like me. Can you entertain the masses? They're all talking about the displays at the gallery. I promised to help Sealy reveal her paintings."

"That's why I'm here. Someone notified Sealy's agent, who notified the press. Funny how quickly news spreads. Apparently, Ogunquit is now the center of the art universe. This will make restaurant owners happy. Tom left his painting and photo and rushed back to feed the hungry crowds."

Louise teased. "You're grinning. Don't tell me you want our small town to grow?"

Paul shook his head. "No, Sealy is telling Chuck and Geordie's story about adoption and promoting the foundation. Tom agreed that his diner and other restaurants would ask the patrons to donate to the cause. I call this double-dipping in a good way."

Louise walked closer to Paul and whispered. "I heard about this morning's incident with Diane. My friend at the hospital told me that Chuck and Geordie are sitting by her. She's on life support. They've even brought in her estate lawyer. Strange isn't it, that her brothers are so dedicated, since they are mortal enemies?"

"I don't think that part of their relationship has changed. All I know is that the two brothers have hearts of gold. I doubt they could do anything different."

"Who knew that they'd be the golden eggs come back to roost. I hope they stay for a bit." Louise waved as she headed to the gallery.

An hour later, the crowds had dwindled, and Paul returned to find Sealy surrounded by a handful of young artists and historians. She motioned Paul over. As he joined her, she continued talking with the group: "You've already talked with Jessica, the owner of the gallery, and this is the town manager, Paul Morris. He'd be happy to answer more questions about the town's history. I'm new here myself, although these last few months I've been enmeshed with the townspeople, chronicling their lives."

Suddenly thrust into the limelight, Paul watched Sealy make her exist to the backroom. Her pace told him something was up. He fielded questions about the legacy of his position, his father's art school, queries about creating a museum, and the new foundation. Most of the remaining locals were at the food table. Paul thanked everyone and went to find Sealy.

He found Sealy with Jessica pouring over the canvas Diane had left. Tears ran down Jessica's face. Paul studied Diane's painting and felt ill. His heart quickened as he realized Diane had entered his home. Not only had she painted the view from the Hawk House, a panorama of the gardens, the gazebo, but also a bird's eye from the inside of his father's upstairs art studio. All of it was too personal, and worse yet, the studio was not in disarray but as he and Sealy had recently reorganized it. He felt violated.

Sealy left Jessica's side and reached for Paul's hand. Paul stood frozen as he looked further. "Did you see what Diane has done?

Not only has she entered my home, but she is also showing us her obsessions and maybe her murders."

Jessica finally spoke. "I don't know, the lady is twisted. She is playing games with us."

Sealy stared at where Diane had placed Richard and her father, Barry, facing a car coming straight at them, a baby in a stroller, and in the distance off a cliff, a baby falling. "Paul, nothing in this is new. Diane is sick. She's taunting you. What she has painted isn't a confession but a wish for power. She is trying to hook you in, like she's done to others. Who knows what she means by the juxtapositions of old news. The only thing for sure is that she is the one who broke into the house."

Paul agreed with Sealy but for the first time he was rattled. "Jessica, what will you do with the painting?"

"Of course I'll return it. The woman is a psycho."

Sealy held his eyes and Paul felt the knot in his stomach dissolve. "Let's clean up and get ready for tonight. Jessica, will your brother be there?"

Jessica gave her a sly look. "Yes, and he'll pick me up and bring Joseph. You know, Joseph thought I had called you after they released him from treatment. He was furious with me. Apparently, I lack social graces and have a problem with sharing emotions."

Paul sighed with a sense of relief. He knew now why his father had kept silent for so long. Why Barry left with his wife and kids. Without someone like Sealy, Diane's vindictive actions would take root again.

As they headed out Paul took Sealy in his arms and said, "I'm ready to enjoy family and friends. I've never felt so lucky."

Sealy mumbled something in his ear. He silenced her with a kiss.

Hours later, Sealy entered the kitchen refreshed by quiet time with Paul and a shower. Danny had assigned Roxie, Reese, and Jeannie's grandkids various jobs. He was having less than success. "Okay, guys, this looks like chaos. At this rate the trays won't be ready by 7:00. The guests will starve." No one responded to his pleas.

Sealy swooped in behind Jeannie's three grandkids, and gave each a kiss, and tickled Roxie and Reese. "How about I give you a break and finish the platters?"

"That would be great. I promised your sister I'd help set up some photos of you and her with your parents. Dad already put out ones with his dad and mom. A celebration this big must include everyone."

Roxie tugged at Danny's pants. "You'll put out one of Mom, too, won't you?"

Reese piped in, "I don't want Amy to feel bad."

Danny washed his hands and swooped Roxie and Reese up in his arms. "Yes! Remember, we picked out a few the other day. Amy will be with us, and we can take more photos of all of us. Tonight is a night to laugh and remember. If you want, you can help me. That is, if Sealy doesn't mind?"

Sealy shooed them away. "Go, I can manage. I'm sure they can all find something to do."

"Okay, but I think you and Jeannie had this planned all along so you can talk." Danny smiled and corralled all the children out of the kitchen.

Jeannie stood at the counter. "Danny's great. But he's right, we need to talk."

Suddenly, Sealy felt weak. She couldn't take any more surprises or upsets in the day. "Are you okay, Jeannie? I mean, we have everyone together. I haven't left you or anyone out, have I?"

"No, don't worry about me or the family. I'm over that and appreciate all the wonderful people you've brought into our life."

Sealy continued setting out the cheese-and-meat platter and then organized the vegetables and dips. "Spit it out, Jeannie. I know you. Either you are hiding something or you're worried. Tell me."

"I remember when you packed up the house to rent. You were the cagey one, obsessed with a photo. I'm feeling that way now and don't want to. I'm purging the rest of our parents' boxes. I brought Dad's boxes for you to see."

Sealy embraced Jeannie. "Good. I'll look at them later. You already sent me enough information. We can't remain on high alert, waiting for the next revelation. I remember when, as a kid, you'd pick at an old scab until it bled. Then you'd run to Mom because you were bleeding."

"You made that up, didn't you?"

Grinning, Sealy continued, "Of course I did. But you'd do stuff to get attention or rehash old wounds. But the story I remember most is when Mom had to go pick you up at the shopping mall."

Jeannie covered her eyes and bent her head. "My friend Sally and I had gone on our own. It was my first time at the mall without Mom. I felt so grown up until I realized Sally was shoplifting. I told her to stop but she wouldn't. I went to call Mom, but before I got to the phone, a guard swooshed me away with Sally. It didn't matter that I hadn't taken anything, I was with her, therefore I was guilty."

Sealy nodded. "I remember Mom's warning. She went on and on about the psychology of bullies and how they keep you silent. She made you promise to stand up for yourself when Sally spun the story differently the next day with her friends."

"Mom was right. The next day, Sally put her arm around me as if we were best friends and started bragging about what happened. In front of everyone, I told her that it was a lie and that only Sally stole. She was furious with me. I walked away."

"Jeannie, no matter what's inside Dad's boxes, we won't get caught up in the lies of the past or any wrongs in the future. We have a moral compass and know better. Mom and Dad learned the lesson the hard way."

Jeannie made one of her twisted faces that always caused Sealy to smile. "Good. Now I have something fun to tell you. John got offered a consulting job in Maine. We've rented a small house nearby."

Sealy burst out laughing. "Couldn't you have started with that news? Now if the gossip wheels start after today, I'll have a buddy to commiserate with."

Paul entered the kitchen. "What have I missed about good news and gossip?"

"Jeannie and her husband rented a cottage close to here. He's got a consulting job." Sealy watched as Paul feigned surprise. "Oh no, you knew and kept it from me. Both of you are in hot water."

Jeannie grinned. "Speaking of hot water, I'm off to shower before the party and make myself beautiful."

Paul stood with Sealy facing the gazebo. "Are you sure you want to do this in front of cameras? You know what will ensue."

"This ceremony isn't just about us, and besides, the bigger news already happened when you invited my agent and press to the event at the gallery." Sealy leaned into Paul. "I think the last of my new works fit perfectly in the gazebo. Each painting covers the open sides and feels like windows looking out."

Sealy twirled her hair in contemplation. "I think my parents would be pleased, even Richard. Before he died, he wanted me to paint his treasured landscapes and all of Hawk House. I hope I've captured the naïve greens, the lightness of eyelashes reflected in the mirrors. I took simple rooms and made them beautiful with sunlight and shadows. My hardest painting was the one with the baby carriage holding triplets. Babies for the ones lost to their mothers like me, the baby who drowned years ago, and your twin." Overwhelmed with emotion Sealy gulped for air as her tears fell along her cheeks.

Paul took Sealy's hand and waited for her emotions to settle.

"Sorry, it's a happy painting, as I've put children skipping together down the road, climbing inside of your wonderful stump house. I've tried to blend our history with the present."

"I can see the joy, especially the little bench along the beach with a hidden drawer. Nice touch, creating more mystery. Your work is always a story to step into. That's why you are so good." Paul removed a piece of paper from his back pocket. "Would you look over this before the guests arrive?"

In mock horror Sealy asked, "Are you going to make a speech?"

"No, this for you. I know you used to dance, and I asked your sister for a list of all your favorite songs."

Twirling her hair, Sealy scanned the playlist. "I feel dated and elated. You chose well. Something for everyone. Thank you for including Jeannie. She so much wants to be part of our life."

Paul nodded. "Yes. The more the merrier. No secrets, no exclusions."

Sealy caught a tear before it dropped. "I hear cars pulling up. Let the fun begin."

Danny rushed in with Louise and Betty. "Dad, can you take over and show Louise and Betty our makeshift stage? I've got to get back to help with parking."

Louise laughed. "You shouldn't worry, seems like you have cute helpers. Besides, we all know the drill. Keep the driveway clear, park on the asphalt, and make sure no one is blocked in."

As Paul showed Louise the setup, Betty patted Sealy's hand. "Thank you for inviting us to this. Louise would never show her emotions, but this is amazing. We've been practicing the songs for weeks. I've never seen Louise so dedicated except for her passions for basketry and pottery. She's alive again, and so am I."

Sealy hugged Betty and took hold of her guitar. "Apparently, Paul has a playlist for you guys. I'm embarrassed by all the oldies, but if you two are playing, I'm sure the renditions will be memorable."

"Better we play the music than dance. Our bones are too rickety. You don't need to help carry the guitar; I can manage."

"I know you can, but I'm fidgety, and you'll be busy up here playing. I may look confident, but I always get nervous before an event."

Betty smiled. "I don't think you need to worry. The town loves you."

"Thanks. Off to greet more guests."

Sealy spotted Jessica with her brother, Jake, and her nephew Joseph. Jessica wore a navy pantsuit with a long silk scarf filled with polka dots in every shade of purple. She looked like the grandmother of a famous star from the Frank Sinatra era. Joseph held on to her elbow and wore a polka dot tie to match. His color had returned, and he'd put on weight. In contrast, Jake wore khaki pants with a green bow tie and a crisp yellow short-sleeved shirt. His eyes roamed until he found Geordie. He was gone before Sealy could make it across the room.

Jessica waved as Sealy approached. Joseph smiled, gave her a big hug, and whispered in her ear, "I owe you my life—I'm so thankful for your existence."

Sealy laughed. "You owe me nothing. Helping you helped me. Hopefully I'll see more of you at the gallery."

"That's the plan if all goes well. I still have chemo treatments for what could be my lifetime, but I'll manage. In the interim, Aunt Jessica will be there."

Jessica nodded. "I haven't firmed up my plans yet. Tonight, however, I'm here to enjoy. What a treat to be here. I haven't been in this house for sixty years. The memories are good. I'm glad today's art show got rid of the more painful ones."

The room had filled up with families from the wharf, old friends of Richard. Sealy relaxed as Paul greeted them and relieved her of some hostess duties.

Jessica pulled her aside. "I'm thrilled with the auction success. We brought in $109,000."

"That's wonderful news. I'm sure Chuck and Geordie will be pleased. What a wonderful campaign for their foundation. Do they know?"

Jessica stared across the room where Chuck stood. "I already told Chuck. He's ecstatic. Sealy, more than a third of it came from your one painting. Are you sure you want to donate that much?"

"Of course I am. I intend to do so annually. We both know how important the adoption foundation will be. Besides, I still owe the gallery a painting. Let's go enjoy the party."

Sealy beamed as the room filled. Jeannie was with her family dancing with her husband, her daughter with her grandkids. Danny and Amy held Roxie and Reese in an embrace swaying to Billy Joel's "Piano Man." From across the room, Paul, Geordie, and Chuck approached.

"You three look serious. What happened?" Sealy asked.

Paul pulled her away from the group. "We have news about Diane, best to go into my office. I told Danny to play host for a bit."

Sealy held Paul's hand. She felt his reassuring squeeze.

Once seated, Chuck began, "The hospital called. They took Diane off life support as her body gave up. This was her wish. We knew it was coming as her lawyer came to the hospital yesterday while we were there. None of us knew how connected we still were."

Geordie interrupted, "We don't need to go into detail. Suffice it to say that our father had a clause in his will stating that if one of us died without a partner or family, their holdings reverted to the original estate. This included any profit they had made in their lifetime."

"What are you saying?" Sealy's mind reeled. "You mean the farm and all her real estate belongs to you two?"

Chuck continued, "Yes, and we've decided to divest the properties. Diane never changed. Maybe she knew about the clause, and that's why she tried so hard to get married. She resented anyone with children. She hated us when we were kids, two orphans who stole love away from her. I guess our parents knew she was vindictive."

Sealy thought how much her parents had loved her, how Jessica had given her up. All done out of love. "What a sad life. I've been lucky."

Sealy felt Paul's gentle touch. His voice filled with emotion. "My mother and father only gave me love. Did they know about your situation?"

"Barry did, so I assume Richard knew too. It doesn't matter. We have the power to change this and right her wrongs."

Sealy couldn't keep still. She rose and came over to Chuck. "I'm sure the monies will help with the foundation."

"We're not using it for the foundation." The two brothers beamed. "Geordie and I decided to make quick claims to the original owners or the renters of her ill-gotten properties. The vineyard is going to Danny if he accepts."

Paul jumped out of his seat. "Do you realize how this will change the town? The impact on everyone is profound."

Geordie put his hand up. "That's why we are going to do this quietly, and individually with each person affected. No newspapers, no publicity. We want to remain on the sidelines. Please help us with this."

Not wanting to ruin the moment, Sealy whispered to Paul, "Remember, no secrets, no hidden agendas, always our best foot forward."

Chuck seemed to have read her mind. "I know you worry about appearances, about hiding things. We will be open to anyone's questions. We'll do it all above board. It's okay if people find out over time, but not now. Too much change would backfire. I know, as an old person who is stuck in the past. You can't make too many waves."

Danny knocked on the door. "Whatever you guys have planned, it's time for the group dance. Our guests are restless."

As they walked out, Louise and Betty sang Joni Mitchell's "Both Sides Now."

Danny stood on the stage and asked everyone to find their partners of choice and raise their hands in love and commitment to a caring town.

Sealy felt Paul's arms gather her in an embrace. They danced eye to eye, lips to lips. Then she whispered, "This is the best."

Acknowledgments

To new friends who walk with me and offer support as I find my way. We may never discuss writing, but the time we pass together offers inspiration.

A special thanks goes to Mary Gillilan from Independent Writers Studio who has been with me through my writing journey, along with Janet Oakley, Janet Bergstrom, and Sephanie Hopkins. These women are talented and generous.

I thank Sara Stamey, a long-time friend who speaks so many truths with her insights. She has my respect and love beyond our lifetime.

To my family that continues to grow and longtime friends who endure my ups and downs, you support me with your steadiness.

And to Teri Bachus, my heart collaborator who remembers all that I forget.

You can find Book Club questions and more information about Abbe Rolnick at her website at abberolnick.com.